When I Was a Witch
& Other Stories

Charlotte Perkins Gilman

This edition is published in 2023 by Flame Tree 451

The text for these stories is based on the original
editions published in *Forerunner*, Volume 1, 1909–10
All other text © copyright 2023 Flame Tree Publishing Ltd

FLAME TREE 451
6 Melbray Mews,
Fulham, London SW3 3NS
United Kingdom
www.flametree451.com

Flame Tree 451 is an imprint of Flame Tree Publishing Ltd
www.flametreepublishing.com

A CIP record for this book is available from the British Library

ISBN: 978-1-80417-580-4

© 2023 Flame Tree Publishing Ltd

Cover image was created by Flame Tree Studio, based
on images courtesy Shutterstock.com

Printed and bound in Great Britain by Clays UK, Elcograf S.p.A.

When I Was a Witch & Other Stories

Charlotte Perkins Gilman

FOUNDATIONS OF FEMINIST FICTION

With a series foreword by Ruth Robbins
And a new introduction by Dr. Catherine J. Golden

451
FLAME TREE

Contents

A Taste for the Fantastic

From mystery to crime, supernatural to horror, fantasy to utopian, dystopian and the foundations of modern speculative fiction, the terrific range of paperbacks and ebooks from Flame Tree 451 offers a healthy diet of werewolves and mechanical men, bloodlusty vampires, dastardly villains, mad scientists, secret worlds, lost civilizations and escapist fantasies. Discover a storehouse of tales gathered specifically for the reader of the fantastic.

Great works by H.G. Wells and Bram Stoker stand shoulder to shoulder with gripping reads by titans of the gothic novel (Algernon Blackwood, Charles Brockden Brown, Arthur Machen), and individual novels by literary giants (Jane Austen, Gustave Flaubert, Charles Dickens, Emily Brontë) mingle with the intensity of H.P. Lovecraft and the pure psychological magic of Edgar Allan Poe.

Of course there are classic Conan Doyle adventures, Wilkie Collins mysteries and the outlandish fantasies of Robert E. Howard, Edgar Rice Burroughs and Mary Shelley, but there are so many other tales to tell: *The White Worm, Black Magic, The Murder Monster, When the World Screamed, The Centaur* and more.

Check our website for regular updates and new additions to our incredible, curated range of speculative fiction at flametreepublishing.com

FANTASTIC TALES

When I Was a Witch
& Other Stories

Charlotte Perkins Gilman

Series Foreword

What did feminism – in fiction and in reality – mean at the turn of the twentieth century? This series of reprints of rare and often forgotten texts from that period answers this question in the widest possible way. For some of its authors, it meant the representation of the New Woman, the sometimes hostile term applied to women who sought the vote, the opportunity for higher education, access to the professions (or just to jobs), or who just wanted their independence from the stifling conventions of the nineteenth century where a woman's place was definitely 'in the home' and where venturing out meant chaperonage or else a risk to reputation. So, some of our chosen texts (for example, *The Job* by Sinclair Lewis) show those women achieving a measure of independence. In the spirit of the realism which was his hallmark, Lewis also shows that getting a job is actually an illusory form of freedom. The daily grind of the office or factory is not the utopian dream that some seekers after female emancipation had hoped. In other terms, and for other reasons, Kate Chopin's *The Awakening* also shows that women could not easily free themselves from standards of sexual propriety: sexual choice is not the route to utopia any more than earning capacity is. Her heroine briefly tastes the pleasure of sexual liberation but cannot escape the judgement of her society: her story does not end well.

For other writers (Charlotte Perkins Gilman, for instance), the representation of *life as it is* that realism demands was also problematic. Realism permitted only the diagnosis of social ills: it could not manage the process of prescribing solutions for the problems it uncovered in the world as it was then constituted. The construction of fantasy worlds, in which current imbalances between the sexes could be redressed in an imagined future was Gilman's solution in *Herland*. This is a speculative fiction, a 'what if?' world rather than a 'what is' world, though in common with all fantasy, it also speaks of the limitations of its own moment of production.

Long ago, Elaine Showalter pointed out, in *A Literature of their Own* (1977), that focusing purely on representation whether realistic or fantastic can be a kind of dead end. If readers only look at false pictures of reality or at impossible visions of futurity, they get stuck: despair or dreamscapes. A third possibility is to look at the woman writer herself, what she does, often slyly and obliquely, with genre and form. Francis Stevens (Gertrude Barrows Bennett), a woman writer cloaked by a male pseudonym, offers another potential meaning for the first wave of feminism: the professional woman writer, using man-made genres for her own ends, both aesthetic and financial. She belongs to a category that frighteningly often overtakes the woman writer – the forgotten novelist. In recovering and reprinting her work, the series shows both her indebtedness to, and her distinctiveness from, the male models of the adventure fiction genre and the weird tale which, along with romance and crime, were the mainstays of the pulp magazines of the early twentieth century. She also made money – an important consideration for the woman who wants independence – in her chosen domain.

If Stevens stands for 'pulp' and popularity, Virginia Woolf is the highbrow novelist par excellence (though she also sold pretty well and was also very interested in the money she could make from her pen as her extended essay *A Room of One's Own* makes clear). Her works span a massive range of reviews, short fiction, novels and polemics, and she often returns to the figure of the woman artist and/or writer to demonstrate the ways in which women can be denied their creativity ('Women can't paint, women can't write', Mr. Tansley says dismissively to the artist Lily Briscoe in *To the Lighthouse*) and opportunity ('Why are women poor?' she asks in *A Room of One's Own*).

For this series, we have brought together texts which showcase women's talents and their frustrations in a historical moment that is not so very long ago. The battles that the New Woman, the Suffragists and Suffragettes, and the founders of women's colleges and union members fought on our behalf may all seem to be won. But they only seem that way. Count the women politicians in the House of Representatives and the House of Commons. Check how much an average woman earns over her lifetime and compare it to the average man's earning capacity. Ask yourself who cleans the bathroom in your house and who does the double shift at work and home. And pay attention to how easily some rights can be lost by the flick of a legislator's pen and a minor political shift.

The feminism of the early years of the twentieth century had its own blind spots: it was not inclusive of women of colour, nor of women from working-class backgrounds, nor of those women for whom heterosexual romance was not their choice, nor of those women who lived at the intersections of multiple disadvantages. Early feminists were also very often conflicted about the 'sex' part of sexual liberation. Nonetheless, those early struggles for white middle-class women's rights have resonance and lessons to teach for the broader struggles for all women, and for other dis-privileged groups. And representation in its broadest sense (of characters, but also of the women writers we might read) is one of our routes to understanding, action and – let us hope – change.

Ruth Robbins

A New Introduction

In his introduction to the 1966 republication of Charlotte Perkins
Gilman's *Women and Economics* (1898), historian Carl Degler calls
Gilman 'the leading intellectual in the women's movement in the
United States during the first two decades of the twentieth century'.
She won international acclaim for *Women and Economics*, a
major contribution to first-wave feminism that denounces women's
financial dependence upon men (the 'sexuo-economic relation'). A
decade later, however, the market for Gilman's writing had lessened.
She refused to cater to publishers and editors or to submit work
to journals run by publishing mogul William Randolph Hearst,
who had sensationalized her separation and divorce from Charles
Walter Stetson. A woman of action, Gilman devised a solution to this
dilemma; as she notes in her autobiography, *The Living of Charlotte
Perkins Gilman* (1935): '"If the editors and publishers will not bring
out my work, I will!" And I did'. In 1909 Gilman founded a monthly
magazine, *Forerunner* (1909–16), to showcase her feminism and
socialism. The 14 stories in this collection appeared in the first
volume of *Forerunner* (November 1909–December 1910).

Gilman is not unique in launching a journal to publish her
work. Charles Dickens, whom she greatly admired, started

Household Words (1850–59) to bring out his serial fiction alongside that of other authors (for example Elizabeth Gaskell and Wilkie Collins). However, Gilman singlehandedly wrote and published every feature of her magazine. Over a seven-year period she filled the issues of *Forerunner* with her poems, editorials, allegories, book reviews, sermons, advertisements and articles on current events. Each issue also contains serial instalments of her theoretical works and novels, as well as short stories to promote what she calls a more 'human world'.

These short stories demonstrate Gilman's unfailing commitment to write with a purpose. In 1896 she told a reporter for the *Topeka State Journal* that her first book of poems, *In This Our World* (1893), was 'a tool box. It was written to drive nails with'. This same metaphor applies to Gilman's *Forerunner* fiction, designed to dismantle patriarchy and improve society. Indeed, in an undated paper from her collected 'Thoughts & Figgerings', Gilman ponders:

> If I can learn to write great stories, it will be a powerful addition to my armory.

To reach a wide audience, she filled her 'armory' with poetry, nonfiction and short stories to emancipate women from the home, freeing them to contribute to the 'world's work'. Such messages were the driving force behind her writing, as critics have acknowledged. 'Gilman gave little attention to her writing as literature, and neither will the reader,' notes Ann J. Lane in her introduction to *The Charlotte Perkins Gilman Reader* (1980).

There are exceptions, however. Gilman's best-known and oft reprinted 'The Yellow Wall-Paper' (1892) has real literary merit. Its denouement is also richly ambiguous, unlike much of her short fiction with pat endings. Critics including Gary Scharnhorst and Lane praise Gilman for her skill in dialogue. Also worthy of note are her older women characters who are resilient, capable and wise. Nevertheless, Gilman wrote much of her fiction hastily to make a deadline, sacrificing artistry to nail a point. Although the writing in her short fiction may seem uneven, these stories reflect her mission to convey 'important truths, needed yet unpopular', as she expresses in her autobiography.

Gilman's 'Mixed Legacy'

Some of Gilman's 'truths' come off as heavy-handed. Worse, her dreams for a better world do not include racial and ethnic minorities, immigrants or the working classes. Gilman focused her agenda on improving the lives of white middle- and upper-class women. Her repugnant nativist views about race, social class, ethnicity and anti-Semitism rear their ugly heads in these stories and will rightly offend readers today. In 'Three Thanksgivings', old Sally, 'a colored lady', cheerfully serves Mrs. Morrison and the white ladies at the women's club. In 'Making a Living', Arnold Blake hires 'an Italian from Tuscany' and 'other sturdy Italians' to build his mill. In 'Boys and the Butter', missionaries travel 'to those dark lands where the heathen go naked, worship idols and throw their children to the crocodiles'. 'Solomon' sounds like a Jewish name in 'According to Solomon', and Mrs. Grey in 'A Word in Season' is described as being 'as rich as a Jew! ...And never spendin' a cent!'. Gilman also stigmatizes physical difference, referring to Mrs. Joyce in 'Martha's Mother' as 'a cripple'.

These prejudices, evident in the work of other Anglo-American writers of her time, lessen our appreciation of Gilman as a feminist visionary. Hers is a 'mixed legacy' – the subject of a book entitled *The Mixed Legacy of Charlotte Perkins Gilman* (2000), edited by Catherine J. Golden and Joanna Schneider Zangrando – and we must approach her oeuvre critically. Radical in her time, Gilman nonetheless remains an influential figure in the history of feminism because she foregrounded previously invisible forms of gender oppression. These *Forerunner* stories offer solutions to problems easily achieved when women and men work together, support each other and use their initiative. They preview Gilman's enlightened feminist and civic agendas, including kitchenless apartments, housekeeping services, public safety, dress reform, responsible journalism and economic independence for women – all ideas she developed in her fiction and nonfiction published before and after them.

The Progressive Era in America

Gilman published *Forerunner* during the Progressive Era in US history (1890–1920). The Gilded Age (*c.* 1877–96), a period of rebuilding following the Civil War, witnessed excessive materialism, corporate growth and wealth for a distinct elite. The Progressive Era, in contrast, aimed to improve the lives of the rapidly growing US population, not just a privileged few. As Judith A. Allen describes in *The Feminism of Charlotte Perkins Gilman* (2009), on

> the lecture circuit, and as an editor, journalist, and publisher, she [Gilman] addressed sex parasitism, "masculism", sexual economics, birth control, eugenics, motherhood, pacifism, food adulteration, humanism and Progressivism itself.

Although Gilman's vision for a more 'human world' was narrower than that of many progressives, it does match the tenor of an era known for vast legislative and social reforms.

Some reforms arose from tragedies in American sweatshops, where workers laboured long hours in overcrowded factories with poor ventilation, inferior lighting and extreme temperatures. Notorious among them is the Triangle Shirtwaist Factory fire of 1911, which led to the deaths of 146 people, many of them young immigrant women, trapped in a burning building that was locked to guard against theft. From this disaster grew a commission to investigate the fire, leading to sweeping changes in New York City (for example fire safety codes and child labour laws) to improve workers' health and safety.

Upton Sinclair's *The Jungle* (1906) proved instrumental to reforming the food industry. Sinclair, a muckraker who began his career investigating labour conditions in Chicago, exposed the unsafe working conditions and unsanitary practices in meat packing factories. His novel sparked public outcry, and an investigation was launched by President Theodore Roosevelt. The result was the passing in 1906 of two pieces of legislation, the Meat Inspection Act and the Pure Food and Drug Act. Gilman supported the latter in the *Woman's Journal* of 1904.

This transitional time in American history also witnessed a widening of the domestic sphere and greater equality between the sexes. Jane Addams, a leading progressive, established Hull House (1889) in Chicago to provide childcare, a community kitchen, a gymnasium and education for the urban poor. Proponents for women's suffrage, including Elizabeth Cady Stanton, Susan B. Anthony and Carrie Chapman Catt, pushed for women's right to vote in US elections, resulting in the Nineteenth Amendment, ratified in 1920. Gilman met both Addams and Stanton when she organized the Woman's Congress in 1895. Addams asked Gilman to visit Hull House, which inspired her utopian writings. Of these, *Herland* (1915), which describes an idyllic society inhabited only by women, is her best known. Stanton invited Gilman to attend the 1896 Women's Suffrage Convention held in Washington, D.C., where she spoke in favour of suffrage to the House Judiciary Committee.

The onset of the First World War saw the decline of the Progressive Era. Nonetheless, the liberal legislation enacted during this period and the social reforms that Gilman supported continued to shape US society.

Gilman's Life up to 1909

When Gilman launched *Forerunner*, she had already been married to Providence artist Charles Walter Stetson (1884), become a mother (1885), separated from Stetson (1888), divorced him (1894) and married her first cousin, George Houghton Gilman (1900). The birth of her only child, Katharine, born ten months after her marriage to Stetson, triggered a debilitating breakdown. An enforced rest cure at the Philadelphia sanitarium of leading nerve specialist Dr. S. Weir Mitchell – whose parting advice, as noted in Gilman's autobiography, was to 'never touch pen, brush or pencil as long as you live' – stirred Gilman to write her autobiographical story 'The Yellow Wall-Paper' (1892), a searing indictment of Mitchell. The nameless narrator of 'The Yellow Wall-Paper', a young wife and mother undergoing a rest cure administered by her husband/physician in a rented country mansion, stays in a former nursery with noxious yellow patterned wallpaper; this at first disgusts and then fascinates her. In the denouement, the narrator rips the wallpaper, allegedly to free a woman trapped behind its pattern (arguably the narrator's double), and crawls over her husband, who faints upon seeing her. Critics have endlessly debated the story's ending. In the 'Afterword' to the 1973 Feminist Press edition, Elaine Hedges argues that the narrator 'has been defeated. She is totally mad'. In contrast Sandra Gilbert and Susan Gubar claim in *The Madwoman in the Attic* (1979) that 'the narrator has enabled this double to escape from her textual/architectural confinement' and that Dr John 'has been temporarily defeated, or at least momentarily stunned'. Stetson, a loving but extremely traditional husband, is the presumed model for Dr. John.

Divorce from Stetson freed Gilman to establish herself as a leading feminist thinker, although she repudiated the term 'feminist', coined in the London *Athenaeum* book review in 1891. Gilman considered herself a 'humanist' whose mission was to promote gender equality. She did not at first plan to remarry, but she went on to wed Houghton, a patent attorney, on the condition that she continue her mission to make a better world. Like activists Stanton and Catt, Gilman this time balanced marriage with a full career of writing and speaking engagements. Houghton, Gilman's unfailing advocate, assisted her research, read her work and attended her lectures. He is arguably the model for the enlightened men who populate her *Forerunner* fiction. Charlton, the name of Gilman's publishing company, fittingly combines their two first names: Charlotte and Houghton.

Gilman brought editorial and writing experience to *Forerunner*, published by the Charlton Company. In 1894 she served as editor, manager and writer for *Impress*, the voice of the Pacific Coast Women's Press Association (PCWPA) based in San Francisco, CA. Hoping to turn *Impress* into 'a good family weekly', as she calls it in her autobiography, Gilman wrote an inventive 'Studies in Style' column. In this she imitated writing by noted authors (for example, Charles Dickens, Mark Twain and George Eliot) to expand her readers' appreciation of literature. The *Impress* was short-lived, however, because the PCPWA was unable to 'surmount the liability of Stetson's [Gilman's] local reputation as a divorced woman and "unnatural mother"', as Scharnhorst notes in *Charlotte Perkins Gilman* (1985). Following her divorce, Gilman had given custody of her then nine-year-old daughter to Stetson, who married Gilman's close friend Grace Ellery Channing. Forward thinking, Gilman considered Grace her co-mother, but she faced harsh criticism for being both a divorcée and an 'unnatural mother', a title she used for a short story. Ever resilient, Gilman left San Francisco and over the next years travelled widely on the lecture circuit, aiming to broaden her audience.

Gilman's position as assistant editor of *Woman's Journal*, the mouthpiece for the National American Woman Suffrage Association, also prepared her for the launch of *Forerunner*. In 1904 Gilman (together with Florence Adkinson and Catharine Wilde) assumed the post of assistant editor of the influential Boston-based woman suffrage magazine founded by Lucy Stone, a leading suffragist and abolitionist. For an entire year Gilman published without pay a weekly column called 'Vital Issues', in which she presented enlightened views on work, the home, childcare, Santa Claus, cremation, maiden names, clean air and water and suffrage.

Forerunner : Importance and Features

In her introduction to the 1968 Greenwood Press republication of the complete *Forerunner*, Madeleine B. Stern notes that in 1909:

> There was no magazine… that combined, as *The Forerunner* would combine, a crusade for women's rights and a plea for socialism.

She aptly calls *Forerunner* a 'literary *tour de force*' and describes it as Gilman's 'greatest single achievement– … It was, in essence, Charlotte Perkins Gilman's Magazine'.

Forerunner ran for seven years and two months. There are 86 monthly issues, initially of 32 pages but then reduced to 28 pages of solid text, beginning in the fourth issue. Scharnhorst notes in *Charlotte Perkins Gilman* (1985) that through *Forerunner* Gilman published 'the equivalent of twenty-eight books'. She published *Forerunner* for a dime an issue or $1.00 for a year's subscription. The magazine's approximately 1,500 subscribers, mainly women, came from across England, Europe and the United States, as well as from Australia and India.

However, the journal's income amounted to only about half of the $3,000 required to produce it. Money problems plagued Gilman her entire life – she and Houghton heavily subsidized *Forerunner* – so Gilman lectured and wrote more in order to make ends meet. She singlehandedly wrote, edited and published *Forerunner*, even writing advertisements for the first issues. In the inaugural issue, she opens with 'Then This', a poem that boldly lambastes 'yellow journalism': 'The news-stands bloom with magazines,/ They flame, they blaze indeed', Gilman proclaims. The initial four lines of the second stanza, in contrast, lay out the mission for her own magazine:

> *Then This: It strives in prose and verse,*
> *Thought, fancy, fact and fun,*
> *To tell the things we ought to know,*
> *To point the way we ought to go.*

Forerunner would indeed 'point the way' that Gilman believed the world 'ought to go'.

This first issue contains 'Three Thanksgivings', a story about a resilient older woman's efforts to support herself; 'How Doth the Hat', a poem lambasting women's taste for enormous hats 'of repugnant shapes!' decorated with bird 'corpses'; the first instalment of *What Diantha Did*, a novel about the resourceful Diantha Bell, who leaves her home and fiancé to launch a professional housekeeping business; the first instalment of *Our Androcentric Culture, or The Man-Made World,* a theoretical treatise arguing that androcentric societies disenfranchise men, women and humanity; and an advertisement for Lowney's chocolates, guaranteeing 'all the Lowney preparations are pure and honest and perfectly reliable'. This issue contains Gilman's advertisements for other products she personally endorsed – Fels-Naptha Soap, Holeproof Hosiery and Moore's Fountain Pen.

Looking across the issues collectively, *Forerunner* – through poetry, fiction and nonfiction – presents Gilman's seemingly tireless commitment to end prostitution, venereal disease, child labour and war alongside her vision for public safety, enhanced sanitation, suffrage, dress reform, housekeeping services and much more. However, by 1916 Gilman could no longer afford to subsidize *Forerunner* and closed the journal. She believed that she had no more to say. In addition, Gilman recognized the US, poised to enter the First World War, was no longer as committed to progressive reform nor as willing to listen to what she had to say.

Forerunner Stories in Context of Gilman's Oeuvre

As Denise D. Knight notes in *Charlotte Perkins Gilman: A Study of the Short Fiction* (1997):

The subjects depicted in Gilman's fiction were the same as those addressed in her essays and lectures – the move toward economic independence for women, the benefits of professional housekeeping, the need for expert child care, the advantages of dress reform, the practical necessity of the kitchenless home, the pervasiveness of yellow journalism, the problem of nonegalitarian marriages.

Grouping the stories according to such themes highlights Gilman's feminist, civic-minded and socialist agendas. Although some stories read as feminist fantasies, and many are dogmatic in tone, all express Gilman's desire to re-educate her readers and improve her – and their – world.

Feminist Fantasy and Restorative Justice

'When I Was a Witch' – the story from which this collection takes its title – cleverly combines fantasy, utopianism, retributive justice and a humanitarian agenda to improve daily living for animals and humans. The unnamed narrator of 'When I Was a Witch' receives a witch's powers on Hallowe'en eve. For several days, many of her wishes come true. Public transportation improves; streetcar drivers stop being rude; boards of directors make beneficial changes to their companies; preachers tell the truth, leading to packed churches; and newspapers adopt color coding to highlight sensationalism and lying. Some wishes function as a punishment to fit the crime: a horse-and-cab driver who cruelly whips his horse, for example, feels the pain intended for the horse.

There is a limit to the narrator's magic when it comes to wishing that women stop being 'blind, chained, untaught, in a treadmill', obliged to do 'the work of servants without even a servant's pay'. The narrator rationalizes this by noting that her wish for women is not granted because it is a positive wish ('white' magic), while those granted serve to harm ('black magic'), even if they may seem justified. But progressive changes do occur in this *Forerunner* story, demonstrating Gilman's belief that institutions can change for the better. In this respect, 'When I Was a Witch' allows us to glimpse the idealism Gilman presents in her three utopian novels including *Herland*, issued in *Forerunner* in 1915.

Stories of Social Consciousness and Children's Rights

Gilman's belief in social justice carries into two other stories in the collection, 'The Boys and the Butter' and 'An Offender'. Disagreeable Miss Jane McCoy in 'The Boys and the Butter' promises her great-nephews, Holdfast and J. Edwards Fernald, a reward of $50 each if they forgo eating butter for an entire year. Miss McCoy reasons that butter is 'Bad for the blood' – is Gilman anticipating current medical knowledge about high cholesterol? – and claims that 'self-denial is good for children'. But deception is not good for children, the point of Gilman's story. When the year of deprivation for the 'butterless boys' finally ends, Miss McCoy does not quite uphold her bargain:

she purchases each great-nephew a $50 life membership to the Missionary Society. The boys are downcast until word gets out about the deception, whereupon the ethical Missionary Society returns the boys their promised 'untold wealth'.

Another story of social consciousness, 'An Offender' does not end happily. Mr. Cortland, president of a streetcar company, is visiting his divorced wife Mary, after an estrangement of seven years. Hoping to reunite with her and their son, Harry, he professes to be 'an older man – and I think wiser', but Mary is uncertain. Cortland had voted against allocating funds for fenders, a much-needed safety feature for streetcars to protect children, who are regularly killed by 'those cars going up and down like roaring lions'. The story ends with a young boy being crushed by 'the great car holding him down like a mouse in a trap' outside their apartment window. Mary Cortland declares, '"your cars commit murder! Child murder!"', and vows never to see Cortland again. As in 'The Boys and the Butter', concern for children's rights and safety lies at the heart of this story.

Stories of Economic Independence for Women

'Three Thanksgivings', 'According to Solomon' and 'Martha's Mother' all present older female characters whose resilience enables them to overcome obstacles and achieve economic independence for themselves and their families. In 'Three Thanksgivings' Delia Morrison, a widow with two adult children, launches a women's club to gain independence. Her son and daughter urge Delia to leave her home and move in with one of them, but visits to her son on the first Thanksgiving and her daughter on the second confirm her commitment to remain self-sufficient. A manipulative former suitor named Mr. Peter Butts assumes Delia's mortgage and pressures her to marry him:

> 'I've always wanted you – and I've always wanted this house, too.'

Undaunted, Delia finds a solution by turning her spacious home into a Saturday women's club. With wise management and a growing number of paying members, she repays her mortgage, frees herself from Mr. Butts and invites her children and their families to spend the third Thanksgiving in her home.

Much as in 'Three Thanksgivings', Gilman uses a holiday as a plot device to structure 'According to Solomon'. Sombre, proverb-spouting Solomon Bankside wonders why he wed Mary, a woman with a 'spirit of incorrigible independence, and a light-mindedness which... he could almost term irreligious'. Gift giving each Christmas brings out their differences. Solomon buys Mary one expensive item when she prefers small presents; her allowance is too meagre to buy much for her husband, family and friends. However, a friend's gift of a loom changes Mary's life for the better. She becomes a talented entrepreneur, taking orders for initialled towels and accepting a commission to make woven belts for a large department store. The following Christmas Mary showers her family with presents bought from money earned by her craft. At first Solomon considers his wife's earning to be '"certainly a most mortifying and painful thing to me – most unprecedented"'. In time, however, he gets 'used to it' and finally 'became proud of it'.

In 'Martha's Mother' Mrs. Joyce, a widow with a disability, thrives when asked to manage a house for union workers. A bifurcated story, 'Martha's Mother' begins with the plight of Martha Joyce, a stenographer and typist living in a small, cold, cramped boarding house; she is also preyed upon by one of her bosses, Mr. Bassett. The focus then shifts to Mrs. Joyce, a once vigorous farmer's wife, now widowed and no longer able bodied: she is reliant on crutches and, as she explains, "'dependent on my sister and children! It galls me terribly!'". Like 'Three Thanksgivings', this story conveys Gilman's enduring commitment to labour unions and women's clubs, where she often lectured. In 'Martha's Mother' the Girls' Trade Union Association asks Mrs. Joyce – who previously managed a hotel and her husband's farm – to run a boarding house for union members including her daughter Martha. "'I guess I can make a livin''", Mrs. Joyce rejoices. And so she does: even better, she protects the working women from unwanted predators. When Mr. Bassett calls again on Martha Joyce, Mrs. Joyce 'blocked his path'.

Women and Economics underpins all three stories about economic independence for women. In her landmark treatise, Gilman deplores what she calls the 'sexuo-economic relation' wherein women are dependent upon men for their very survival. As Gilman notes *in Women and Economics*, when 'the mate becomes also the master' a woman loses her autonomy – something that Delia Morrison, Mrs. Bankside and Mrs. Joyce regain by earning their own livelihood. Despite their differences in marital status and ability, all three heroines, as in many Gilman stories, achieve a happy ending.

Stories of Women Empowering Women

The narrator of 'A Coincidence' is an unnamed older woman who proclaims 'I love problems, human problems'. She solves the difficulties of a widow named Emma Ordway, preyed upon by gluttonous Mirabella Vlack, who comes for a visit and remains for five years. Mirabella, overcome by indigestion on an afternoon outing, is advised by the narrator and a sage woman doctor to stop at her sister's home close by (where she previously lived), 'and in five minutes we had her in bed in what used to be her room'. With the 'Incubus' removed, Emma Ordway regains her health, takes control of her life and begins to travel. The narrator in 'A Coincidence' thus resembles Gilman's older, wiser Mrs. Joyce at the end of 'Martha's Mother'. She also anticipates the unnamed older woman narrator who saves a fellow female train traveller from ruin in 'The Girl in the Pink Hat' (1916), as well as Mary Yale, an older, wealthy woman in *Mag-Marjorie* (1912) who helps a 16-year-old maid move beyond an unfortunate experience and become a successful doctor.

'A Word in Season' introduces a disagreeable older woman akin to 'A Coincidence's' Mirabella Vlack. Wealthy Mrs. Grey lives off her son and his family. Dozing fitfully one day, she eavesdrops on the goings-on of the household and hears 'no good of herself' from the servants, her kind daughter-in-law's sister and even her dearly loved granddaughter, who proclaims "'Grandma spoils everything'". Mrs. Grey, a healthy 65-year-old, becomes 'angry, but impressed' and vows to make a change. On Christmas morning she leaves notes and much-needed presents for her family and sets off on a year-long world tour. The empowered travelling widows of 'A Word in Season' and 'A Coincidence' anticipate the happy fate of the independent-minded widow Mrs. McPherson in 'The Widow's Might' (1911), another *Forerunner* story from Gilman's 'tool box'.

'Mr. Robert Grey, Sr.' takes a different approach to empowerment: a young woman resists pressures to marry and instead rescues herself. The heroine Jenny and her family experience a run of misfortunes straight out of the Book of Job. When her beloved, Jimmy Young, seemingly disappears at sea, Jenny finds herself pursued by Mr. Robert Grey Sr., a lecherous old widower who has harassed her since childhood. Mr. Grey offers powerful bribes, proposing financial support for her family if she marries him, but resilient Jenny holds firm despite her parents' wishes. She grows a garden, sells her produce and keeps her family afloat until Jimmy miraculously returns to marry her. This story has Gilman's preferred happy ending although for readers today the marriage plot undercuts the autonomy that Jenny has achieved.

Stories of the 'New Woman' and the 'New Man'

In contrast to Gilman's stories where a young mother cannot cope with the demands of home and motherhood – 'The Yellow Wall-Paper' (1892) and 'Making a Change' (1911) *par excellence* – in 'My Astonishing Dodo' she creates a 'New Woman', an independent woman who breaks with traditional domesticity to pursue education and a career. Astonishing Dorothy (Dodo) Howland professionalizes housekeeping for her family of seven in the fashion of Diantha Bell in *What Diantha Did*. She views motherhood and household management as a career path, advising her husband Morton to 'leave the housekeeping business to me'. Introducing ideas from Gilman's nonfiction 'armory', *The Home: Its Work and Influence* (1903) and *Concerning Children* (1900), Dodo takes lessons in 'child culture' and 'domestic economy'. She gains skills in child rearing and running an efficient home, even personally training a paid domestic to help with the housework.

'A Middle-Sized Artist' features another 'New Woman' who challenges notions of traditional femininity in a different way. Rosamond, an educated, independent career woman, vows to become an illustrator after the fashion of John Tenniel for Lewis Carroll's *Alice in Wonderland* (1865). At 21 she falls in love with Mr. Allen G. Goddard, an aspiring writer at her father's publishing house, who calls her a 'selfish heartless creature' when she declines his marriage proposal. Gilman delays the marriage to allow her heroine to develop a profession. Studying art in Paris, Rosamond becomes an accomplished artist. On returning home, she accepts a commission to illustrate a book that we later learn Goddard wrote about Rosamond.

'A Middle-Sized Artist' story concludes happily with Allen Goddard declaring Rosamond an '"immeasurably clever darling'". The Howland family thrives because of Dodo's efficiency and Mr. Morton Howland is enormously proud of her, but neither Goddard nor Howland is a 'New Man' as we witness in three stories in this collection: 'Making a Living', 'Her Housekeeper' and 'The Cottagette'. Gilman was keenly aware that a 'New Woman' needed an enlightened 'New Man' – one willing to forsake traditional male roles, demonstrate sensitivity and at times assume domestic responsibilities. In 'Making a Living', Arnold Blake loves poetry and studies agriculture. He refuses to enter his father's business as his traditional younger brother has done, moving instead to a summer home on land belonging to his beloved late mother. Choosing a simple lifestyle, Arnold turns the fine chestnut trees on his land into a nourishing product called Hill Mill Meal, which he then successfully markets with his own rhyming advertisements. Anticipating today's green movement, Arnold preserves a good portion of the land, rather than expand to become 'a Millionaire'. He also earns the love of Ella Sutherland, who chooses this sensitive 'New Man' over his conventional brother.

'Her Housekeeper' tells the story of young, widowed Mrs. Leland, an attractive actress living comfortably with her son in a boarding house. Mrs. Leland loves acting and hates housekeeping. The more interesting character, though, is Arthur Olmstead, her admirer and fellow boarding house resident; he invites her to tea and earns her trust and friendship. Meeting her every objection to his marriage proposal (for example, he wants her to keep on acting and not to keep house), Arthur admits that he is in the boarding house business; for the past three years he has made changes in the cooking, housekeeping and accommodations to please Mrs. Leland's taste. To Mrs. Leland, running a boarding house "'seems such a funny business – for a man'", but Arthur runs them as efficiently as Diantha Bell. The story ends with the actress, now remarried, proclaiming she never dreamed marriage could be 'like this'.

'Was there ever a man like this?' Gilman concludes 'The Cottagette', a better-known story that features another quintessential new man. In it Ford Mathews, an aspiring writer, courts an artist named Malda. She rents a small kitchenless cottage with her older friend Lois, taking meals at the nearby boarding house and devoting her days to embroidery and drawing. When Lois realizes Malda loves Ford, she unwisely advises putting a kitchen onto their cottage since men prize domesticity. Malda's bliss quickly becomes ruined by 'the call of the kitchen'. Gilman solves the problem by Mathews revealing that he is a professional cook; he will marry Malda on the condition that she return to her art and give up cooking. Ford Mathews the cook, Arnold Blake the eco-conscious poet and Arthur Olmstead the professional house manager: these three characters collectively demonstrate qualities of the 'New Man'.

Gilman wrote these *Forerunner* stories when women did not have the vote and domesticity was sacrosanct. Today, many women have been freed from the drudgery of housework. Gilman, who found real comfort in a woman doctor, would be pleased by the number of women in medicine and other previously male-dominated professions.

Some of her enlightened men anticipate today's 'house husbands' whose wives contribute to the 'world's work'. In our ageist society we still need Gilman's inspiring older women characters who open women's clubs, run boarding houses, leave undeserving men and develop their talents. Gender inequalities have also survived. Gilman's vision as a feminist thinker and social reformer – influential to her time – is still unrealized today.

Dr. Catherine J. Golden

Further Reading

Allen, Judith A., *The Feminism of Charlotte Perkins Gilman* (University of Chicago Press, 2009)

Bergman, Jill, ed., *Charlotte Perkins Gilman and a Woman's Place in America* (University of Alabama Press, 2017)

Degler, Carl N., 'Introduction', in Charlotte Perkins Gilman, *Women and Economics* (Harper & Row, 1966), vi–xxxv

Gilbert, Sandra and Susan Gubar, *The Madwoman in the Attic* (Yale University Press, 1979)

Gilman, Charlotte Perkins, *The Living of Charlotte Perkins Gilman: An Autobiography* (Appleton-Century, 1935; reprinted by University of Wisconsin Press, 1990)

Gilman, Charlotte Perkins, 'Thoughts & Figgerings', Folder 16 (1883–1918), Schlesinger Library

Gilman, Charlotte Perkins, *Topeka State Journal*, vol. 7 (15 June 1896)

Golden, Catherine J., ed., *Charlotte Perkins Gilman's The Yellow Wall-Paper: A Sourcebook and Critical Edition* (Routledge, 2004)

Golden, Catherine J. and Joanna Schneider Zangrando, *The Mixed Legacy of Charlotte Perkins Gilman* (University of Delaware Press, 2000)

Hedges, Elaine R., 'Afterword', in Charlotte Perkins Gilman, *The Yellow Wallpaper* (Feminist Press, 1973), 37–62

Knight, Denise D., *Charlotte Perkins Gilman: A Study of the Short Fiction* (Twayne, 1997)

Knight, Denise D., ed., *The Diaries of Charlotte Perkins Gilman*, 2 vols (University of Virginia Press, 1994)

Knight, Denise D. and Jennifer S. Tuttle, eds, *The Select Letters of Charlotte Perkins Gilman* (University of Alabama Press, 2009).

Lane, Ann J., 'Introduction', *Charlotte Perkins Gilman Reader* (Pantheon, 1980)

Rudd, Jill and Val Gough, eds, *Charlotte Perkins Gilman: Optimist Reformer* (University of Iowa Press, 1999)

Scharnhorst, Gary, *Charlotte Perkins Gilman* (Twayne, 1985)

Scharnhorst, Gary, *Charlotte Perkins Gilman: A Bibliography* (Scarecrow Press, 1985)

Stern, Madeleine, 'Introduction', *Forerunner*, vols 1–7 (1909–16) (Greenwood, 1968), v–xii

Tuttle, Jennifer S. and Carol Farley Kessler, eds, *Charlotte Perkins Gilman: New Texts, New Contexts* (Ohio State University Press, 2011)

When I Was a Witch
& Other Stories

Charlotte Perkins Gilman

According to Solomon

"**He that rebuketh** a man afterwards shall find more favor than he that flattereth with his tongue,'" said Mr. Solomon Bankside to his wife Mary.

"Its the other way with a woman, I think;" she answered him, "you might put that in."

"Tut, tut, Molly," said he; "'Add not unto his words,' – do not speak lightly of the wisdom of the great king."

"I don't mean to, dear, but – when you hear it all the time—"

"'He that turneth away his ear from the law, even his prayer shall be an abomination,'" answered Mr. Bankside.

"I believe you know every one of those old Proverbs by heart," said his wife with some heat. "Now that's not disrespectful! – they *are* old! – and I do wish you'd forget some of them!"

He smiled at her quizzically, tossing back his heavy silver-gray hair with the gesture she had always loved. His eyes were deep blue and bright under their bushy brows; and the mouth was kind – in its iron way. "I can think of at least three to squelch you with, Molly," said he, "but I won't."

"O I know the one you want! 'A continual dropping in a very rainy day and a contentions woman are alike!' I'm *not* contentious, Solomon!"

"No, you are not," he frankly admitted. "What I really had in mind was this – 'A prudent wife is from the Lord,' and 'He that findeth a wife findeth a good thing; and obtaineth favor of the Lord.'"

She ran around the table in the impulsive way years did not alter, and kissed him warmly.

"I'm not scolding you, my dear," he continued: "but if you had all the money you'd like to give away – there wouldn't be much left!"

"But look at what you spend on me!" she urged.

"That's a wise investment – as well as a deserved reward," her husband answered calmly. "'There is that scattereth and yet increaseth,' you know, my dear; 'And there is that withholdeth more than is meet – and it tendeth to poverty!' Take all you get my dear – its none too good for you."

He gave her his goodby kiss with special fondness, put on his heavy satin-lined overcoat and went to the office.

Mr. Solomon Bankside was not a Jew; though his last name suggested and his first seemed to prove it; also his proficiency in the Old Testament gave color to the idea. No, he came from Vermont; of generations of unbroken New England and old English Puritan ancestry, where the Solomons and Isaacs and Zedekiahs were only mitigated by the Standfasts and Praise-the-Lords. Pious, persistent pigheaded folk were they, down all the line.

His wife had no such simple pedigree. A streak of Huguenot blood she had (some of the best in France, though neither of them knew that), a grandmother from Albany with a Van to her name; a great grandmother with a Mac; and another with an O'; even a German cross came in somewhere. Mr. Bankside was devoted to genealogy, and had been at some pains to dig up these facts – the more he found the worse he felt, and the lower ran his opinion of Mrs. Bankside's ancestry.

She had been a fascinating girl; pretty, with the dash and piquancy of an oriole in a May apple-tree; clever and efficient in everything her swift hands touched; quite a spectacular housekeeper; and the sober, long-faced young downeasterner had married her with a sudden decision that he often wondered about in later years. So did she.

What he had not sufficiently weighed at the time, was her spirit of incorrigible independence, and a light-mindedness which, on maturer judgment, he could almost term irreligious. His conduct was based on principle, all of it; built firmly into habit and buttressed by scriptural quotations. Hers seemed to him as inconsequent as the flight of a moth. Studying it, in his solemn conscientious way, in the light of his genealogical researches, he felt that all her uncertainties were accounted for, and that the error was his – in having married too many kinds of people at once.

They had been, and were, very happy together none the less: though sometimes their happiness was a little tottery. This was one of the times. It was the day after Christmas, and Mrs. Bankside entered the big drawing room, redolent of popcorn and evergreen, and walked slowly to the corner where the fruits of yesterday were lovingly arranged; so few that she had been able to give – so many that she had received.

There were the numerous pretty interchangeable things given her by her many friends; "presents," suitable to any lady. There were the few perfectly selected ones given by the few who knew her best. There was the rather perplexing gift of Mrs. MacAvelly. There was her brother's stiff white envelope enclosing a check. There were the loving gifts of children and grand-children.

Finally there was Solomon's.

It was his custom to bestow upon her one solemn and expensive object, a boon as it were, carefully selected, after much thought and balancing of merits; but the consideration was spent on the nature of the gift – not on the desires of the recipient. There was the piano she could not play, the statue she did not admire, the set of Dante she never read, the heavy gold bracelet, the stiff diamond brooch – and all the others. This time it was a set of sables, costing even more than she imagined.

Christmas after Christmas had these things come to her; and she stood there now, thinking of that procession of unvalued valuables, with an expression so mixed and changeful it resembled a kaleidoscope. Love for Solomon, pride in Solomon, respect for Solomon's judgment and power to pay, gratitude for his unfailing kindness and generosity, impatience with his always giving her this one big valuable permanent thing, when he knew so well that she much preferred small renewable cheap ones; her personal dislike of furs, the painful conviction that brown was not becoming to her – all these and more filled the little woman with what used to be called "conflicting emotions."

She smoothed out her brother's check, wishing as she always did that it had come before Christmas, so that she might buy more presents for her beloved people. Solomon liked to spend money on her – in his own way; but he did not like to have her spend money on him – or on anyone for that matter. She had asked her brother once, if he would mind sending her his Christmas present beforehand.

"Not on your life, Polly!" he said. "You'd never see a cent of it! You can't buy 'em many things right on top of Christmas, and it'll be gone long before the next one."

She put the check away and turned to examine her queerest gift. Upon which scrutiny presently entered the donor.

"I'm ever so much obliged, Benigna," said Mrs. Bankside. "You know how I love to do things. It's a loom, isn't it? Can you show me how it works?"

"Of course I can, my dear; that's just what I ran in for – I was afraid you wouldn't know. But you are so clever with your hands that I'm sure you'll enjoy it. I do."

Whereat Mrs. MacAvelly taught Mrs. Bankside the time-honored art of weaving. And Mrs. Bankside enjoyed it more than any previous handicraft she had essayed.

She did it well, beginning with rather coarse and simple weaves; and gradually learning the finer grades of work. Despising as she did the more modern woolens, she bought real wool yarn of a lovely red – and made some light warm flannelly stuff in which she proceeded to rapturously enclose her little grandchildren.

Mr. Bankside warmly approved, murmuring affectionately, "'She seeketh wool and flax – she worketh willingly with her hands.'"

He watched little Bob and Polly strenuously "helping" the furnace man to clear the sidewalk, hopping about like red-birds in their new caps and coats; and his face beamed with the appositeness of his quotation, as he remarked, "She is not afraid of the snow for her household, for all her household are clothed with scarlet!" and he proffered an extra, wholly spontaneous kiss, which pleased her mightily.

"You dear man!" she said with a hug; "I believe you'd rather find a proverb to fit than a gold mine!"

To which he triumphantly responded: "'Wisdom is better than rubies; and all the things that may be desired are not to be compared to it.'"

She laughed sweetly at him. "And do you think wisdom stopped with that string of proverbs?"

"You can't get much beyond it," he answered calmly. "If we lived up to all there is in that list we shouldn't be far out, my dear!"

Whereat she laughed again smoothed his gray mane, and kissed him in the back of his neck. "You *dear* thing!" said Mrs. Bankside.

She kept herself busy with the new plaything as he called it. Hands that had been rather empty were now smoothly full. Her health was better, and any hint of occasional querulousness disappeared entirely; so that her husband was moved to fresh admiration of her sunny temper, and quoted for the hundredth time, "'She openeth her mouth with wisdom, and in her tongue is the law of kindness.'"

Mrs. MacAvelly taught her to make towels. But Mrs. Bankside's skill outstripped hers; she showed inventive genius and designed patterns of her own. The fineness and quality of the work increased; and she joyfully replenished her linen chest with her own handiwork.

"I tell you, my dear," said Mrs. MacAvelly, "if you'd be willing to sell them you could get almost any price for those towels. With the initials woven in. I know I could get you orders – through the Woman's Exchange, you know!"

Mrs. Bankside was delighted. "What fun!" she said. "And I needn't appear at all?"

"No, you needn't appear at all – do let me try."

So Mrs. Bankside made towels of price, soft, fine, and splendid, till she was weary of them; and in the opulence of constructive genius fell to devising woven belts of elaborate design.

These were admired excessively. All her women friends wanted one, or more; the Exchange got hold of it, there was a distinct demand; and finally Mrs. MacAvelly came in one day with a very important air and a special order.

"I don't know what you'll think, my dear," she said, "but I happen to know the Percy's very well – the big store people, you know; and Mr. Percy was talking about those belts of yours to me; – of course he didn't know they are yours; but he said (the Exchange people told him I knew, you see) he said, 'If you can place an order with that woman, I can take all she'll make and pay her full price for them. Is she poor?' he asked. 'Is she dependent on her work?' And I told him, 'Not altogether.' And I think he thinks it an interesting case! Anyhow, there's the order. Will you do it?'

Mrs. Bankside was much excited. She wanted to very much, but dreaded offending her husband. So far she had not told him of her quiet trade in towels; but hid and saved this precious money – the first she had ever earned.

The two friends discussed the pros and cons at considerable length; and finally with some perturbation, she decided to accept the order.

"You'll never tell, Benigna!" she urged. "Solomon would never forgive me, I'm afraid."

"Why of course I won't – you needn't have a moment's fear of it. You give them to me – I'll stop with the carriage you see; and I take them to the Exchange – and he gets them from there."

"It seems like smuggling!" said Mrs. Bankside delightedly. "I always did love to smuggle!"

"They say women have no conscience about laws, don't they?" Mrs. MacAvelly suggested.

"Why should we?" answered her friend. "We don't make 'em – nor God – nor nature. Why on earth should we respect a set of silly rules made by some men one day and changed by some more the next?"

"Bless us, Polly! Do you talk to Mr. Bankside like that?"

"Indeed I don't!" answered her hostess, holding out a particularly beautiful star-patterned belt to show to advantage. "There are lots of things I don't say to Mr. Bankside—'A man of understanding holdeth his peace' you know – or a woman."

She was a pretty creature, her hair like that of a powdered marchioness, her rosy cheeks and firm slight figure suggesting a charmer in Dresden china.

Mrs. MacAvelly regarded her admiringly. "'Where there is no wood the fire goeth out; so where there is no tale bearer the strife ceaseth,'" she proudly offered, "I can quote that much myself."

But Mrs. Bankside had many misgivings as she pursued her audacious way; the busy hours flying away from her, and the always astonishing checks flying toward her in gratifying accumulation. She came down to her well-planned dinners gracious and sweet; always effectively dressed; spent the cosy quiet evenings with her husband, or went out with him, with a manner of such increased tenderness and charm that his heart warmed anew to the wife of his youth; and he even relented a little toward her miscellaneous ancestors.

As the days shortened and darkened she sparkled more and more; with little snatches of song now and then; gay ineffectual strumming on the big piano; sudden affectionate darts at him, with quaintly distributed caresses.

"Molly!" said he, "I don't believe you're a day over twenty! What makes you act so?"

"Don't you like it, So?" she asked him. That was the nearest she ever would approximate to his name.

He did like it, naturally, and even gave her an extra ten dollars to buy Christmas presents with; while he meditated giving her an electric runabout; – to her! – who was afraid of a wheelbarrow!

When the day arrived and the family were gathered together, Mrs. Bankside, wearing the diamond brooch, the gold bracelet, the point lace handkerchief – everything she could carry of his accumulated generosity – and such an air of triumphant mystery that the tree itself was dim beside her; handed out to her astonished relatives such an assortment of desirable articles that they found no words to express their gratitude.

"Why, *Mother!*" said Jessie, whose husband was a minister and salaried as such, "Why, *Mother* – how did you know we wanted just that kind of a rug! – and a sewing-machine *too! An*d this lovely suit – and – and – why *Mother!*"

But her son-in-law took her aside and kissed her solemnly. He had wanted that particular set of sociological books for years – and never hoped to get them; or that bunch of magazines either.

Nellie had "married rich;" she was less ostentatiously favored; but she had shown her thankfulness a week ago – when her mother had handed her a check.

"Sh, sh! my dear!" her mother had said, "Not one word. I know! What pleasant weather we're having."

This son-in-law was agreeably surprised, too; and the other relatives, married and single; while the children rioted among their tools and toys, taking this Christmas like any other, as a season of unmitigated joy.

Mr. Solomon Bankside looked on with growing amazement, making computations in his practiced mind; saying nothing whatever. Should he criticize his wife before others?

But when his turn came – when gifts upon gifts were offered to him – sets of silken handkerchiefs (he couldn't bear the touch of a silk handkerchief!), a cabinet of cards and chips and counters of all sorts (he never played cards), an inlaid chess-table and ivory men (the game was unknown to him), a gorgeous scarf-pin (he abominated jewelery), a five pound box of candy (he never ate it), his feelings so mounted within him, that since he would not express, and could not repress them, he summarily went up stairs to his room.

She found him there later, coming in blushing, smiling, crying a little too – like a naughty but charming child.

He swallowed hard as he looked at her; and his voice was a little strained.

"I can take a joke as well as any man, Molly. I guess we're square on that. But – my dear! – where did you get it?"

"Earned it," said she, looking down, and fingering her lace handkerchief.

"Earned it! My wife, earning money! How – if I may ask?"

"By my weaving, dear – the towels and the belts – I sold 'em. Don't be angry – nobody knows – my name didn't appear at all! Please don't be angry! – It isn't wicked, and it was such fun!"

"No – it's not wicked, I suppose," said he rather grimly. "But it is certainly a most mortifying and painful thing to me – most unprecedented."

"Not so unprecedented, Dear," she urged, "Even the woman you think most of did it! Don't you remember 'She maketh fine linen and selleth it – and delivereth girdles unto the merchants!'"

Mr. Bankside came down handsomely.

He got used to it after a while, and then he became proud of it. If a friend ventured to suggest a criticism, or to sympathize, he would calmly respond, "'The heart of her husband doth safely trust in her, so that he shall have no need of spoil. Give her of the fruit of her hands, and let her own works praise her in the gates.'"

The Boys and the Butter

Young Holdfast and J. Edwards Fernald sat grimly at their father's table, being seen and not heard, and eating what was set before them, asking no questions for conscience' sake, as they had been duly reared. But in their hearts were most unchristian feelings toward a venerable guest, their mother's aunt, by name Miss Jane McCoy.

They knew, with the keen observation of childhood, that it was only a sense of hospitality, and duty to a relative, which made their father and mother polite to her – polite, but not cordial.

Mr. Fernald, as a professed Christian, did his best to love his wife's aunt, who came as near being an "enemy" as anyone he knew. But Mahala, his wife, was of a less saintly nature, and made no pretense of more than decent courtesy.

"I don't like her and I won't pretend to; it's not honest!" she protested to her husband, when he remonstrated with her upon her want of natural affection. "I can't help her being my aunt – we are not commanded to honor our aunts and uncles, Jonathan E."

Mrs. Fernald's honesty was of an iron hardness and heroic mould. She would have died rather than have told a lie, and classed as lies any form of evasion, deceit, concealment or even artistic exaggeration.

Her two sons, thus starkly reared, found their only imaginative license in secret converse between themselves, sacredly guarded by a pact of mutual faith, which was stronger than any outward compulsion. They kicked each other under the table, while enduring this visitation, exchanged dark glances concerning the object of their common dislike, and discussed her personal peculiarities with caustic comment later, when they should have been asleep.

Miss McCoy was not an endearing old lady. She was heavily built, and gobbled her food, carefully selecting the best. Her clothing was elaborate, but not beautiful, and on close approach aroused a suspicion of deferred laundry bills.

Among many causes for dislike for her aunt, Mrs. Fernald cherished this point especially. On one of these unwelcome visits she had been at some pains to carry up hot water for the Saturday evening bath, which was all the New England conscience of those days exacted, and the old lady had neglected it not only once but twice.

"Goodness sake, Aunt Jane! aren't you ever going to take a bath?"

"Nonsense!" replied her visitor. "I don't believe in all this wetting and slopping. The Scripture says, 'Whoso washeth his feet, his whole body shall be made clean.'"

Miss McCoy had numberless theories for other people's conduct, usually backed by well-chosen texts, and urged them with no regard for anybody's feelings. Even the authority of parents had no terrors for her.

Sipping her tea from the saucer with deep swattering inhalations, she fixed her prominent eyes upon the two boys as they ploughed their way through their bread and butter. Nothing must be left on the plate, in the table ethics of that time. The meal was simple in the extreme. A New Hampshire farm furnished few luxuries, and the dish of quince preserves had already been depleted by her.

"Mahala," she said with solemn determination, "those boys eat too much butter."

Mrs. Fernald flushed up to the edging of her cap. "I think I must be the judge of what my children eat at my table, Aunt Jane," she answered, not too gently.

Here Mr. Fernald interposed with a "soft answer." (He had never lost faith in the efficacy of these wrath turners, even on long repeated failure. As a matter of fact, to his wife's temper, a soft answer, especially an intentionally soft answer, was a fresh aggravation.) "The missionary, now, he praised our butter; said he never got any butter in China, or wherever 'tis he lives."

"He is a man of God," announced Miss McCoy. "If there is anybody on this poor earth deserving reverence, it is a missionary. What they endure for the Gospel is a lesson for us all. When I am taken I intend to leave all I have to the Missionary Society. You know that."

They knew it and said nothing. Their patience with her was in no way mercenary.

"But what I am speaking of is children," she continued, not to be diverted from her fell purpose. "Children ought not to eat butter."

"They seem to thrive on it," Mrs. Fernald replied tartly. And in truth both the boys were sturdy little specimens of humanity, in spite of their luxurious food.

"It's bad for them. Makes them break out. Bad for the blood. And self-denial is good for children. 'It is better to bear the yoke in thy youth.'"

The youth in question spread its butter more thickly, and ate it with satisfaction, saying nothing.

"Here, boys!" she suddenly assailed them. "If you will go without butter for a year – a whole year, till I come round again – I'll give each of you fifty dollars!"

This was an overwhelming proposition.

Butter was butter – almost the only alleviation of a dry and monotonous bill of fare, consisting largely of bread. Bread without butter! Brown bread without butter! No butter on potatoes! No butter on anything! The young imagination recoiled. And this measureless deprivation was to cover a whole year. A ninth or an eleventh of a lifetime to them respectively. About a fifth of all they could really remember. Countless days, each having three meals; weeks, months, the long dry butterless vista stretched before them like Siberian exile to a Russian prisoner.

But, on the other hand, there was the fifty dollars. Fifty dollars would buy a horse, a gun, tools, knives – a farm, maybe. It could be put in the bank, and drawn on for life, doubtless. Fifty dollars at that time was like five hundred to-day, and to a child it was a fortune.

Even their mother wavered in her resentment as she considered the fifty dollars, and the father did not waver at all, but thought it a Godsend.

"Let 'em choose," said Miss McCoy.

Stern is the stock of the Granite State. Self-denial is the essence of their religion; and economy, to give it a favorable name, is for them Nature's first law.

The struggle was brief. Holdfast laid down his thick-spread slice. J. Edwards laid down his. "Yes, ma'am," said one after the other. "Thank you, ma'am. We'll do it."

* * *

It was a long year. Milk did not take the place of it. Gravy and drippings, freely given by their mother, did not take the place of it, nor did the infrequent portions of preserves. Nothing met the same want. And if their health was improved by the abstinence it was in no way visible to the naked eye. They were well, but they were well before.

As to the moral effect – it was complex. An extorted sacrifice has not the same odor of sanctity as a voluntary one. Even when made willingly, if the willingness is purchased, the effect seems somewhat confused. Butter was not renounced, only postponed, and as the year wore on the young ascetics, in their secret conferences, indulged in wild visions of oleaginous excess so soon as the period of dearth should be over.

But most they refreshed their souls with plans for the spending and the saving of the hard-earned wealth that was coming to them. Holdfast was for saving his, and being a rich man – richer than Captain Briggs or Deacon Holbrook. But at times he wavered, spurred by the imagination of J. Edwards, and invested that magic sum in joys unnumbered.

The habit of self-denial was perhaps being established, but so was the habit of discounting the future, of indulging in wild plans of self-gratification when the ship came in.

* * *

Even for butterless boys, time passes, and the endless year at last drew to a close. They counted the months, they counted the weeks, they counted the days. Thanksgiving itself shone pale by contrast with this coming festival of joy and triumph. As it drew nearer and nearer their excitement increased, and they could not forget it even in the passing visit of a real missionary, a live one, who had been to those dark lands where the heathen go naked, worship idols and throw their children to the crocodiles.

They were taken to hear him, of course, and not only so, but he came to supper at their house and won their young hearts by the stories he told them. Gray of hair and beard was the preacher and sternly devout; but he had a twinkling eye none the less, and told tales of wonder and amazement that were sometimes almost funny and always interesting.

"Do not imagine, my young friends," he said, after filling them with delicious horror at the unspeakable wickedness of those "godless lands," "that the heathen are wholly without morality. The Chinese, among whom I have labored for many years, are more honest than some Christians. Their business honor is a lesson to us all. But works alone cannot save." And he questioned them as to their religious state, receiving satisfactory answers.

The town turned out to hear him; and, when he went on circuit, preaching, exhorting, describing the hardships and dangers of missionary life, the joys of soul-saving, and urging his hearers to contribute to this great duty of preaching the Gospel to all creatures, they had a sort of revival season; and arranged for a great missionary church meeting with a special collection when he should return.

The town talked missionary and thought missionary; dreamed missionary, it might well be; and garrets were ransacked to make up missionary boxes to send to the heathen. But Holdfast and J. Edwards mingled their interest in those unfortunate savages with a passionate desire for butter, and a longing for money such as they had never known before.

Then Miss McCoy returned.

They knew the day, the hour. They watched their father drive down to meet the stage, and tormented their mother with questions as to whether she would give it to them before supper or after.

"I'm sure I don't know!" she snapped at last. "I'll be thankful when it's over and done with, I'm sure. A mighty foolish business, I think!"

Then they saw the old chaise turn the corner. What? Only one in it!

The boys rushed to the gate – the mother, too.

"What is it, Jonathan? Didn't she come?"

"Oh, father!"

"Where is she, father?"

"She's not coming," said Mr. Fernald. "Says she's going to stay with

Cousin Sarah, so's to be in town and go to all the missionary doin's.

But she's sent it."

Then he was besieged, and as soon as the horse was put up, by three pairs of busy hands, they came to the supper table, whereon was a full two pounds of delicious butter, and sat down with tingling impatience.

The blessing was asked in all due form – a blessing ten miles long, it seemed to the youngsters, and then the long, fat envelope came out of Mr. Fernald's pocket.

"She must have written a lot," he said, taking out two folded papers, and then a letter.

"My dear great-nephews," ran the epistle, "as your parents have assured me that you have kept your promise, and denied yourselves butter for the space of a year, here is the fifty dollars I promised to each of you – wisely invested."

Mr. Fernald opened the papers. To Holdfast Fernald and to J. Edwards Fernald, duly made out, receipted, signed and sealed, were two $50 life memberships in the Missionary society!

Poor children! The younger one burst into wild weeping. The older seized the butter dish and cast it on the floor, for which he had to be punished, of course, but the punishment added nothing to his grief and rage.

When they were alone at last, and able to speak for sobbing, those gentle youths exchanged their sentiments; and these were of the nature of blasphemy and rebellion against God. They had learned at one fell blow the hideous lesson of human depravity. People lied – grown people – religious people – they lied! You couldn't trust them! They had been deceived, betrayed, robbed! They had lost the actual joy renounced, and the potential joy promised and withheld. The money they might some day earn, but not heaven itself could give back that year of butter. And all this in the name of religion – and of missionaries! Wild, seething outrage filled their hearts at first; slower results would follow.

* * *

The pious enthusiasm of the little town was at its height. The religious imagination, rather starved on the bald alternatives of Calvinism, found rich food in these glowing tales of danger, devotion, sometimes martyrdom; while the spirit of rigid economy, used to daylong saving from the cradle to the grave, took passionate delight in the success of these noble evangelists who went so far afield to save lost souls.

Out of their narrow means they had scraped still further; denied themselves necessaries where no pleasures remained; and when the crowning meeting was announced, the big collection meeting, with the wonderful brother from the Church in Asia to address them again, the meeting house was packed in floor and gallery.

Hearts were warm and open, souls were full of enthusiasm for the great work, wave on wave of intense feeling streamed through the crowded house.

Only in the Fernalds' pew was a spirit out of tune.

Fernald, good man though he was, had not yet forgiven. His wife had not tried.

"Don't talk to me!" she had cried passionately, when he had urged a reconciliation. "Forgive your enemies! Yes, but she hasn't done any harm to *me!*. *I*t's my boys she's hurt! It don't say one word about forgiving other people's enemies!"

Yet Mrs. Fernald, for all her anger, seemed to have some inner source of consolation, denied her husband, over which she nodded to herself from time to time, drawing in her thin lips, and wagging her head decisively.

Vengeful bitterness and impotent rage possessed the hearts of Holdfast and J. Edwards.

This state of mind in young and old was not improved when, on arriving at the meeting a little late, they had found the head of the pew was occupied by Miss McCoy.

It was neither the time nor the place for a demonstration. No other seats were vacant, and Mrs. Fernald marched in and sat next to her, looking straight at the pulpit. Next came the boys, and murder was in their hearts. Last, Mr. Fernald, inwardly praying for a more Christian spirit, but not getting it.

Holdfast and young J. Edwards dared not speak in church or make any protest; but they smelled the cardamum seeds in the champing jaws beyond their mother, and they cast black looks at each other and very secretly showed clenched fists, held low.

In fierce inward rebellion they sat through the earlier speeches, and when the time came for the address of the occasion, even the deep voice of the brother from Asia failed to stir them. Was he not a missionary, and were not missionaries and all their works proved false?

But what was this?

The address was over; the collection, in cash, was in the piled plates at the foot of the pulpit. The collection in goods was enumerated and described with full names given.

Then the hero of the hour was seen to confer with the other reverend brothers, and to rise and come forward, raising his hand for silence.

"Dearly beloved brethren and sisters," he said, "in this time of thanksgiving for gifts spiritual and temporal I wish to ask your patience for a moment more, that we may do justice. There has come to my ears a tale concerning one of our recent gifts which I wish you to hear, that judgment may be done in Israel.

"One among us has brought to the House of the Lord a tainted offering – an offering stained with cruelty and falsehood. Two young children of our flock were bribed a year ago to renounce one of the scant pleasures of their lives for a year's time – a whole long year of a child's life. They were bribed with a promise – a promise of untold wealth to a child, of fifty dollars each."

The congregation drew a long breath.

Those who knew of the Fernald boys' endeavor (and who in that friendly radius did not?) looked at them eagerly. Those who recognized Miss McCoy looked at her, too, and they were many. She sat, fanning herself, with a small, straight-handled palmleaf fan, striving to appear unconscious.

"When the time was up," the clear voice went on remorselessly, "the year of struggle and privation, and the eager hearts of childhood expected the reward; instead of keeping the given word, instead of the money promised, each child was given a paid life membership in our society!"

Again the house drew in its breath. Did not the end justify the means?

He went on:

"I have conferred with my fellow members, and we are united in our repudiation of this gift. The money is not ours. It was obtained by a trick which the heathen themselves would scorn."

There was a shocked pause. Miss McCoy was purple in the face, and only kept her place for fear of drawing more attention if she strove to escape.

"I name no names," the speaker continued, "and I regret the burden laid upon me to thus expose this possibly well-meant transaction, but what we have at stake to-night is not this handful of silver, nor the feelings of one sinner, but two children's souls. Are we to have their sense of justice outraged in impressionable youth? Are they to believe with the Psalmist that all men are liars? Are they to feel anger and blame for the great work to which our lives are given because in its name they were deceived and robbed? No, my brothers, we clear our skirts of this ignominy. In the name of the society, I shall return this money to its rightful owners. 'Whoso offendeth one of these little ones, it were better that a millstone be hanged about his neck and he cast into the depths of the sea.'"

A Coincidence

"O that! It was a fortunate coincidence, wasn't it? All things work together for good with those who love the Lord, you know, and Emma Ordway is the most outrageously Christian woman I ever knew. It did look that Autumn as if there was no way out of it, but things do happen, sometimes.

I dropped in rather late one afternoon to have a cup of tea with Emma, hoping against hope that Mirabella Vlack wouldn't be on hand; but she was, of course, and gobbling. There never was such a woman for candy and all manner of sweet stuff. I can remember her at school, with those large innocent eyes, and that wide mouth, eating Emma's nicest tidbits even then.

Emma loves sweets but she loves her friends better, and never gets anything for herself unless there is more than enough for everybody. She is very fond of a particular kind of fudge I make, has been fond of it for thirty years, and I love to make it for her once in a while, but after Mirabella came – I might as well have made it for her to begin with.

I devised the idea of bringing it in separate boxes, one for each, but bless you! Mirabella kept hers in her room, and ate Emma's!

"O I've left mine up stairs!" she'd say; "Let me go up and get it; "—and of course Emma wouldn't hear of such a thing. Trust Emma!

I've loved that girl ever since she was a girl, in spite of her preternatural unselfishness. And I've always hated those Vlack girls, both of them, Mirabella the most. At least I think so when I'm with her. When I'm with Arabella I'm not so sure. She married a man named Sibthorpe, just rich.

They were both there that afternoon, the Vlack girls I mean, and disagreeing as usual. Arabella was lean and hard and rigorously well dressed, she meant to have her way in this world and generally got it. Mirabella was thick and soft. Her face was draped puffily upon its unseen bones, and of an unwholesome color because of indigestion. She was the type that suggests cushioned upholstery, whereas Arabella's construction was evident.

"You don't look well, Mirabella," said she.

"I am well," replied her sister, "Quite well I assure you."

Mirabella was at that time some kind of a holy thoughtist. She had tried every variety of doctor, keeping them only as long as they did not charge too much, and let her eat what she pleased; which necessitated frequent change.

Mrs. Montrose smiled diplomatically, remarking "What a comfort these wonderful new faiths are!" She was one of Emma's old friends, and was urging her to go out to California with them and spend the winter. She dilated on the heavenly beauty and sweetness of the place till it almost made my mouth water, and Emma! – she loved travel better than anything, and California was one of the few places she had not seen.

Then that Vlack girl began to perform. "Why don't you go, Emma?" she said. "I'm not able to travel myself," (she wouldn't admit she was pointedly left out), "but that's no reason you should miss such a delightful opportunity. I can be housekeeper for you in your absence." This proposition had been tried once. All Emma's old servants left, and she had to come back in the middle of her trip, and re-organize the household.

Thus Mirabella, looking saintly and cheerful. And Emma – I could have shaken her soundly where she sat – Emma smiled bravely at Mrs. Montrose and thanked her warmly; she'd love it above all things, but there were many reasons why she couldn't leave home that winter. And we both knew there was only one, a huge thing in petticoats sitting gobbling there.

One or two other old friends dropped in, but they didn't stay long; they never did any more, and hardly any men came now. As I sat there drinking my pale tea I heard these people asking Emma why she didn't do this any more, and why she didn't come to that any more, and Emma just as dignified and nice as you please, telling all sorts of perforated paper fibs to explain and decline. One can't be perfect, and nobody could be as absolutely kind and gracious and universally beloved as Emma if she always told the plain truth.

I'd brought in my last protege that day, Dr. Lucy Barnes, a small quaint person, with more knowledge of her profession than her looks would indicate. She was a very wise little creature altogether. I had been studying chemistry with her, just for fun. You never know when yon may want to know a thing.

It was fine to see Dr. Lucy put her finger on Mirabella's weakness.

There that great cuckoo sat and discoursed on the symptoms she used to have, and would have now if it wasn't for "science "; and there I sat and watched Emma, and I declare she seemed to age visibly before my eyes.

Was I to keep quiet and let one of the nicest women that ever breathed be worn into her grave by that – Incubus? Even if she hadn't been a friend of mine, even if she hadn't been too good for this world, it would have been a shame. As it was the outrage cried to heaven. – and nobody could do anything.

Here was Emma, a widow, and in her own house; you couldn't coerce her. And she could afford it, as far as money went, you couldn't interfere that way. She had been so happy! She'd got over being a widow – I mean got used to it, and was finding her own feet. Her children were all married and reasonably happy, except the youngest, who was unreasonably happy; but time would make that all right. The Emma really began to enjoy life. Her health was good; she'd kept her looks wonderfully; and all the vivid interests of her girlhood cropped up again. She began to study things; to go to lectures and courses of lectures; to travel every year to a new place; to see her old friends and make new ones. She never liked to keep house, but Emma was so idiotically unselfish that she never would enjoy herself as long as there was anybody at home to give up to.

And then came Mirabella Vlack.

She came for a visit, at least she called one day with her air of saintly patience, and a miserable story of her loneliness and unhappiness, and how she couldn't bear to be dependent on Arabella – Arabella was so unsympathetic! – and that misguided Emma invited her to visit her for awhile.

That was five years ago. Five years! And here she sat, gobbling, forty pounds fatter and the soul of amiability, while Emma grew old.

Of course we all remonstrated – after it was too late.

Emma had a right to her own visitors – nobody ever dreamed that the thing was permanent, and nobody could break down that adamantine wall of Christian virtue she suffered behind, not owning that she suffered.

It was a problem.

But I love problems, human problems, better even than problems in chemistry, and they are fascinating enough.

First I tried Arabella. She said she regretted that poor Mirabella would not come to her loving arms. You see Mirabella had tried them, for about a year after her husband died, and preferred Emma's.

"It really doesn't look well," said Arabella. "Here am I alone in these great halls, and there is my only sister preferring to live with a comparative stranger! Her duty is to live with me, where I can take care of her."

Not much progress here. Mirabella did not want to be taken care of by a fault-finding older sister – not while Emma was in reach. It paid, too. Her insurance money kept her in clothes, and she could save a good deal, having no living expenses. As long as she preferred living with Emma Ordway, and Emma let her – what could anybody do?

It was getting well along in November, miserable weather.

Emma had a cough that hung on for weeks and weeks, she couldn't seem to gather herself together and throw it off, and Mirabella all the time assuring her that she had no cough at all!

Certain things began to seem very clear to me.

One was the duty of a sister, of two sisters. One was the need of a change of climate for my Emma.

One was that ever opening field of human possibilities which it has been the increasing joy of my lifetime to study.

I carried two boxes of my delectable fudge to those ladies quite regularly, a plain white one for Emma, a pretty colored one for the Incubus.

"Are you sure it is good for you?" I asked Mirabella; "I love to make it and have it appreciated, but does your Doctor think it is good for you?"

Strong in her latest faith she proudly declared she could eat anything. She could – visibly. So she took me up short on this point, and ate several to demonstrate immunity – out of Emma's box.

Nevertheless, in spite of all demonstration she seemed to grow somewhat – queasy – shall we say? – and drove poor Emma almost to tears trying to please her in the matter of meals.

Then I began to take them both out to ride in my motor, and to call quite frequently on Arabella; they couldn't well help it, you see, when I stopped the car and hopped out. "Mrs. Sibthorpe's sister" I'd always say to the butler or maid, and she'd always act as if she owned the house – that is if Arabella was out.

Then I had a good talk with Emma's old doctor, and he quite frightened her.

"You ought to close up the house," he said, "and spend the winter in a warm climate. You need complete rest and change, for a long time, a year at least," he told her. I urged her to go.

"Do make a change," I begged. "Here's Mrs. Sibthorpe perfectly willing to keep Mirabella – she'd be just as well off there; and you do really need a rest."

Emma smiled that saintly smile of hers, and said, "Of course, if Mirabella would go to her sister's awhile I could leave? But I can't ask her to go."

I could. I did. I put it to her fair and square, – the state of Emma's health, her real need to break up housekeeping, and how Arabella was just waiting for her to come there. But what's the use of talking to that kind? Emma wasn't sick, couldn't be sick, nobody could. At that very moment she paused suddenly, laid a fat hand on a fat side with an expression that certainly looked like pain; but she changed it for one of lofty and determined faith, and seemed to feel better. It made her cross though, as near it as she ever gets. She'd have been rude I think, but she likes my motor, to say nothing of my fudge.

I took them both out to ride that very afternoon, and Dr. Lucy with us.

Emma, foolish thing, insisted on sitting with the driver, and Mirabella made for her pet corner at once. I put Dr. Lucy in the middle, and encouraged Mirabella in her favorite backsliding, the discussion of her symptoms – the symptoms she used to have – or would have now if she gave way to "error."

Dr. Lucy was ingeniously sympathetic. She made no pretence of taking up the new view, but was perfectly polite about it.

"Judging from what you tell me ", she said, "and from my own point of view, I should say that you had a quite serious digestive trouble; that you had a good deal of pain now and then; and were quite likely to have a sudden and perhaps serious attack. But that is all nonsense to you I suppose."

"Of course it is!" said Mirabella, turning a shade paler.

We were running smoothly down the to avenue where Arabella lived.

"Here's something to cheer you up," I said, producing my two boxes of fudge. One I passed around in front to Emma; she couldn't share it with us. The other I gave Mirabella.

She fell upon it at once; perfunctorily offering some to Dr. Lucy, who declined; and to me. I took one for politeness's sake, and casually put it in my pocket.

We had just about reached Mrs. Sibthorpe's gate when Mirabella gave in.

"Oh I have such a terrible pain!" said she. "Oh Dr. Lucy! What shall I do?"

"Shall I take you down to your healer?" I suggested; but Mirabella was feeling very badly indeed.

"I think I'd better go in here a moment," she said; and in five minutes we had her in bed in what used to be her room.

Dr. Lucy seemed averse to prescribe.

"I have no right to interfere with your faith, Mrs. Vlack," she said. "I have medicines which I think would relieve you, but you do not believe in them. I think you should summon your – practitioner, at once."

"Oh Dr. Lucy!" gasped poor Mirabella, whose aspect was that of a small boy in an August orchard. "Don't leave me! Oh do something for me quick!"

"Will you do just what I say?"

"I will! I will; I'll do *anything*!" said Mirabella, curling up in as small a heap as was possible to her proportions, and Dr. Lucy took the case.

We waited in the big bald parlors till she came down to tell us what was wrong. Emma seemed very anxious, but then Emma is a preternatural saint.

Arabella came home and made a great todo. "So fortunate that she was near my door!" she said. "Oh my poor sister! I am so glad she has a real doctor!"

The real doctor came down after a while. "She is practically out of pain," she said, "and resting quietly. But she is extremely weak, and ought not to be moved for a long time."

"She shall not be!" said Arabella fervently. "My own sister! I am so thankful she came to me in her hour of need!"

I took Emma away. "Let's pick up Mrs. Montrose," I said. "She's tired out with packing – the air will do her good."

She was glad to come. We all sat back comfortably in the big seat and had a fine ride; and then Mrs. Montrose had us both come in and take dinner with her. Emma ate better than I'd seen her in months, and before she went home it was settled that she leave with Mrs. Montrose on Tuesday.

Dear Emma! She was as pleased as a child. I ran about with her, doing a little shopping. "Don't bother with anything," I said, "You can get things out there. Maybe you'll go on to Japan next spring with the James's."

"If we could sell the house I would!" said Emma. She brisked and sparkled – the years fell off from her – she started off looking fairly girlish in her hope and enthusiasm.

I drew a long sigh of relief.

Mr. MacAvelly has some real estate interests.

The house was sold before Mirabella was out of bed.

The Cottagette

"Why not?" said Mr. Mathews "It is far too small for a house, too pretty for a hut, too – unusual – for a cottage."

"Cottagette, by all means," said Lois, seating herself on a porch chair.

"But it is larger than it looks, Mr. Mathews. How do you like it,

Malda?"

I was delighted with it. More than delighted. Here this tiny shell of fresh unpainted wood peeped out from under the trees, the only house in sight except the distant white specks on far off farms, and the little wandering village in the river-threaded valley. It sat right on the turf, – no road, no path even, and the dark woods shadowed the back windows.

"How about meals?" asked Lois.

"Not two minutes walk," he assured her, and showed us a little furtive path between the trees to the place where meals were furnished.

We discussed and examined and exclaimed, Lois holding her pongee skirts close about her – she needn't have been so careful, there wasn't a speck of dust, – and presently decided to take it.

Never did I know the real joy and peace of living, before that blessed summer at "High Court." It was a mountain place, easy enough to get to, but strangely big and still and far away when you were there.

The working basis of the establishment was an eccentric woman named Caswell, a sort of musical enthusiast, who had a summer school of music and the "higher things." Malicious persons, not able to obtain accommodations there, called the place "High C."

I liked the music very well, and kept my thoughts to myself, both high and low, but "The Cottagette" I loved unreservedly. It was so little and new and clean, smelling only of its fresh-planed boards – they hadn't even stained it.

There was one big room and two little ones in the tiny thing, though from the outside you wouldn't have believed it, it looked so small; but small as it was it harbored a miracle – a real bathroom with water piped from mountain springs. Our windows opened into the green shadiness, the soft brownness, the bird-inhabited quiet flower-starred woods. But in front we looked across whole counties – over a far-off river-into another state. Off and down and away – it was like sitting on the roof of something – something very big.

The grass swept up to the door-step, to the walls – only it wasn't just grass of course, but such a procession of flowers as I had never imagined could grow in one place.

You had to go quite a way through the meadow, wearing your own narrow faintly marked streak in the grass, to reach the town-connecting road below. But in the woods was a little path, clear and wide, by which we went to meals.

For we ate with the highly thoughtful musicians, and highly musical thinkers, in their central boarding-house nearby. They didn't call it a boarding-house, which is neither high nor musical; they called it "The Calceolaria." There was plenty of that growing about, and I didn't mind what they called it so long as the food was good – which it was, and the prices reasonable – which they were.

The people were extremely interesting – some of them at least; and all of them were better than the average of summer boarders.

But if there hadn't been any interesting ones it didn't matter while Ford Mathews was there. He was a newspaper man, or rather an ex-newspaper man, then becoming a writer for magazines, with books ahead.

He had friends at High Court – he liked music – he liked the place – and he liked us. Lois liked him too, as was quite natural. I'm sure I did.

He used to come up evenings and sit on the porch and talk.

He came daytimes and went on long walks with us. He established his workshop in a most attractive little cave not far beyond far beyond us – the country there is full of rocky ledges and hollows, and sometimes asked us over to an afternoon tea, made on a gipsy fire.

Lois was a good deal older than I, but not really old at all, and she didn't look her thirty-five by ten years. I never blamed her for not mentioning it, and I wouldn't have done so, myself, on any account. But I felt that together we made a safe and reasonable household. She played beautifully, and there was a piano in our big room. There were pianos in several other little cottages about – but too far off for any jar of sound. When the wind was right we caught little wafts of music now and then; but mostly it was still – blessedly still, about us. And yet that Calceolaria was only two minutes off – and with raincoats and rubbers we never minded going to it.

We saw a good deal of Ford and I got interested in him, I couldn't help it. He was big. Not extra big in pounds and inches, but a man with big view and a grip – with purpose and real power. He was going to do things. I thought he was doing them now, but he didn't – this was all like cutting steps in the ice-wall, he said. It had to be done, but the road was long ahead. And he took an interest in my work too, which is unusual for a literary man.

Mine wasn't much. I did embroidery and made designs.

It is such pretty work! I like to draw from flowers and leaves and things about me; conventionalize them sometimes, and sometimes paint them just as they are, – in soft silk stitches.

All about up here were the lovely small things I needed; and not only these, but the lovely big things that make one feel so strong and able to do beautiful work.

Here was the friend I lived so happily with, and all this fairy land of sun and shadow, the free immensity of our view, and the dainty comfort of the Cottagette. We never had to think of ordinary things till the soft musical thrill of the Japanese gong stole through the trees, and we trotted off to the Calceolaria.

I think Lois knew before I did.

We were old friends and trusted each other, and she had had experience too.

"Malda," she said, "let us face this thing and be rational."
It was a strange thing that Lois should be so rational and yet
so musical – but she was, and that was one reason I liked her
so much.

"You are beginning to love Ford Mathews – do you
know it?"

I said yes, I thought I was.

"Does he love you?"

That I couldn't say. "It is early yet," I told her. "He is a
man, he is about thirty I believe, he has seen more of life
and probably loved before – it may be nothing more than
friendliness with him."

"Do you think it would be a good marriage?" she asked. We
had often talked of love and marriage, and Lois had helped
me to form my views – hers were very clear and strong.

"Why yes – if he loves me," I said. "He has told me quite
a bit about his family, good western farming people, real
Americans. He is strong and well – you can read clean living
in his eyes and mouth." Ford's eyes were as clear as a girl's,
the whites of them were clear. Most men's eyes, when you
look at them critically, are not like that. They may look at
you very expressively, but when you look at them, just as
features, they are not very nice.

I liked his looks, but I liked him better.

So I told her that as far as I knew it would be a good
marriage – if it was one.

"How much do you love him?" she asked.

That I couldn't quite tell, – it was a good deal, – but I didn't
think it would kill me to lose him.

"Do you love him enough to do something to win him – to really put yourself out somewhat for that purpose?"

"Why – yes – I think I do. If it was something I approved of. What do you mean?"

Then Lois unfolded her plan. She had been married, – unhappily married, in her youth; that was all over and done with years ago; she had told me about it long since; and she said she did not regret the pain and loss because it had given her experience. She had her maiden name again – and freedom. She was so fond of me she wanted to give me the benefit of her experience – without the pain.

"Men like music," said Lois; "they like sensible talk; they like beauty of course, and all that,—"

"Then they ought to like you!" I interrupted, and, as a matter of fact they did. I knew several who wanted to marry her, but she said "once was enough." I don't think they were "good marriages" though.

"Don't be foolish, child," said Lois, "this is serious. What they care for most after all is domesticity. Of course they'll fall in love with anything; but what they want to marry is a homemaker. Now we are living here in an idyllic sort of way, quite conducive to falling in love, but no temptation to marriage. If I were you – if I really loved this man and wished to marry him, I would make a home of this place."

"Make a home? – why it *is* a home. I never was so happy anywhere in my life. What on earth do you mean, Lois?"

"A person might be happy in a balloon, I suppose," she replied, "but it wouldn't be a home. He comes here and sits talking with us, and it's quiet and feminine and attractive

– and then we hear that big gong at the Calceolaria, and off we go stopping through the wet woods – and the spell is broken. Now you can cook." I could cook. I could cook excellently. My esteemed Mama had rigorously taught me every branch of what is now called "domestic science;" and I had no objection to the work, except that it prevented my doing anything else. And one's hands are not so nice when one cooks and washes dishes, – I need nice hands for my needlework. But if it was a question of pleasing Ford Mathews—

Lois went on calmly. "Miss Caswell would put on a kitchen for us in a minute, she said she would, you know, when we took the cottage. Plenty of people keep house up here – we, can if we want to."

"But we don't want to," I said, "we never have wanted to. The very beauty of the place is that it never had any house-keeping about it. Still, as you say, it would be cosy on a wet night, we could have delicious little suppers, and have him stay—"

"He told me he had never known a home since he was eighteen," said Lois.

That was how we came to install a kitchen in the Cottagette. The men put it up in a few days, just a lean-to with a window, a sink and two doors. I did the cooking. We had nice things, there is no denying that; good fresh milk and vegetables particularly, fruit is hard to get in the country, and meat too, still we managed nicely; the less you have the more you have to manage – it takes time and brains, that's all.

Lois likes to do housework, but it spoils her hands for practicing, so she can't; and I was perfectly willing to do it

– it was all in the interest of my own heart. Ford certainly enjoyed it. He dropped in often, and ate things with undeniable relish. So I was pleased, though it did interfere with my work a good deal. I always work best in the morning; but of course housework has to be done in the morning too; and it is astonishing how much work there is in the littlest kitchen. You go in for a minute, and you see this thing and that thing and the other thing to be done, and your minute is an hour before you know it.

When I was ready to sit down the freshness of the morning was gone somehow. Before, when I woke up, there was only the clean wood smell of the house, and then the blessed out-of-doors: now I always felt the call of the kitchen as soon as I woke. An oil stove will smell a little, either in or out of the house; and soap, and – well you know if you cook in a bedroom how it makes the room feel differently? Our house had been only bedroom and parlor before.

We baked too – the baker's bread was really pretty poor, and Ford did enjoy my whole wheat, and brown, and especially hot rolls and gems. it was a pleasure to feed him, but it did heat up the house, and me. I never could work much – at my work – baking days. Then, when I did get to work, the people would come with things, – milk or meat or vegetables, or children with berries; and what distressed me most was the wheelmarks on our meadow. They soon made quite a road – they had to of course, but I hated it – I lost that lovely sense of being on the last edge and looking over – we were just a bead on a string like other houses. But it was quite true that I loved this man, and would do more than this to please him. We couldn't go off so freely on excursions as we used, either; when meals are to be prepared someone has to be there, and to take in things when they come. Sometimes Lois stayed in, she always asked to, but mostly I did. I couldn't let her spoil her summer on my account. And Ford certainly liked it.

He came so often that Lois said she thought it would look better if we had an older person with us; and that her mother could come if I wanted her, and she could help with the work of course. That seemed reasonable, and she came. I wasn't very fond of Lois's mother, Mrs. Fowler, but it did seem a little conspicuous, Mr. Mathews eating with us more than he did at the Calceolaria.

There were others of course, plenty of them dropping in, but I didn't encourage it much, it made so much more work. They would come in to supper, and then we would have musical evenings. They offered to help me wash dishes, some of them, but a new hand in the kitchen is not much help, I preferred to do it myself; then I knew where the dishes were.

Ford never seemed to want to wipe dishes; though I often wished he would.

So Mrs. Fowler came. She and Lois had one room, they had to, – and she really did a lot of the work, she was a very practical old lady.

Then the house began to be noisy. You hear another person in a kitchen more than you hear yourself, I think, – and the walls were only boards. She swept more than we did too. I don't think much sweeping is needed in a clean place like that; and she dusted all the time; which I know is unnecessary. I still did most of the cooking, but I could get off more to draw, out-of-doors; and to walk. Ford was in and out continually, and, it seemed to me, was really coming nearer. What was one summer of interrupted work, of noise and dirt and smell and constant meditation on what to eat next, compared to a lifetime of love? Besides – if he married me – I should have to do it always, and might as well get used to it.

Lois kept me contented, too, telling me nice things that Ford said about my cooking. "He does appreciate it so," she said.

One day he came around early and asked me to go up Hugh's Peak with him. It was a lovely climb and took all day. I demurred a little, it was Monday, Mrs. Fowler thought it was cheaper to have a woman come and wash, and we did, but it certainly made more work.

"Never mind," he said, "what's washing day or ironing day or any of that old foolishness to us? This is walking day – that's what it is." It was really, cool and sweet and fresh, – it had rained in the night, – and brilliantly clear.

"Come along!" he said. "We can see as far as Patch Mountain I'm sure.

There'll never be a better day."

"Is anyone else going?" I asked.

"Not a soul. It's just us. Come."

I came gladly, only suggesting – "Wait, let me put up a lunch."

"I'll wait just long enough for you to put on knickers and a short skirt," said he. "The lunch is all in the basket on my back. I know how long it takes for you women to 'put up' sandwiches and things."

We were off in ten minutes, light-footed and happy, and the day was all that could be asked. He brought a perfect lunch, too, and had made it all himself. I confess it tasted better to me than my own cooking; but perhaps that was the climb.

When we were nearly down we stopped by a spring on a broad ledge, and supped, making tea as he liked to do out-of-doors. We saw the round sun setting at one end of a world view, and the round moon rising at the other; calmly shining each on each.

And then he asked me to be his wife—

We were very happy.

"But there's a condition!" said he all at once, sitting up straight and looking very fierce. "You mustn't cook!"

"What!" said I. "Mustn't cook?"

"No," said he, "you must give it up – for my sake."

I stared at him dumbly.

"Yes, I know all about it," he went on, "Lois told me. I've seen a good deal of Lois – since you've taken to cooking. And since I would talk about you, naturally I learned a lot. She told me how you were brought up, and how strong your domestic instincts were – but bless your artist soul dear girl, you have some others!" Then he smiled rather queerly and murmured, "surely in vain the net is spread in the sight of any bird."

"I've watched you, dear, all summer;" he went on, "it doesn't agree with you.

"Of course the things taste good – but so do my things! I'm a good cook myself. My father was a cook, for years – at good wages. I'm used to it you see.

"One summer when I was hard up I cooked for a living – and saved money instead of starving."

"O ho!" said I, "that accounts for the tea – and the lunch!"

"And lots of other things," said he. "But you haven't done half as much of your lovely work since you started this kitchen business, and – you'll forgive me, dear – it hasn't been as good. Your work is quite too good to lose; it is a beautiful and distinctive art, and I don't want you to let it go. What would you think of me if I gave up my hard long years of writing for the easy competence of a well-paid cook!"

I was still too happy to think very clearly. I just sat and looked at him. "But you want to marry me?" I said.

"I want to marry you, Malda, – because I love you – because you are young and strong and beautiful – because you are wild and sweet and – fragrant, and – elusive, like the wild flowers you love. Because you are so truly an artist in your special way, seeing beauty and giving it to others. I love you because of all this, because you are rational and highminded and capable of friendship, – and in spite of your cooking!"

"But – how do you want to live?"

"As we did here – at first," he said. "There was peace, exquisite silence. There was beauty – nothing but beauty. There were the clean wood odors and flowers and fragrances and sweet wild wind. And there was you – your fair self, always delicately dressed, with white firm fingers sure of touch in delicate true work. I loved you then. When you took to cooking it jarred on me. I have been a cook, I tell you, and I know what it is. I hated it – to see my wood-flower in a kitchen. But Lois told me about how you were brought up to it and loved it – and I said to myself, 'I love this woman; I will wait and see if I love her even as a cook.' And I do, Darling: I withdraw the condition. I will love you always, even if you insist on being my cook for life!"

"O I don't insist!" I cried. "I don't want to cook – I want to draw!

But I thought – Lois said – How she has misunderstood you!"

"It is not true, always, my dear," said he, "that the way to a man's heart is through his stomach; at least it's not the only way. Lois doesn't know everything, she is young yet! And perhaps for my sake you can give it up. Can you sweet?"

Could I? Could I? Was there ever a man like this?

Her Housekeeper

On the top floor of a New York boarding-house lived a particularly attractive woman who was an actress. She was also a widow, not divorcee, but just plain widow; and she persisted in acting under her real name, which was Mrs. Leland. The manager objected, but her reputation was good enough to carry the point.

"It will cost you a great deal of money, Mrs. Leland," said the manager.

"I make money enough," she answered.

"You will not attract so many – admirers," said the manager.

"I have admirers enough," she answered; which was visibly true.

She was well under thirty, even by daylight – and about eighteen on the stage; and as for admirers – they apparently thought Mrs. Leland was a carefully selected stage name.

Besides being a widow, she was a mother, having a small boy of about five years; and this small boy did not look in the least like a "stage child," but was a brown-skinned, healthy little rascal of the ordinary sort.

With this boy, an excellent nursery governess, and a maid, Mrs. Leland occupied the top floor above mentioned, and enjoyed it. She had a big room in front, to receive in; and a small room with a skylight, to sleep in. The boy's room and the governess' rooms were at the back, with sunny south windows, and the maid slept on a couch in the parlor. She was a colored lady, named Alice, and did not seem to care where she slept, or if she slept at all.

"I never was so comfortable in my life," said Mrs. Leland to her friends. "I've been here three years and mean to stay. It is not like any boarding-house I ever saw, and it is not like any home I ever had. I have the privacy, the detachment, the carelessness of a boarding-house, and 'all the comforts of a home.' Up I go to my little top flat as private as you like. My Alice takes care of it – the housemaids only come in when I'm out. I can eat with the others downstairs if I please; but mostly I don't please; and up come my little meals on the dumbwaiter – hot and good."

"But – having to flock with a lot of promiscuous boarders!" said her friends.

"I don't flock, you see; that's just it. And besides, they are not promiscuous – there isn't a person in the house now who isn't some sort of a friend of mine. As fast as a room was vacated I'd suggest somebody – and here we all are. It's great."

"But do you *like* a skylight room?" Mrs. Leland's friends further inquired of her?"

"By no means!" she promptly replied. "I hate it. I feel like a mouse in a pitcher!"

"Then why in the name of reason—?"

"Because I can sleep there! *Sleep*! – It's the only way to be quiet in New York, and I have to sleep late if I sleep at all. I've fixed the skylight so that I'm drenched with air – and not drenched with rain! – and there I am. Johnny is gagged and muffled as it were, and carried downstairs as early as possible. He gets his breakfast, and the unfortunate Miss Merton has to go out and play with him – in all weathers – except kindergarten time. Then Alice sits on the stairs and keeps everybody away till I ring."

Possibly it was owing to the stillness and the air and the sleep till near lunchtime that Mrs. Leland kept her engaging youth, her vivid uncertain beauty. At times you said of her, "She has a keen intelligent face, but she's not pretty." Which was true. She was not pretty. But at times again she overcame you with her sudden loveliness.

All of which was observed by her friend from the second floor who wanted to marry her. In this he was not alone; either as a friend, of whom she had many, or as a lover, of whom she had more. His distinction lay first in his opportunities, as a co-resident, for which he was heartily hated by all the more and some of the many; and second in that he remained a friend in spite of being a lover, and remained a lover in spite of being flatly refused.

His name in the telephone book was given "Arthur Olmstead, real estate;" office this and residence that – she looked him up therein after their first meeting. He was rather a short man, heavily built, with a quiet kind face, and a somewhat quizzical smile. He seemed to make all the money he needed, occupied the two rooms and plentiful closet space of his floor in great contentment, and manifested most improper domesticity of taste by inviting friends to tea. "Just like a woman!" Mrs. Leland told him.

"And why not? Women have so many attractive ways – why not imitate them?" he asked her.

"A man doesn't want to be feminine, I'm sure," struck in a pallid, overdressed youth, with openwork socks on his slim feet, and perfumed handkerchief.

Mr. Olmstead smiled a broad friendly smile. He was standing near the young man, a little behind him, and at this point he put his hands just beneath the youth's arms, lifted and set him aside as if he were an umbrella-stand. "Excuse me, Mr. Masters," he said gravely, but you were standing on Mrs. Leland's gown."

Mr. Masters was too much absorbed in apologizing to the lady to take umbrage at the method of his removal; but she was not so oblivious. She tried doing it to her little boy afterwards, and found him very heavy.

When she came home from her walk or drive in the early winter dusk, this large quietly furnished room, the glowing fire, the excellent tea and delicate thin bread and butter were most restful. "It is two more stories up before I can get my own;" she would say – "I must stop a minute."

When he began to propose to her the first time she tried to stop him. "O please don't!" she cried. "*Please* don't! There are no end of reasons why I will not marry anybody again. Why can't some of you men be nice to me and not – that! Now I can't come in to tea any more!"

"I'd like to know why not," said he calmly. "You don't have to marry me if you don't want to; but that's no reason for cutting my acquaintance, is it?"

She gazed at him in amazement.

"I'm not threatening to kill myself, am I? I don't intend going to the devil. I'd like to be your husband, but if I can't – mayn't I be a brother to you?"

She was inclined to think he was making fun of her, but no – his proposal had had the real ring in it. "And you're not – you're not going to—?" it seemed the baldest assumption to think that he was going to, he looked so strong and calm and friendly.

"Not going to annoy you? Not going to force an undesired affection on you and rob myself of a most agreeable friendship? Of course not. Your tea is cold, Mrs. Leland – let me give you another cup. And do you think Miss Rose is going to do well as 'Angelina?'"

So presently Mrs. Leland was quite relieved in her mind, and free to enjoy the exceeding comfortableness of this relation. Little Johnny was extremely fond of Mr. Olmstead; who always treated him with respect, and who could listen to his tales of strife and glory more intelligently than either mother or governess. Mr. Olmstead kept on hand a changing supply of interesting things; not toys – never, but real things not intended for little boys to play with. No little boy would want to play with dolls for instance; but what little boy would not be fascinated by a small wooden lay figure, capable of unheard-of contortions. Tin soldiers were common, but the flags of all nations – real flags, and true stories about them, were interesting. Noah's arks were cheap and unreliable scientifically; but Barye lions, ivory elephants, and Japanese monkeys in didactic groups of three, had unfailing attraction. And the books this man had – great solid books that could be opened wide on the floor, and a little boy lie down to in peace and comfort!

Mrs. Leland stirred her tea and watched them until Johnny was taken upstairs.

"Why don't you smoke?" she asked suddenly. "Doctor's orders?"

"No – mine," he answered. "I never consulted a doctor in my life."

"Nor a dentist, I judge," said she.

"Nor a dentist."

"You'd better knock on wood!" she told him.

"And cry 'Uncle Reuben?' he asked smilingly.

"You haven't told me why you don't smoke!" said she suddenly.

"Haven't I?" he said. "That was very rude of me. But look here. There's a thing I wanted to ask you. Now I'm not pressing any sort of inquiry as to myself; but as a brother, would you mind telling me some of those numerous reasons why you will not marry anybody?"

She eyed him suspiciously, but he was as solid and calm as usual, regarding her pleasantly and with no hint of ulterior purpose. "Why – I don't mind," she began slowly. "First – I have been married – and was very unhappy. That's reason enough."

He did not contradict her; but merely said, "That's one," and set it down in his notebook.

"Dear me, Mr. Olmstead! You're not a reporter, are you!"

"O no – but I wanted to have them clear and think about them," he explained. "Do you mind?" And he made as if to shut his little book again.

"I don't know as I mind," she said slowly. "But it looks so – businesslike."

"This is a very serious business, Mrs. Leland, as you must know. Quite aside from any personal desire of my own, I am truly 'your sincere friend and well-wisher,' as the Complete Letter Writer has it, and there are so many men wanting to marry you."

This she knew full well, and gazed pensively at the toe of her small flexible slipper, poised on a stool before the fire.

Mr. Olmstead also gazed at the slipper toe with appreciation.

"What's the next one?" he said cheerfully.

"Do you know you are a real comfort," she told him suddenly. "I never knew a man before who could – well leave off being a man for a moment and just be a human creature."

"Thank you, Mrs. Leland," he said in tones of pleasant sincerity. "I want to be a comfort to you if I can. Incidentally wouldn't you be more comfortable on this side of the fire – the light falls better – don't move." And before she realized what he was doing he picked her up, chair and all, and put her down softly on the other side, setting the footstool as before, and even daring to place her little feet upon it – but with so businesslike an air that she saw no opening for rebuke. It is a difficult matter to object to a man's doing things like that when he doesn't look as if he was doing them.

"That's better," said he cheerfully, taking the place where she had been. "Now, what's the next one?"

"The next one is my boy."

"Second – Boy," he said, putting it down. "But I should think he'd be a reason the other way. Excuse me – I wasn't going to criticize – yet! And the third?"

"Why should you criticize at all, Mr. Olmstead?"

"I shouldn't – on my own account. But there may come a man you love." He had a fine baritone voice. When she heard him sing Mrs. Leland always wished he were taller, handsomer, more distinguished looking; his voice sounded as if he were. And I should hate to see these reasons standing in the way of your happiness," he continued.

"Perhaps they wouldn't," said she in a revery.

"Perhaps they wouldn't – and in that case it is no possible harm that you tell me the rest of them. I won't cast it up at you. Third?"

"Third, I won't give up my profession for any man alive."

"Any man alive would be a fool to want you to," said he setting down,

"Third – Profession."

"Fourth – I like *Freedom*!" she said with sudden intensity. "You don't know! – they kept me so tight! – so *tight* – when I was a girl! Then – I was left alone, with a very little money, and I began to study for the stage – that was like heaven! And then – O what *idiots* women are!" She said the word not tragically, but with such hard-pointed intensity that it sounded like a gimlet. "Then I married, you see – I gave up all my new-won freedom to *marry*! – and he kept me tighter than ever." She shut her expressive mouth in level lines – stood up suddenly and stretched her arms wide and high. "I'm free again, free – I can do exactly as I please!" The words were individually relished. "I have the work I love. I can earn all I need – am saving something for the boy. I'm perfectly independent!"

"And perfectly happy!" he cordially endorsed her. "I don't blame you for not wanting to give it up."

"O well – happy!" she hesitated. "There are times, of course, when one isn't happy. But then – the other way I was unhappy all the time."

"He's dead – unfortunately," mused Mr. Olmstead.

"Unfortunately? – Why?"

He looked at her with his straightforward, pleasant smile. "I'd have liked the pleasure of killing him," he said regretfully.

She was startled, and watched him with dawning alarm. But he was quite quiet – even cheerful. "Fourth – Freedom," he wrote. "Is that all?"

"No – there are two more. Neither of them will please you. You won't think so much of me any more. The worst one is this. I like – lovers! I'm very much ashamed of it, but I do! I try not to be unfair to them – some I really try to keep away from me – but honestly I like admiration and lots of it."

"What's the harm of that?" he asked easily, setting down,

"Fifth – Lovers."

"No harm, so long as I'm my own mistress," said she defiantly. "I take care of my boy, I take care of myself – let them take care of themselves! Don't blame me too much!"

"You're not a very good psychologist, I'm afraid," said he.

"What do you mean?" she asked rather nervously.

"You surely don't expect a man to blame you for being a woman, do you?"

"All women are not like that," she hastily asserted. "They are too conscientious. Lots of my friends blame me severely."

"Women friends," he ventured.

"Men, too. Some men have said very hard things of me."

"Because you turned 'em down. That's natural."

"You don't!"

"No, I don't. I'm different. ".

"How different?" she asked.

He looked at her steadily. His eyes were hazel, flecked with changing bits of color, deep, steady, with a sort of inner light that grew as she watched till presently she thought it well to consider her slipper again; and continued, "The sixth is as bad as the other almost. I hate – I'd like to write a dozen tragic plays to show how much I hate – Housekeeping! There! That's all!"

"Sixth – Housekeeping," he wrote down, quite unmoved. "But why should anyone blame you for that – it's not your business."

"No – thank goodness, it's not! And never will be! I'm *free*, I tell you and I stay free! – But look at the clock!" And she whisked away to dress for dinner.

He was not at table that night – not at home that night – not at home for some days – the landlady said he had gone out of town; and Mrs. Leland missed her afternoon tea.

She had it upstairs, of course, and people came in – both friends and lovers; but she missed the quiet and cosiness of the green and brown room downstairs.

Johnny missed his big friend still more. "Mama, where's Mr. Olmstead? Mama, why don't Mr. Olmstead come back?

Mama! When is Mr. Olmstead coming back? Mama! Why don't you write to Mr. Olmstead and tell him to come back? Mama! – can't we go in there and play with his things?"

As if in answer to this last wish she got a little note from him saying simply, "Don't let Johnny miss the lions and monkeys – he and Miss Merton and you, of course, are quite welcome to the whole floor. Go in at any time."

Just to keep the child quiet she took advantage of this offer, and Johnnie introduced her to all the ins and outs of the place. In a corner of the bedroom was a zinc-lined tray with clay in it, where Johnnie played rapturously at making "making country." While he played his mother noted the quiet good taste and individuality of the place.

"It smells so clean!" she said to herself. "There! he hasn't told me yet why he doesn't smoke. I never told him I didn't like it."

Johnnie tugged at a bureau drawer. "He keeps the water in here!" he said, and before she could stop him he had out a little box with bits of looking-glass in it, which soon became lakes and rivers in his clay continent.

Mrs. Leland put them back afterward, admiring the fine quality and goodly number of garments in that drawer, and their perfect order. Her husband had been a man who made a chowder of his bureau drawers, and who expected her to find all his studs and put them in for him.

"A man like this would be no trouble at all," she thought for a moment – but then she remembered other things and set her mouth hard. "Not for mine!" she said determinedly.

By and by he came back, serene as ever, friendly and unpresuming.

"Aren't you going to tell me why you don't smoke?" she suddenly demanded of him on another quiet dusky afternoon when tea was before them.

He seemed so impersonal, almost remote, though nicer than ever to Johnny; and Mrs. Leland rather preferred the personal note in conservation.

"Why of course I am," he replied cordially. "That's easy," and he fumbled in his inner pocket.

"Is that where you keep your reasons?" she mischievously inquired.

"It's where I keep yours," he promptly answered, producing the little notebook. "Now look here – I've got these all answered – you won't be able to hold to one of 'em after this. May I sit by you and explain?"

She made room for him on the sofa amiably enough, but defied him to convince her. "Go ahead," she said cheerfully.

"First," he read off, "Previous Marriage. This is not a sufficient objection. Because you have been married you now know what to choose and what to avoid. A girl is comparatively helpless in this matter; you are armed. That your first marriage was unhappy is a reason for trying it again. It is not only that you are better able to choose, but that by the law of chances you stand to win next time. Do you admit the justice of this reasoning?"

"I don't admit anything," she said. "I'm waiting to ask you a question."

"Ask it now."

"No – I'll wait till you are all through. Do go on."

"'Second – The Boy,'" he continued. "Now Mrs. Leland, solely on the boy's account I should advise you to marry again. While he is a baby a mother is enough, but the older he grows the more he will need a father. Of course you should select a man the child could love – a man who could love the child."

"I begin to suspect you of deep double-dyed surreptitious designs, Mr. Olmstead. You know Johnnie loves you dearly. And you know I won't marry you," she hastily added.

"I'm not asking you to – now, Mrs. Leland. I did, in good faith, and I would again if I thought I had the shadow of a chance – but I'm not at present. Still, I'm quite willing to stand as an instance. Now, we might resume, on that basis. Objection one does not really hold against me – now does it?"

He looked at her cheerily, warmly, openly; and in his clean, solid strength and tactful kindness he was so unspeakably different from the dark, fascinating slender man who had become a nightmare to her youth, that she felt in her heart he was right – so far. "I won't admit a thing," she said sweetly. "But, pray go on."

He went on, unabashed. "'Second – Boy,' Now if you married me I should consider the boy as an added attraction. Indeed – if you do marry again – someone who doesn't want the boy – I wish you'd give him to me. I mean it. I think he loves me, and I think I could be of real service to the child."

He seemed almost to have forgotten her, and she watched him curiously.

"Now, to go on," he continued. "'Third-Profession.' As to your profession," said he slowly, clasping his hands over one knee and gazing at the dark soft-colored rug, "if you married me, and gave up your profession I should find it a distinct loss, I should lose my favorite actress."

She gave a little start of surprise.

"Didn't you know how much I admire your work?" he said. "I don't hang around the stage entrance – there are plenty of chappies to do that; and I don't always occupy a box and throw bouquets – I don't like a box anyhow. But I haven't missed seeing you in any part you've played yet – some of 'em I've seen a dozen times. And you're growing – you'll do better work still. It is sometimes a little weak in the love parts – seems as if you couldn't quite take it seriously – couldn't let yourself go – but you'll grow. You'll do better – I really think – after you're married"

She was rather impressed by this, but found it rather difficult to say anything; for he was not looking at her at all. He took up his notebook again with a smile.

"So – if you married me, you would be more than welcome to go on with your profession. I wouldn't stand in your way any more than I do now. 'Fourth – Freedom,'" he read slowly. "That is easy in one way – hard in another. If you married me," – She stirred resentfully at this constant reference to their marriage; but he seemed purely hypothetical in tone; "*I* wouldn't interfere with your freedom any. Not of my own will. But if you ever grew to love me – or if there were children – it would make *some* difference. Not much. There mightn't be any children, and it isn't likely you'd ever love me enough to have that stand in your way. Otherwise than that you'd have freedom – as much as now. A little more; because if you wanted to make a foreign tour, or anything like that, I'd take care of Johnnie. 'Fifth – Lovers.'" Here he paused leaning forward with his chin in his hands, his eyes bent down. She could see the broad heavy shoulders, the smooth fit of the well-made, coat, the spotless collar, and the fine, strong, clean-cut neck. As it happened she particularly disliked the neck of the average man – either the cordy, the beefy or the adipose, and particularly liked this kind, firm and round like a Roman's, with the hair coming to a clean-cut edge and stopping there.

"As to lovers," he went on – "I hesitate a little as to what to say about that. I'm afraid I shall shock you. Perhaps I'd better leave out that one."

"As insuperable?" she mischievously asked.

"No, as too easy," he answered.

"You'd better explain," she said.

"Well then – it's simply this: as a man – I myself admire you more because so many other men admire you. I don't sympathize with them, any! – Not for a minute. Of course, if you loved any one of them you wouldn't be my wife. But if you were my wife—"

"Well?" said she, a little breathlessly. "You're very irritating! What would you do? Kill 'em all? Come – If I were your wife? —"

"If you were my wife —" he turned and faced her squarely, his deep eyes blazing steadily into hers, "In the first place the more lovers you had that you didn't love the better I'd be pleased."

"And if I did?" she dared him.

"If you were my wife," he purused with perfect quietness, "you would never love anyone else."

There was a throbbing silence.

"'Sixth – Housekeeping,'" he read.

At this she rose to her feet as if released. "Sixth and last and all-sufficient!" she burst out, giving herself a little shake as if to waken. "Final and conclusive and admitting no reply! "—I will not keep house for any man. Never! Never!! Never!!!"

"Why should you?" he said, as he had said it before; "Why not board?"

"I wouldn't board on any account!"

"But you are boarding now. Aren't you comfortable here?"

"O yes, perfectly comfortable. But this is the only boarding-house I ever saw that was comfortable."

"Why not go on as we are – if you married me?"

She laughed shrilly. "With the other boarders round them and a whole floor laid between," she parodied gaily. "No, sir! *If I* ever married again – and I wont – I'd want a home of my own – a whole house – and have it run as smoothly and perfectly as this does. With no more care than I have now!"

"If I could give you a whole house, like this, and run it for you as smoothly and perfectly as this one – then would you marry me?" he asked.

"O, I dare say I would," she said mockingly.

"My dear," said he, "I have kept this house – for you – for three years."

"What do you mean?" she demanded, flushingly.

"I mean that it is my business," he answered serenely. "Some men run hotels and some restaurants: I keep a number of boarding houses and make a handsome income from them. All the people are comfortable – I see to that. I planned to have you use these rooms, had the dumbwaiter run to the top so you could have meals comfortably there. You didn't much like the first housekeeper. I got one you liked better; cooks to please you, maids to please you. I have most seriously tried to make you comfortable. When you didn't like a boarder I got rid of him – or her – they are mostly all your friends now. Of course if we were married, we'd fire 'em all." His tone was perfectly calm and business like. "You should keep your special apartments on top; you should also have the floor above this, a larger bedroom, drawing-room, and bath and private parlor for you; – I'd stay right here as I am now – and when you wanted me – I'd be here."

She stiffened a little at this rather tame ending. She was stirred, uneasy, dissatisfied. She felt as if something had been offered and withdrawn; something was lacking.

"It seems such a funny business – for a man," she said.

"Any funnier than Delmonico's?" he asked. "It's a business that takes some ability – witness the many failures. It is certainly useful. And it pays – amazingly."

"I thought it was real estate," she insisted.

"It is. I'm in a real estate office. I buy and sell houses – that's how

I came to take this up!"

He rose up, calmly and methodically, walked over to the fire, and laid his notebook on it. "There wasn't any strength in any of those objections, my dear," said he. "Especially the first one. Previous marriage, indeed! You have never been married before. You are going to be – now."

It was some weeks after that marriage that she suddenly turned upon him – as suddenly as one can turn upon a person whose arms are about one – demanding.

"And why don't you smoke? – You never told me!"

"I shouldn't like to kiss you so well if you smoked! "— said he.

"I never had any idea," she ventured after a while, "that it could be – like this."

Making a Living

"There won't be any litigation and chicanery to help you out, young man. I've fixed that. Here are the title deeds of your precious country-place; you can sit in that hand-made hut of yours and make poetry and crazy inventions the rest of your life! The water's good – and I guess you can live on the chestnuts!"

"Yes, sir," said Arnold Blake, rubbing his long chin dubiously. "I guess I can."

His father surveyed him with entire disgust. "If you had wit enough you might rebuild that old saw-mill and make a living off it!"

"Yes, sir," said Arnold again. "I had thought of that."

"You had, had you?" sneered his father. "Thought of it because it rhymed, I bet you! Hill and mill, eh? Hut and nut, trees and breeze, waterfall – beat-'em-all? I'm something of a poet myself, you see! Well, – there's your property. And with what your Mother left you will buy books and writing paper! As for my property – that's going to Jack. I've got the papers for that too. Not being an idiot I've saved out enough for myself – no Lear business for mine! Well, boy – I'm sorry you're a fool. But you've got what you seem to like best."

"Yes, sir," said Arnold once more. "I have, and I'm really much obliged to you, Father, for not trying to make me take the business."

Then young John Blake, pattern and image of his father, came into possession of large assets and began to use them in the only correct way; to increase and multiply without end.

Then old John Blake, gazing with pride on his younger son, whose acumen almost compensated him for the bitter disappointment of being father to a poet; set forth for a season of rest and change.

"I'm going to see the world! I never had time before!" quoth he; and started off for Europe, Asia, and Africa.

Then Arnold Blake, whose eyes were the eyes of a poet, but whose mouth had a touch of resemblance to his father's, betook himself to his Hill.

But the night before they separated, he and his brother both proposed to Ella Sutherland. John because he had made up his mind that it was the proper time for him to marry, and this was the proper woman; and Arnold because he couldn't help it.

John got to work first. He was really very fond of Ella, and made hot love to her. It was a painful surprise to him to be refused. He argued with her. He told her how much he loved her.

"There are others!" said Miss Ella.

He told her how rich he was.

"That isn't the point," said Ella.

He told her how rich he was going to be.

"I'm not for sale!" said Ella, "even on futures!"

Then he got angry and criticised her judgement.

"It's a pity, isn't it," she said, "for me to have such poor judgment – and for you to have to abide by it!"

"I won't take your decision," said John. "You're only a child yet. In two years' time you'll be wiser. I'll ask you again then."

"All right," said Ella. "I'll answer you again then."

John went away, angry, but determined.

Arnold was less categorical.

"I've no right to say a word," he began, and then said it. Mostly he dilated on her beauty and goodness and his overmastering affection for her.

"Are you offering marriage?" she inquired, rather quizzically.

"Why yes – of course!" said he, "only – only I've nothing to offer."

"There's you!" said Ella.

"But that's so little!" said Arnold. "O! if you will wait for me! – I will work!—"

"What will you work at?" said Ella.

Arnold laughed. Ella laughed. "I love to camp out!" said she.

"Will you wait for me a year?" said Arnold.

"Ye-es," said Ella. "I'll even wait two – if I have to. But no longer!"

"What will you do then?" asked Arnold miserably.

"Marry you," said Ella.

So Arnold went off to his Hill.

What was one hill among so many? There they arose about him, far green, farther blue, farthest purple, rolling away to the real peaks of the Catskills. This one had been part of his mother's father's land; a big stretch, coming down to them from an old Dutch grant. It ran out like a promontory into the winding valley below; the valley that had been a real river when the Catskills were real mountains. There was some river there yet, a little sulky stream, fretting most of the year in its sunken stony bed, and losing its temper altogether when the spring floods came.

Arnold did not care much for the river – he had a brook of his own; an ideal brook, beginning with an over-flowing spring; and giving him three waterfalls and a lake on his own land. It was a very little lake and handmade. In one place his brook ran through a narrow valley or valleyette – so small it was; and a few weeks of sturdy work had damned the exit and made a lovely pool. Arnold did that years ago, when he was a great hulking brooding boy, and used to come up there with his mother in summer; while his father stuck to the office and John went to Bar Harbor with his chums. Arnold could work hard even if he was a poet.

He quarried stone from his hill – as everyone did in those regions; and built a small solid house, adding to it from year to year; that was a growing joy as long as the dear mother lived.

This was high up, near the dark, clear pool of the spring; he had piped the water into the house – for his mother's comfort. It stood on a level terrace, fronting south-westward; and every season he did more to make it lovely. There was a fine smooth lawn there now and flowering vines and bushes; every pretty wild thing that would grow and bloom of itself in that region, he collected about him.

That dear mother had delighted in all the plants and trees; she studied about them and made observations, while he enjoyed them – and made poems. The chestnuts were their common pride. This hill stood out among all the others in the flowering time, like a great pompon, and the odor of it -

was by no means attractive – unless you happened to like it, as they did.

The chestnut crop was tremendous; and when Arnold found that not only neighboring boys, but business expeditions from the city made a practice of rifling his mountain garden, he raged for one season and acted the next. When the first frost dropped the great burrs, he was on hand, with a posse of strong young fellows from the farms about. They beat and shook and harvested, and sack upon sack of glossy brown nuts were piled on wagons and sent to market by the owner instead of the depredator.

Then he and his mother made great plans, the eager boy full of ambition. He studied forestry and arboriculture; and grafted the big fat foreign chestnut on his sturdy native stocks, while his father sneered and scolded because he would not go into the office.

Now he was left to himself with his plans and hopes. The dear mother was gone, but the hill was there – and Ella might come some day; there was a chance.

"What do you think of it?" he said to Patsy. Patsy was not Irish. He was an Italian from Tuscany; a farmer and forester by birth and breeding, a soldier by compulsion, an American citizen by choice.

"Fine!" said Patsy. "Fine. Ver' good. You do well."

They went over the ground together. "Could you build a little house here?" said Arnold. "Could you bring your wife? Could she attend to my house up there? – and could you keep hens and a cow and raise vegetables on this patch here – enough for all of us? – you to own the house and land – only you cannot sell it except to me?"

Then Patsy thanked his long neglected saints, imported his wife and little ones, took his eldest daughter out of the box factory, and his eldest son out of the printing office; and by the end of the summer they were comfortably established and ready to attend to the chestnut crop.

Arnold worked as hard as his man. Temporarily he hired other sturdy Italians, mechanics of experience; and spent his little store of capital in a way that would have made his father swear and his brother jeer at him.

When the year was over he had not much money left, but he had by his second waterfall a small electrical plant, with a printing office attached; and by the third a solid little mill, its turbine wheel running merrily in the ceaseless pour. Millstones cost more money than he thought, but there they were – brought up by night from the Hudson River – that his neighbors might not laugh too soon. Over the mill were large light rooms, pleasant to work in; with the shade of mighty trees upon the roof; and the sound of falling water in the sun.

By next summer this work was done, and the extra workmen gone. Whereat our poet refreshed himself with a visit to his Ella, putting in some lazy weeks with her at Gloucester, happy and hopeful, but silent.

"How's the chestnut crop?" she asked him.

"Fine. Ver' good," he answered. "That's what Patsy says – and Patsy knows."

She pursued her inquiries. "Who cooks for you? Who keeps your camp in order? Who washes your clothes?"

"Mrs. Patsy," said he. "She's as good a cook as anybody need want."

"And how is the prospect?" asked Ella.

Arnold turned lazily over, where he lay on the sand at her feet, and looked at her long and hungrily. "The prospect," said he, "is divine."

Ella blushed and laughed and said he was a goose; but he kept on looking.

He wouldn't tell her much, though. "Don't, dear," he said when she urged for information. "It's too serious. If I should fail—"

"You won't fail!" she protested. "You can't fail! And if you do – why – as I told you before, I like to camp out!"

But when he tried to take some natural advantage of her friendliness she teased him – said he was growing to look just like his father! Which made them both laugh.

Arnold returned and settled down to business. He purchased stores of pasteboard, of paper, of printers ink, and a little machine to fold cartons. Thus equipped he retired to his fastness, and set dark-eyed Caterlina to work in a little box factory of his own; while clever Guiseppe ran the printing press, and Mafalda pasted. Cartons, piled flat, do not take up much room, even in thousands.

Then Arnold loafed deliberately.

"Why not your Mr. Blake work no more?" inquired Mrs. Patsy of her spouse.

"O he work – he work hard," replied Patsy. "You women – you not understand work!"

Mrs. Patsy tossed her head and answered in fluent Italian, so that her husband presently preferred out of doors occupation; but in truth Arnold Blake did not seem to do much that summer. He loafed under his great trees, regarding them lovingly; he loafed by his lonely upper waterfall, with happy dreaming eyes; he loafed in his little blue lake – floating face to the sky, care free and happy as a child. And if he scribbled a great deal – at any sudden moment when the fit seized him, why that was only his weakness as a poet.

Toward the end of September, he invited an old college friend up to see him; now a newspaper man – in the advertising department. These two seemed to have merry times together. They fished and walked and climbed, they talked much; and at night were heard roaring with laughter by their hickory fire.

"Have you got any money left?" demanded his friend.

"About a thou—" said Arnold. "And that's got to last me till next spring, you know."

"Blow it in – blow in every cent – it'll pay you. You can live through the winter somehow. How about transportation?"

"Got a nice electric dray – light and strong. Runs down hill with the load to tidewater, you see, and there's the old motorboat to take it down. Brings back supplies."

"Great! – It's simply great! Now, you save enough to eat till spring and give me the rest. Send me your stuff, all of it! and as soon as you get in a cent above expenses – send me that – I'll 'tend to the advertising!"

He did. He had only $800 to begin with. When the first profits began to come in he used them better; and as they rolled up he still spent them. Arnold began to feel anxious, to want to save money; but his friend replied: "You furnish the meal – I'll furnish the market!" And he did.

He began it in the subway in New York; that place of misery where eyes, ears, nose, and common self-respect are all offended, and even an advertisement is some relief.

"Hill" said the first hundred dollars, on a big blank space for a week.

"Mill" said the second. "Hill Mill Meal," said the third.

The fourth was more explicit.

> *"When tired of every cereal*
> *Try our new material –*
> *Hill Mill Meal."*

The fifth –

> *"Ask your grocer if you feel*
> *An interest in Hill Mill Meal.*
> *Samples free."*

The sixth –

> *"A paradox! Surprising! True!*
> *Made of chestnuts but brand new!*
> *Hill Mill Meal."*

And the seventh –

> *"Solomon said it couldn't be done,*
> *There wasn't a new thing under the sun –*
> *He never ate Hill Mill Meal!"*

Seven hundred dollars went in this one method only; and meanwhile diligent young men in automobiles were making arrangements and leaving circulars and samples with the grocer. Anybody will take free samples and everybody likes chestnuts. Are they not the crown of luxury in turkey stuffing? The gem of the confection as *marron glaces*? The sure profit of the corner-merchant with his little charcoal stove, even when they are half scorched and half cold? Do we not all love them, roast, or boiled – only they are so messy to peel.

Arnold's only secret was his process; but his permanent advantage was in the fine quality of his nuts, and his exquisite care in manufacture. In dainty, neat, easily opened cartons (easily shut too, so they were not left gaping to gather dust), he put upon the market a sort of samp, chestnuts perfectly shelled and husked, roasted and ground, both coarse and fine. Good? You stood and ate half a package out of your hand, just tasting of it. Then you sat down and ate the other half.

He made pocket-size cartons, filled with whole ones, crafty man! And they became "The Business Man's Lunch" forthwith. A pocketful of roast chestnuts – and no mess nor trouble! And when they were boiled – well, we all know how good boiled chestnuts are. As to the meal, a new variety of mush appeared, and gems, muffins, and pancakes that made old epicures feel young again in the joys of a fresh taste, and gave America new standing in the eyes of France.

The orders rolled in and the poetry rolled out. The market for a new food is as wide as the world; and Jim Chamberlin was mad to conquer it, but Arnold explained to him that his total output was only so many bushels a year.

"Nonsense!" said Jim. "You're a – a – well, a *poet*! Come! Use your imagination! Look at these hills about you – they could grow chestnuts to the horizon! Look at this valley, that rattling river, a bunch of mills could run here! You can support a fine population – a whole village of people – there's no end to it, I tell you!"

"And where would my privacy be then and the beauty of the place?" asked Arnold, "I love this green island of chestnut trees, and the winding empty valley, just freckled with a few farms. I'd hate to support a village!"

"But you can be a Millionaire!" said Jim.

"I don't want to be a Millionaire," Arnold cheerfully replied.

Jim gazed at him, opening and shutting his mouth in silence.

"You – confounded old – *poet*!" he burst forth at last.

"I can't help that," said Arnold.

"You'd better ask Miss Sutherland about it, I think," his friend drily suggested.

"To be sure! I had forgotten that – I will," the poet replied.

Then he invited her to come up and visit his Hill, met her at the train with the smooth, swift, noiseless, smell-less electric car, and held her hand in blissful silence as they rolled up the valley road. They wound more slowly up his graded avenue, green-arched by chestnut boughs.

He showed her the bit of meadowy inlet where the mill stood, by the heavy lower fall; the broad bright packing rooms above, where the busy Italian boys and girls chattered gaily as they worked. He showed her the second fall, with his little low-humming electric plant; a bluestone building, vine-covered, lovely, a tiny temple to the flower-god.

"It does our printing," said Arnold, "gives us light, heat and telephones. And runs the cars."

Then he showed her the shaded reaches of his lake, still, starred with lilies, lying dark under the curving boughs of water maples, doubling the sheer height of flower-crowned cliffs.

She held his hand tighter as they wound upward, circling the crown of the hill that she might see the splendid range of outlook; and swinging smoothly down a little and out on the green stretch before the house.

Ella gasped with delight. Gray, rough and harmonious, hung with woodbine and wildgrape, broad-porched and wide-windowed, it faced the setting sun. She stood looking, looking, over the green miles of tumbling hills, to the blue billowy far-off peaks swimming in soft light.

"There's the house," said Arnold, "furnished – there's a view room built on – for you, dear; I did it myself. There's the hill – and the little lake and one waterfall all for us! And the spring, and the garden, and some very nice Italians. And it will earn – my Hill and Mill, about three or four thousand dollars a year – above *all* expenses!"

"How perfectly splendid!" said Ella. "But there's one thing you've left out!"

"What's that?" he asked, a little dashed.

"*You!*" she answered. "Arnold Blake! My Poet!"

"Oh, I forgot," he added, after some long still moments. "I ought to ask you about this first. Jim Chamberlain says I can cover all these hills with chestnuts, fill this valley with people, string that little river with a row of mills, make breakfast for all the world – and be a Millionaire. Shall I?"

"For goodness sake – *No!*" said Ella. "Millionaire, indeed? And spoil the most perfect piece of living I ever saw or heard of!"

Then there was a period of bliss, indeed there was enough to last indefinitely.

But one pleasure they missed. They never saw even the astonished face, much less the highly irritated mind, of old John Blake, when he first returned from his two years of travel. The worst of it was he had eaten the stuff all the way home-and liked it! They told him it was Chestnut Meal – but that meant nothing to him. Then he began to find the jingling advertisements in every magazine; things that ran in his head and annoyed him.

> *"When corn or rice no more are nice,*
> *When oatmeal seems to pall,*
> *When cream of wheat's no longer sweet*
> *And you abhor them all—"*
> *"I do abhor them all!" the old man would*
> *vow, and take up a newspaper, only to read:*
> *"Better than any food that grows*
> *Upon or in the ground,*
> *Strong, pure and sweet*
> *And good to eat*
> *Our tree-born nuts are found."*
> *"Bah!" said Mr. Blake, and tried*
> *another, which only showed him:*
> *"Good for mother, good for brother,*
> *Good for child;*
> *As for father – well, rather!*

He's just wild."
He was. But the truth never dawned
upon him till he came to this one:
"About my hut
There grew a nut
Nutritious;
I could but feel
'Twould make a meal
Delicious.
I had a Hill,
I built a Mill
Upon it.
And hour by hour
I sought for power
To run it.
To burn my trees
Or try the breeze
Seemed crazy;
To use my arm
Had little charm –
I'm lazy!
The nuts are here,
But coal! – Quite dear
We find it!
We have the stuff.
Where's power enough
To grind it?
What force to find
My nuts to grind?

I've found it!
The Water-fall
Could beat 'em all –
And ground it!

PETER POETICUS."

"Confound your impudence!" he wrote to his son. "And confound your poetic stupidity in not making a Big Business now you've got a start! But I understand you do make a living, and I'm thankful for that."

* * *

Arnold and Ella, watching the sunset from their hammock, laughed softly together, and lived.

Martha's Mother

It was nine feet long.

It was eight feet high.

It was six feet wide.

There was a closet, actually! – a closet one foot deep – that was why she took this room. There was the bed, and the trunk, and just room to open the closet door part way – that accounted for the length. There was the bed and the bureau and the chair – that accounted for the width. Between the bedside and the bureau and chair side was a strip extending the whole nine feet. There was room to turn around by the window. There was room to turn round by the door. Martha was thin.

One, two, three, four – turn.

One, two, three, four – turn.

She managed it nicely.

"It is a stateroom," she always said to herself. "It is a luxurious, large, well-furnished stateroom with a real window. It is *not* a cell."

Martha had a vigorous constructive imagination. Sometimes it was the joy of her life, her magic carpet, her Aladdin's lamp. Sometimes it frightened her – frightened her horribly, it was so strong.

The cell idea had come to her one gloomy day, and she had foolishly allowed it to enter – played with it a little while. Since then she had to keep a special bar on that particular intruder, so she had arranged a stateroom "set," and forcibly kept it on hand.

Martha was a stenographer and typewriter in a real estate office. She got $12 a week, and was thankful for it. It was steady pay, and enough to live on. Seven dollars she paid for board and lodging, ninety cents for her six lunches, ten a day for carfare, including Sundays; seventy-five for laundry; one for her mother – that left one dollar and sixty-five cents for clothes, shoes, gloves, everything. She had tried cheaper board, but made up the cost in doctor's bills; and lost a good place by being ill.

"Stone walls do not a prison make, nor hall bedrooms a cage," said she determinedly. "Now then – here is another evening – what shall I do? Library? No. My eyes are tired. Besides, three times a week is enough. 'Tisn't club night. Will *not* sit in the parlor. Too wet to walk. Can't sew, worse'n reading – O good *land*! I'm almost ready to go with Basset!"

She shook herself and paced up and down again.

Prisoners form the habit of talking to themselves – this was the suggestion that floated through her mind – that cell idea again.

"I've got to get out of this!" said Martha, stopping short. "It's enough to drive a girl crazy!"

The driving process was stayed by a knock at the door. "Excuse me for coming up," said a voice. "It's Mrs. MacAvelly."

Martha knew this lady well. She was a friend of Miss Podder at the Girls' Trade Union Association. "Come in. I'm glad to see you!" she said hospitably. "Have the chair – or the bed's really more comfortable!"

"I was with Miss Podder this evening and she was anxious to know whether your union has gained any since the last meeting – I told her I'd find out – I had nothing else to do. Am I intruding?"

"Intruding!" Martha, gave a short laugh. "Why, it's a godsend, Mrs.

MacAvelly! If you knew how dull the evenings are to us girls!"

"Don't you – go out much? To – to theaters – or parks?" The lady's tone was sympathetic and not inquisitive.

"Not very much," said Martha, rather sardonically. "Theaters – two girls, two dollars, and twenty cents carfare. Parks, twenty cents – walk your feet off, or sit on the benches and be stared at. Museums – not open evenings."

"But don't you have visitors – in the parlor here?"

"Did you see it?" asked Martha.

Mrs. MacAvelly had seen it. It was cold and also stuffy. It was ugly and shabby and stiff. Three tired girls sat there, two trying to read by a strangled gaslight overhead; one trying to entertain a caller in a social fiction of privacy at the other end of the room.

"Yes, we have visitors – but mostly they ask us out. And some of us don't go," said Martha darkly.

"I see, I see!" said Mrs. MacAvelly, with a pleasant smile; and Martha wondered whether she did see, or was just being civil.

"For instance, there's Mr. Basset," the girl pursued, somewhat recklessly; meaning that her visitor should understand her.

"Mr. Basset?"

"Yes, 'Pond & Basset' – one of my employers."

Mrs. MacAvelly looked pained. "Couldn't you – er – avoid it?" she suggested.

"You mean shake him?" asked Martha. "Why, yes – I could. Might lose my job. Get another place – another Basset, probably."

"I see!" said Mrs. MacAvelly again. "Like the Fox and the Swarm of Flies! There ought to be a more comfortable way of living for all you girls! And how about the union—I have to be going back to Miss Podder."

Martha gave her the information she wanted, and started to accompany her downstairs. They heard the thin jangle of the door-bell, down through the echoing halls, and the dragging feet of the servant coming up. A kinky black head was thrust in at the door.

"Mr. Basset, callin' on Miss Joyce," was announced formally.

Martha stiffened. "Please tell Mr. Basset I am not feeling well to-night – and beg to be excused.

She looked rather defiantly at her guest, as Lucy clattered down the long stairs; then stole to the railing and peered down the narrow well. She heard the message given with pompous accuracy, and then heard the clear, firm tones of Mr. Basset:

"Tell Miss Joyce that I will wait."

Martha returned to her room in three long steps, slipped off her shoes and calmly got into bed. "Good-night, Mrs. MacAvelly," she said. "I'm so sorry, but my head aches and

I've gone to bed! Would you be so very good as to tell Lucy so as you're going down."

Mrs. MacAvelly said she would, and departed, and Martha lay conscientiously quiet till she heard the door shut far below.

She was quiet, but she was not contented.

* * *

Yet the discontent of Martha was as nothing to the discontent of Mrs. Joyce, her mother, in her rural home. Here was a woman of fifty-three, alert, vigorous, nervously active; but an automobile-agitated horse had danced upon her, and her usefulness, as she understood it, was over. She could not get about without crutches, nor use her hands for needlework, though still able to write after a fashion. Writing was not her *forte*, however, at the best of times.

She lived with a widowed sister in a little, lean dusty farmhouse by the side of the road; a hill road that went nowhere in particular, and was too steep for those who were going there.

Brisk on her crutches, Mrs. Joyce hopped about the little house, there was nowhere else to hop to. She had talked her sister out long since – Mary never had never much to say. Occasionally they quarreled and then Mrs. Joyce hopped only in her room, a limited process.

She sat at the window one day, staring greedily out at the lumpy rock-ribbed road; silent, perforce, and tapping the arms of her chair with nervous intensity. Suddenly she called out, "Mary! Mary Ames! Come here quick! There's somebody coming up the road!"

Mary came in, as fast as she could with eggs in her apron. "It's Mrs.

Holmes!" she said. "And a boarder, I guess."

"No, it ain't," said Mrs. Joyce, eagerly. "It's that woman that's visiting the Holmes – she was in church last week, Myra Slater told me about her. Her name's MacDowell, or something."

"It ain't MacDowell," said her sister. "I remember; it's MacAvelly."

This theory was borne out by Mrs. Holmes' entrance and introduction of her friend.

"Have you any eggs for us, Mrs. Ames?" she said.

"Set down – set down," said Mrs. Ames cordially. "I was just getting in my eggs – but here's only about eight yet. How many was you wantin'?"

"I want all you can find," said Mrs. Holmes. "Two dozen, three dozen – all I can carry."

"There's two hens layin' out – I'll go and look them up. And I ain't been in the woodshed chamber yet. I'll go'n hunt. You set right here with my sister." And Mrs. Ames bustled off.

"Pleasant view you have here," said Mrs. MacAvelly politely, while Mrs.

Holmes rocked and fanned herself.

"Pleasant! Glad you think so, ma'am. Maybe you city folks wouldn't think so much of views if you had nothing else to look at!"

"What would you like to look at?"

"Folks!" said Mrs. Joyce briefly. "Lots of folks! Somethin' doin'."

"You'd like to live in the city?"

"Yes, ma'am – I would so! I worked in the city once when I was a girl. Waitress. In a big restaurant. I got to be cashier – in two years! I like the business!"

"And then you married a farmer?" suggested Mrs. Holmes.

"Yes, I did. And I never was sorry, Mrs. Holmes. David Joyce was a mighty good man. We was engaged before I left home – I was workin' to help earn, so 't we could marry."

"There's plenty of work on a farm, isn't there?" Mrs. MacAvelly inquired.

Mrs. Joyce's eager eyes kindled. "There is *so!*" she agreed. "Lots to do. And lots to manage! We kept help then, and the farm hands, and the children growin' up. And some seasons we took boarders."

"Did you like that?"

"I did. I liked it first rate. I like lots of people, and to do for 'em. The best time I ever had was one summer I ran a hotel."

"Ran a hotel! How interesting!"

"Yes'm – it was interesting! I had a cousin who kept a summer hotel up here in the mountains a piece – and he was short-handed that summer and got me to go up and help him out. Then he was taken sick, and I had the whole thing on my shoulders! I just enjoyed it! And the place cleared more that summer'n it ever did! He said 'twas owin' to his advantageous buyin'. Maybe 'twas! But I could 'a bought more advantageous than he did – I could a' told him that. Point o' fact, I did tell him that – and he wouldn't have me again."

"That was a pity!" said Mrs. Holmes. "And I suppose if it wasn't for your foot you would do that now – and enjoy it!"

"Of course I could!" protested Mrs. Joyce. "Do it better 'n ever, city or country! But here I am, tied by the leg! And dependent on my sister and children! It galls me terribly!"

Mrs. Holmes nodded sympathetically. "You are very brave, Mrs. Joyce," she said. "I admire your courage, and—" she couldn't say patience, so she said, "cheerfulness."

Mrs. Ames came in with more eggs. "Not enough, but some," she said, and the visitors departed therewith.

Toward the end of the summer, Miss Podder at the Girls' Trade Union Association, sweltering in the little office, was pleased to receive a call from her friend, Mrs. MacAvelly.

"I'd no idea you were in town," she said.

"I'm not, officially," answered her visitor, "just stopping over between visits. It's hotter than I thought it would be, even on the upper west side."

"Think what it is on the lower east side!" answered Miss Podder, eagerly. "Hot all day – and hot at night! My girls do suffer so! They are so crowded!"

"How do the clubs get on?" asked Mrs. MacAvelly. "Have your girls any residence clubs yet?"

"No – nothing worth while. It takes somebody to run it right, you know. The girls can't; the people who work for money can't meet our wants – and the people who work for love, don't work well as a rule."

Mrs. McAvelly smiled sympathetically. "You're quite right about that," she said. "But really – some of those 'Homes' are better than others, aren't they?"

"The girls hate them," answered Miss Podder. "They'd rather board – even two or three in a room. They like their independence. You remember Martha Joyce?"

Mrs. MacAvelly remembered. "Yes," she said, "I do – I met her mother this summer."

"She's a cripple, isn't she?" asked Miss Podder. "Martha's told me about her."

"Why, not exactly. She's what a Westerner might call 'crippled up some,' but she's livelier than most well persons." And she amused her friend with a vivid rehearsal of Mrs. Joyce's love of the city and her former triumphs in restaurant and hotel.

"She'd be a fine one to run such a house for the girls, wouldn't she?" suddenly cried Miss Podder.

"Why – if she could," Mrs. MacAvelly admitted slowly.

"*Could! Wh*y not? You say she gets about easily enough. All she's have to do is *manage, yo*u see. She could order by 'phone and keep the servants running!"

"I'm sure she'd like it," said Mrs. MacAvelly. "But don't such things require capital?"

Miss Podder was somewhat daunted. "Yes – some; but I guess we could raise it. If we could find the right house!"

"Let's look in the paper," suggested her visitor. "I've got a *Herald.*"

"There's one that reads all right," Miss Podder presently proclaimed. "The location's good, and it's got a lot of rooms – furnished. I suppose it would cost too much."

Mrs. MacAvelly agreed, rather ruefully.

"Come," she said, "it's time to close here, surely. Let's go and look at that house, anyway. It's not far."

They got their permit and were in the house very shortly. "I remember this place," said Miss Podder. "It was for sale earlier in the summer."

It was one of those once spacious houses, not of "old," but at least of "middle-aged" New York; with large rooms arbitrarily divided into smaller ones."p"It's been a boarding-house, that's clear," said Mrs. MacAvelly.

"Why, of course," Miss Podder answered, eagerly plunging about and examining everything. "Anybody could see that! But it's been done over – most thoroughly. The cellar's all whitewashed, and there's a new furnace, and new range, and look at this icebox!" It was an ice-closet, as a matter of fact, of large capacity, and a most sanitary aspect.

"Isn't it too big?" Mrs. MacAvelly inquired.

"Not for a boarding-house, my dear," Miss Podder enthusiastically replied. "Why, they could buy a side of beef with that ice-box! And look at the extra ovens! Did you ever see a place better furnished – for what we want? It looks as if it had been done on purpose!"

"It does, doesn't it?" said Mrs. MacAvelley.

Miss Podder, eager and determined, let no grass grow under her feet.

The rent of the place was within reason.

"If they had twenty boarders – and some "mealers," I believe it could be done! she said. "It's a miracle – this house. Seems as if somebody had done it just for us!"

* * *

Armed with a list of girls who would agree to come, for six and seven dollars a week, Miss Podder made a trip to Willettville and laid the matter before Martha's mother.

"What an outrageous rent!" said that lady.

"Yes – New York rents *are* rather inconsiderate," Miss Podder admitted. "But see, here's a guaranteed income if the girls stay – and I'm sure they will; and if the cooking's good you could easily get table boarders besides."

Mrs. Joyce hopped to the bureau and brought out a hard, sharp-pointed pencil, and a lined writing tablet.

"Let's figger it out," said she. "You say that house rents furnished at $3,200. It would take a cook and a chambermaid!"

"And a furnace man," said Miss Podder. "They come to about fifty a year. The cook would be thirty a month, the maid twenty-five, if you got first-class help, and you'd need it."

"That amounts to $710 altogether," stated Mrs. Joyce.

"Fuel and light and such things would be $200," Miss Podder estimated, "and I think you ought to allow $200 more for breakage and extras generally."

"That's $4,310 already," said Mrs. Joyce.

Then there's the food," Miss Podder went on. "How much do you think it would cost to feed twenty girls, two meals a day, and three Sundays?"

"And three more," Mrs. Joyce added, "with me, and the help, twenty-three. I could do it for $2.00 a week apiece."

"Oh!" said Miss Podder. "*Could yo*u? At New York prices?"

"See me do it!" said Mrs. Joyce.

"That makes a total expense of $6,710 a year. Now, what's the income, ma'am?"

The income was clear – if they could get it. Ten girls at $6.00 and ten at $7.00 made $130.00 a week – $6,700.00 a year.

"There you are!" said Mrs. Joyce triumphantly. "And the 'mealers' – if my griddle-cakes don't fetch 'em I'm mistaken! If I have ten – at $5.00 a week and clear $3.00 off 'em – that'll be another bit – $1,560.00 more. Total income $8,320.00. More'n one thousand clear! Maybe I can feed 'em a little higher – or charge less!"

The two women worked together for an hour or so; Mrs. Ames drawn in later with demands as to butter, eggs, and "eatin' chickens."

"There's an ice-box as big as a closet," said Miss Podder.

Mrs. Joyce smiled triumphantly. "Good!" she said. "I can buy my critters of Judson here and have him freight 'em down. I can get apples here and potatoes, and lots of stuff."

"You'll need, probably, a little capital to start with," suggested Miss Podder. "I think the Association could – "

"It don't have to, thank you just the same," said Mrs. Joyce. "I've got enough in my stocking to take me to New York and get some fuel. Besides, all my boarders is goin' to pay in advance – that's the one sure way. The mealers can buy tickets!"

Her eyes danced. She fairly coursed about the room on her nimble crutches.

"My!" she said, "it will seem good to have my girl to feed again."

* * *

The house opened in September, full of eager girls with large appetites long unsatisfied. The place was new-smelling, fresh-painted, beautifully clean. The furnishing was cheap, but fresh, tasteful, with minor conveniences dear to the hearts of women.

The smallest rooms were larger than hall bedrooms, the big ones were shared by friends. Martha and her mother had a chamber with two beds and space to spare!

The dining-room was very large, and at night the tables were turned into "settles" by the wall and the girls could dance to the sound of a hired pianola. So could the "mealers," when invited; and there was soon a waiting list of both sexes.

"I guess I can make a livin'," said Mrs. Joyce, "allowin' for bad years."

"I don't understand how you feed us so well – for so little," said Miss

Podder, who was one of the boarders.

"'Sh!" said Mrs. Joyce, privately. "Your breakfast don't really cost more'n ten cents – nor your dinner fifteen – not the way I order! Things taste good 'cause they're *cooked* good – that's all!"

"And you have no troubles with your help?"

"'Sh!" said Mrs. Joyce again, more privately. "I work 'em hard – and pay 'em a bonus – a dollar a week extra, as long as they give satisfaction. It reduces my profits some – but it's worth it!"

"It's worth it to us, I'm sure!" said Miss Podder.

Mrs. MacAvelly called one evening in the first week, with warm interest and approval. The tired girls were sitting about in comfortable rockers and lounges, under comfortable lights, reading and sewing. The untired ones were dancing in the dining-room, to the industrious pianola, or having games of cards in the parlor.

"Do you think it'll be a success?" she asked her friend.

"It *is* a success!" Miss Podder triumphantly replied. "I'm immensely proud of it!"

"I should think you would be," aid Mrs. MacAvelly.

The doorbell rang sharply.

Mrs. Joyce was hopping through the hall at the moment, and promptly opened it.

"Does Miss Martha Joyce board here?" inquired a gentleman.

"She does."

"I should like to see her," said he, handing in his card.

Mrs. Joyce read the card and looked at the man, her face setting in hard lines. She had heard that name before.

"Miss Joyce is engaged," she replied curtly, still holding the door.

He could see past her into the bright, pleasant rooms. He heard the music below, the swing of dancing feet, Martha's gay laugh from the parlor.

The little lady on crutches blocked his path.

"Are you the housekeeper of this place?" he asked sharply.

"I'm more'n that!" she answered. "I'm Martha's mother."

Mr. Basset concluded he would not wait.

A Middle-Sized Artist

When Rosamond's brown eyes seemed almost too big for her brilliant little face, and her brown curls danced on her shoulders, she had a passionate enthusiasm for picture books. She loved "the reading," but when the picture made what her young mind was trying to grasp suddenly real before her, the stimulus reaching the brain from two directions at once, she used to laugh with delight and hug the book.

The vague new words describing things she never saw suggested "castle," a thing of gloom and beauty; and then upon the page came The Castle itself, looming dim and huge before her, with drooping heavy banners against the sunset calm.

How she had regretted it, scarce knowing why, when the pictures were less real than the description; when the princess, whose beauty made her the Rose of the World (her name was Rosamond, too!), appeared in visible form no prettier, no, not as pretty, as The Fair One with The Golden Locks in the other book! And what an outcry she made to her indifferent family when first confronted by the unbelievable blasphemy of an illustration that differed from the text!

"But, Mother – see!" she cried. "It says, 'Her beauty was crowned by rich braids of golden hair, wound thrice around her shapely head,' and this girl has black hair – in curls! Did the man forget what he just said?"

Her mother didn't seem to care at all. "They often get them wrong," she said. "Perhaps it was an old plate. Run away, dear, Mama is very busy."

But Rosamond cared.

She asked her father more particularly about this mysterious "old plate," and he, being a publisher, was able to give her much information thereanent. She learned that these wonderful reinforcements of her adored stories did not emanate direct from the brain of the beneficent author, but were a supplementary product by some draughtsman, who cared far less for what was in the author's mind than for what was in his own; who was sometimes lazy, sometimes arrogant, sometimes incompetent; sometimes all three. That to find a real artist, who could make pictures and was willing to make them like the picture the author saw, was very unusual.

"You see, little girl," said Papa, "the big artists are too big to do it – they'd rather make their own pictures; and the little artists are too little – they can't make real ones of their own ideas, nor yet of another's."

"Aren't there any middle-sized artists?" asked the child.

"Sometimes," said her father; and then he showed her some of the perfect illustrations which leave nothing to be desired, as the familiar ones by Teniel and Henry Holiday, which make Alice's Adventures and the Hunting of the

Snark so doubly dear, Dore and Retsch and Tony Johannot and others.

"When I grow up," said Rosamond decidedly, "I'm going to be a middle-sized artist!"

Fortunately for her aspirations the line of study required was in no way different at first from that of general education. Her parents explained that a good illustrator ought to know pretty much everything. So she obediently went through school and college, and when the time came for real work at her drawing there was no objection to that.

"It is pretty work," said her mother, "a beautiful accomplishment. It will always be a resource for her."

"A girl is better off to have an interest," said her father, "and not marry the first fool that asks her. When she does fall in love this won't stand in the way; it never does; with a woman. Besides – she may need it sometime."

So her father helped and her mother did not hinder, and when the brown eyes were less disproportionate and the brown curls wreathed high upon her small fine head, she found herself at twenty-one more determined to be a middle-sized artist than she was at ten.

Then love came; in the person of one of her father's readers; a strenuous new-fledged college graduate; big, handsome, domineering, opinionative; who was accepting a salary of four dollars a week for the privilege of working in a publishing house, because he loved books and meant to write them some day.

They saw a good deal of each other, and were pleasantly congenial. She sympathized with his criticisms of modem fiction; he sympathized with her criticisms of modern illustration; and her young imagination began to stir with sweet memories of poetry and romance; and sweet hopes of beautiful reality.

There are cases where the longest way round is the shortest way home; but Mr. Allen G. Goddard chose differently. He had read much about women and about love, beginning with a full foundation from the ancients; but lacked an understanding of the modern woman, such as he had to deal with.

Therefore, finding her evidently favorable, his theories and inclinations suiting, he made hot love to her, breathing, "My Wife!" into her ear before she had scarce dared to think "my darling!" and suddenly wrapping her in his arms with hot kisses, while she was still musing on "The Hugenot Lovers" and the kisses she dared dream of came in slow gradation as in the Sonnets From the Portuguese.

He was in desperate earnest. "O you are so beautiful!" he cried. "So unbelievably beautiful! Come to me, my Sweet!" for she had sprung away and stood panting and looking at him, half reproachful, half angry.

"You love me, Dearest! You cannot deny it!" he cried. "And I love you – Ah! You shall know!"

He was single-hearted, sincere; stirred by a very genuine overwhelming emotion. She on the contrary was moved by many emotions at once; – a pleasure she was half ashamed of; a disappointment she could not clearly define; as if some one had told her the whole plot of a promising new novel; a sense of fear of the new hopes she had been holding, and of startled loyalty to her long-held purposes.

"Stop!" she said – for he evidently mistook her agitation, and thought her silence was consent. "I suppose I do – love you – a little; but you've no right to kiss me like that!"

His eyes shone. "You Darling! *My* Darling!" he said. "You will give me the right, won't you? Now, Dearest – see! I am waiting!" And he held out his arms to her.

But Rosamond was more and more displeased. "You will have to wait. I'm sorry; but I'm not ready to be engaged, yet! You know my plans. Why I'm going to Paris this year! I'm going to work! It will be ever so long before I'm ready to – to settle down."

"As to that," he said more calmly, "I cannot of course offer immediate marriage, but we can wait for that – together! You surely will not leave me – if you love me!"

"I think I love you," she said conscientiously, "at least I did think so. You've upset it all, somehow – you hurry me so! – no – I can't bind myself yet."

"Do you tell me to wait for you?" he asked; his deep voice still strong to touch her heart. "How long, Dearest?"

"I'm not asking you to wait for me – I don't want to promise anything – nor to have you. But when I have made a place – am really doing something – perhaps then—"

He laughed harshly. "Do not deceive yourself, child, nor me! If you loved me there would be none of this poor wish for freedom – for a career. You don't love me – that's all!"

He waited for her to deny this. She said nothing. He did not know how hard it was for her to keep from crying – and from running to his arms.

"Very well," said he. "Goodby!" – And he was gone.

All that happened three years ago.

Allen Goddard took it very hard; and added to his earlier ideas about women another, that "the new woman" was a selfish heartless creature, indifferent to her own true nature.

He had to stay where he was and work, owing to the pressure of circumstances, which made it harder; so he became something of a mysogynyst; which is not a bad thing when a young man has to live on very little and build a place for himself.

In spite of this cynicism he could not remove from his mind those softly brilliant dark eyes; the earnest thoughtful lines of the pure young face; and the changing lights and shadows in that silky hair. Also, in the course of his work, he was continually reminded of her; for her characteristic drawings appeared more and frequently in the magazines, and grew better, stronger, more convincing from year to year.

Stories of adventure she illustrated admirably; children's stories to perfection; fairy stories – she was the delight of thousands of children, who never once thought that the tiny quaint rose in a circle that was to be found in all those charming pictures meant a name. But he noticed that she never illustrated love stories; and smiled bitterly, to himself.

And Rosamond?

There were moments when she was inclined to forfeit her passage money and throw herself unreservedly into those strong arms which had held her so tightly for a little while. But a bud picked open does not bloom naturally; and her tumultuous feelings were thoroughly dissipated by a long strong attack of *mal de mer*. She derived two advantages from her experience: one a period of safe indifference to all advances from eager fellow students and more cautious older admirers; the other a facility she had not before aspired to in the making of pictures of love and lovers.

She made pictures of him from memory – so good, so moving, that she put them religiously away in a portfolio by themselves; and only took them out – sometimes. She illustrated, solely for her own enjoyment some of her girlhood's best loved poems and stories. "The Rhyme of the Duchess May," "The Letter L," "In a Balcony," "In a Gondola." And hid them from herself even – they rather frightened her.

After three years of work abroad she came home with an established reputation, plenty of orders, and an interest that would not be stifled in the present state of mind of Mr. Allen Goddard.

She found him still at work, promoted to fifteen dollars a week by this time, and adding to his income by writing political and statistical articles for the magazines. He talked, when they met, of this work, with little enthusiasm, and asked her politely about hers.

"Anybody can see mine!" she told him lightly. "And judge it easily."

"Mine too," he answered. "It to-day is – and to-morrow is cast into the waste-basket. He who runs may read – if he runs fast enough."

He told himself he was glad he was not bound to this hard, bright creature, so unnaturally self-sufficient, and successful.

She told herself that he had never cared for her, really, that was evident.

Then an English publisher who liked her work sent her a new novel by a new writer, "A. Gage." "I know this is out of your usual line," he said, "but I want a woman to do it, and I want you to be the woman, if possible. Read it and see what you think. Any terms you like."

The novel was called "Two and One;" and she began it with languid interest, because she liked that publisher and wished to give full reasons for refusing. It opened with two young people who were much in love with one another; the girl a talented young sculptor with a vivid desire for fame; and another girl, a cousin of the man, ordinary enough, but pretty and sweet, and with no desires save those of romance and domesticity. The first couple broke off a happy engagement because she insisted on studying in Paris, and her lover, who could neither go with her, nor immediately marry her, naturally objected.

Rosamond sat up in bed; pulled a shawl round her, swung the electric light nearer, and went on.

The man was broken-hearted; he suffered tortures of loneliness, disappointment, doubt, self-depreciation. He waited, held at his work by a dependent widowed mother; hoping against hope that his lost one would come back. The girl meanwhile made good in her art work; she was not a great sculptor but a popular portraitist and maker of little genre groups. She had other offers, but refused them, being hardened in her ambitions, and, possibly, still withheld by her early love.

The man after two or three years of empty misery and hard grinding work, falls desperately ill; the pretty cousin helps the mother nurse him, and shows her own affection. He offers the broken remnants of his heart, which she eagerly undertakes to patch up; and they become tolerably happy, at least she is.

But the young sculptor in Paris! Rosamond hurried through the pages to the last chapter. There was the haughty and triumphant heroine in her studio. She had been given a medal – she had plenty of orders – she had just refused a Count. Everyone had gone, and she sat alone in her fine studio, self-satisfied and triumphant.

Then she picks up an old American paper which was lying about; reads it idly as she smokes her cigarette – and then both paper and cigarette drop to the floor, and she sits staring.

Then she starts up – her arms out – vainly. "Wait! O Wait!" she cries – "I was coining back, "—and drops into her chair again. The fire is out. She is alone.

Rosamond shut the book and leaned back upon her pillow. Her eyes were shut tight; but a little gleaming line showed on either cheek under the near light. She put the light out and lay quite still.

* * *

Allen G. Goddard, in his capacity as "reader" was looking over some popular English novels which his firm wished to arrange about publishing in America. He left "Two and One" to the last. It was the second edition, the illustrated one which he had not seen yet; the first he had read before. He regarded it from time to time with a peculiar expression.

"Well," he said to himself, "I suppose I can stand it if the others do. "

And he opened the book.

The drawing was strong work certainly, in a style he did not know. They were striking pictures, vivid, real, carrying out in last detail the descriptions given, and the very spirit of the book, showing it more perfectly than the words. There was the tender happiness of the lovers, the courage, the firmness, the fixed purpose in the young sculptor insisting on her freedom, and the gay pride of the successful artist in her work.

There was beauty and charm in this character, yet the face was always turned away, and there was a haunting suggestion of familiarity in the figure. The other girl was beautiful, and docile in expression; well-dressed and graceful; yet somehow unattractive, even at her best, as nurse; and the man was extremely well drawn, both in his happy ardor as a lover, and his grinding misery when rejected. He was very good-looking; and here too was this strong sense of resemblance.

"Why he looks like *me*!" suddenly cried the reader – springing to his feet. "Confound his impudence!" he cried. "How in thunder!" Then he looked at the picture again, more carefully, a growing suspicion in his face; and turned hurriedly to the title page, – seeing a name unknown to him.

This subtle, powerful convincing work; this man who undeniably suggested him; this girl whose eyes he could not see; he turned from one to another and hurried to the back of the book.

"The fire was out – she was alone." And there, in the remorseless light of a big lamp before her fireless hearth, the crumpled newspaper beside her, and all hope gone from a limp, crouching little figure, sat – why, he would know her among a thousand – even if her face was buried in her hands, and sunk on the arm of the chair – it was Rosamond!

* * *

She was in her little downtown room and hard at work when he entered; but she had time to conceal a new book quickly.

He came straight to her; he had a book in his hand, open – he held it out.

"Did you do this?" he demanded. "Tell me – tell me!" His voice was very unreliable.

She lifted her eyes slowly to his; large, soft, full of dancing lights, and the rich color swept to the gold-lighted borders of her hair.

"Did you?" she asked.

He was taken aback. "I!" said he. "Why it's by –" he showed her the title-page. "By A. Gage," he read.

"Yes," said she, "Go on," and he went on, 'Illustrated by A. N. Other.'"

"It's a splendid novel," she said seriously. "Real work – great work. I always knew you'd do it, Allen. I'm so proud of you!" And she held out her hand in the sincere intelligent appreciation of a fellow craftsman.

He took it, still bewildered.

"Thank you," he said. "I value your opinion – honestly I do! And – with a sudden sweep of recognition. "And yours is great work! Superb! Why you've put more into that story than I knew was there! You make the thing live and breathe! You've put a shadow of remorse in that lonely ruffian there that I was too proud to admit! And you've shown the – unconvincingness of that Other Girl; marvellously. But see here – no more fooling!"

He took her face between his hands, hands that quivered strongly, and forced her to look at him. "Tell me about that last picture! Is it – true?"

Her eyes met his, with the look he longed for. "It is true," she said.

* * *

After some time, really it was a long time, but they had not noticed it, he suddenly burst forth. "But how did you *know*?"

She lifted a flushed and smiling face: and pointed to the title page again.

"'A. Gage.' – You threw it down."

"And you –" He threw back his head and laughed delightedly. "You threw down A-N-Other! O you witch! You immeasurably clever darling! How well our work fits. By Jove! What good times we'll have!"

And they did.

Mr. Robert Grey Sr.

I thought I knew what trouble was when Jimmy went away. It was bad enough when he was clerking in Barstow and I only saw him once a week; but now he'd gone to sea.

He said he'd never earn much as a clerk, and he hated it too. He'd saved every cent he could of his wages and taken a share in the Mary Jenks, and I shouldn't see him again for a year maybe, – maybe more. She was a sealer.

O dear! I'd have married him just as he was; but he said he couldn't keep me yet, and if they had luck he'd make 400 per cent. on his savings that voyage, – and it was all for me. My blessed Jimmy!

He hadn't been gone but a bare fortnight when "unmerciful disaster followed fast and followed faster" on our poor heads. First father broke his arm. There was the doctor to pay, and all that plaster cast thing, and of course I had to do the milking and all the work. I didn't mind that a bit. We hadn't any horse then, to take care of, and Rosy, our cow, was a dear; gentle as a kitten, and sweet-breathed as a baby. But it put back all the farm work, of course; we couldn't hire, and there wasn't enough to go shares on. Mother was pretty wretched, and no wonder.

And then Rosy was stolen! That did seem the last straw. As long as

Rosy was there and I could milk her, we shouldn't starve.

Poor father! There he sat, with that plaster arm in the sling – the other one looking so discouraged and nerveless, and his head bowed on his breast; the hand hanging, the strong busy fingers laxly open.

"I'll go and look," he said, starting up, "where's my hat?"

"It's no use looking, father," said I, "the halter's gone, there are big footprints beside her hoof-marks out to the road, and then quite a stamped place, and then wagon wheels and her nice little clean tracks going off after the wagon. Plain stolen."

He sat down again and groaned.

"Thought I heard a wagon in the middle of the night," said mother, weakly. Her face was flushed, and her eyes ran over. "I can't sleep much you know. I ought to have spoken, but you need your sleep."

I ran to her and kissed her.

"Now mother dear! Don't you fret over it, – please don't! We'll find Rosy. I'll get Mrs. Clark to 'phone for me at once."

"'Phone where?" said father. "It's no use 'phoning. Its those gypsies. And they got to town hours ago – and Rosy's beef by this time." He set his jaw hard; but there were tears in his eyes, too.

I was nearly distracted myself. "If only Jimmy were here," I said, "he'd find her!"

"I don't doubt he'd make a try," said father, "but it's too late."

I ran over to Mrs. Clark, and we 'phoned to the police in Barstow, and sure enough they found the hide and horns! It didn't do us any good. They arrested some gypsies, but couldn't prove anything; shut one of 'em up for vagrancy, too, – but that didn't do us any good, either. And if they'd proved it and convicted him it wouldn't have brought back Rosy, – or given us another cow.

Then mother got sick. It was pure discouragement as much as anything, I think, and she missed Rosy's milk, – she used to half live on it. After she was sick she missed it more, there were so few things she could eat, – and not many of those I could get for her.

O how I did miss Jimmy! If he'd been there he'd have helped me to *see over it* all. "Sho!" he'd have said. "It's hard lines, little girl, now; but bless you, a broken arm's only temporary; your father'll be as good as ever soon. And your mother'll get well; she's a strong woman. I never saw a stronger woman of her age. And as to the food – just claim you're 'no breakfast' people, and believe in fasting for your health!"

That's the way Jimmy met things, and I tried to say it all to myself, and keep my spirits up, – and theirs. But Jimmy was at sea.

Well, father couldn't work, it had to be his right arm, of course. And mother couldn't work either; she was just helpless and miserable, and the more she worried the sicker she got, and the sicker she got the more she worried. My patience! How I did work! No time to read, no time to study, no time to sew on any of the pretty white things I was gradually accumulating. I got up before daylight, almost; kept the house as neat as I could, and got breakfast, such as it was. Father could dress himself after a fashion, and he could sit with mother when I was outside working in the garden. I began that garden just as an experiment, the day after father broke his arm. The outlay was only thirty cents for lettuce and radish seed, but it took a lot of work.

Then there was mother to do for, and father to cheer up (which was hardest of all), and dinner and supper to get, – and nothing to get them with, practically.

The doctor didn't push us any, but father hates a debt as he hates poison, and mother is a natural worrier. "She is killing herself with worry," the doctor said; and he had no anti-toxin for that, apparently.

And then, as if that wasn't enough, that Mr. Robert Grey Sr. took advantage of our misfortunes and began to make up to me again.

I never liked the old man since I was a little girl. He was always picking me up and kissing me, when I didn't want to in the least. When I got older he'd pinch my checks, and offer me a nickle if I'd kiss him.

Mother liked him, for he stood high in the church, and was a charitable soul. Father liked him because he was successful – father always admired successful men; – and Mr. Grey got his money honestly, too, father said. He was a kind old soul. He offered to send me to college, and I was awfully tempted; but father couldn't bear a money obligation, – and I couldn't bear Mr. Grey.

There was a Robert Grey Jr., who was disagreeable enough; a thin, pimply, sanctimonious young fellow, with a class of girls in sunday-school. He was sickly enough, but Mr. Robert Grey Sr. was worse. He sort of tottered and threw his feet about as he walked; and kind or not kind, I couldn't bear him. But he came around now all the time.

He brought mother nice things to eat, – you can't refuse gifts to the sick, – and they were awfully nice; he has a first class cook. And he brought so much that there was enough for father too. We had to eat it to save it, you see, – but I hated every mouthful. I lived on our potatoes mostly, and they were poor enough – in June – and no milk to go with them.

He came every day, bringing his basket of delicacies for mother, and he'd chat awhile with her – she liked it; and he'd sit and talk with father – he liked it; and then he'd hang around me – and I had to be civil to him! But I did not like it a bit. I couldn't bear the old man with his thin grey whiskers, and his watery gray eyes, and his big pink mouth – color of an old hollyhock.

But he came and came, and nobody could fail to see what he wanted; but O dear me! How I wished for Jimmy. My big, strong, brisk boy, with the jolly laugh and the funny little swears that he invented himself! I watched the shipping news, and waited and hoped; he might come back any time now, if they'd had luck. But he didn't come. Mr. Robert Grey Sr. was there every day – and Jimmy didn't come.

I tried not to cry. I needed all my strength and courage to keep some heart in father and mother, and I tried always to

MR. ROBERT GREY SR.

remember what Jimmy would have said; how he'd have faced it. "Don't be phazed by *anything*," he used to say. "Everything goes by – give it time. Don't holler! Don't give a jam!" (People always looked so surprised when Jimmy said "Jam! ") "Just hang on and do the square thing. You're not responsible for other people's sorrows. Hold up your own end."

Jimmy was splendid! He used to read to me about an old philosopher called Euripides, and I got to appreciate him too. But when the papers were full of "Storms at sea" – "Terrible weather in the north" – "Gales" – "High winds" – "Losses in shipping" – it did seem as if I couldn't bear it.

Then at last it came, in a terrible list of wrecks. The Mary Jenks – lost, with all on board.

O what was the use of living! What did anything matter! Why couldn't I die! Why couldn't I die!

But I didn't. My health was as good as ever; I could even sleep – when I wasn't crying. Working hard out of doors and not eating very much makes you sleep I guess, heart or no heart. And I had to keep on working; my lettuce was up and coming on finely, rows upon rows of it, just as I had planted it, two days apart. And the radishes too, they were eatable, and we tried them.

But father laughed grimly at my small garden. "A lot of good that'll do us, child!" he said. "O Jenny – there's more than that you can do for your poor mother! I know you feel badly, and ordinarily I wouldn't say a word, but – you see how it is."

I saw how it was well enough, but it seemed to me too horrible to think of. To thrust that tottering old philanthropist right into my poor bleeding heart! I couldn't bear it.

Mother never said a word. But she looked. She'd lie there with her big hollow eyes following me around the room; and when I came to do anything for her she'd look in my face so! It was more effective than all father's talks. For father had made up his mind now, and urged me all the time.

"We might as well face the facts, Jenny," he said. "James Young is gone, and I'm sorry; and you are naturally broken-hearted. But even if you were a widow I'd say the same thing. Here is this man who has been good to you since you were a child; he will treat you well, you'll have a home, you'll be provided for when he dies. I know you're not in love with him. I don't expect it. He don't either. He has spoken to me. He don't expect miracles. Here we are, absolutely living on his food! It – it is *terrible* to me, Jennie! But I couldn't refuse, for your mother's sake. Now if I could pocket my pride for her sake, can't you pocket your grief? You can't bring back the dead."

"O father, don't!" I said. "How can you talk so! O Jimmy! Jimmy! – If you were here!"

"He isn't here – he never will be!" said father steadily. "But your mother is here, and sick. Mr. Grey wants to send her to a sanitarium – 'as a friend.' I can't let him do that, – it would cost hundreds of dollars. But – as a son-in-law I could."

Mother didn't say a thing – dear mother. But she looked at me.

They made me feel like a brute, between them; at least father did. He kept right on talking.

"Mr. Grey is a good man," he said, "an unusually good man. If he was a bad man I'd never say a word."

"He was when he was young, old Miss Green says," I answered.

"I am ashamed of you, Jennie," said father, "to listen to such scandalous gossip! How – how unmaidenly of you! I dare say he was a little wild, – forty years ago. Most young fellows are, and he was rich and handsome. But he has been a shining light in this community for forty years. – A good husband – a good father."

"What'd his wife die of?" I asked suddenly.

"An operation, – but he did everything for her. She had the best doctors and nurses. She was a good deal of an invalid, I believe, after Robert Jr. was born."

"He's not much!" said I.

"No, Robert Jr. has been a great disappointment to his father – the great disappointment of his life, I may say; though he was very fond of his wife. But he won't trouble you any, Jenny; his father is going to send him to Europe for a long time – for his health. Now Jenny, all this is ancient history. Here is a good kind man who loves you dearly, and wants to marry you at once. If you do it you may save your mother's life, – and set me on my feet again for what remains of mine. I never said a word while you were engaged to Jimmy Young, but now it's a plain duty."

That night Mr. Grey Sr. came as usual. He had sent round his car and got mother to take a ride that afternoon. It did her good, too. And when he came father went out and sat with her, and left me to him: – and he asked me to marry him.

He told me all the things he'd do for me – for mother – for father. He said he shouldn't live very long anyway, and then I could be my own mistress, with plenty of money. And I couldn't say a word, yes or no.

I sat there, playing with the edge of the lamp-mat – and thinking of Jimmy.

And then Mr. Robert Grey Sr. made a mistake. He got a hold of my hand and fingered it. He came and took me in his arms – and kissed my mouth.

I jerked away from him – he almost fell over. "No! O NO!" I cried. "I can't do it Mr. Grey. I simply *can't*!"

He turned the color of ashes.

"Why not?" he said.

"Because it isn't decent," said I firmly. "I can't bear to have you touch me – never could. I will be a servant to you – I will work for you – nurse you – but to be your wife! – I'm sorry Mr. Grey, but I can't do it."

I ran upstairs, and cried and cried; and I had reason to cry, for father was a living thundercloud after that, and mother was worse; and they wouldn't take any more of Mr. Grey's kindnesses, either of them.

My lettuce and radishes kept us alive until the potatoes were ripe. I sold them, fresh every day. Walked three miles with a big basket full every morning, to one of the summer hotels. It was awfully heavy, especially when it rained. They didn't pay much, but it kept us – a dollar a day, sometimes more.

Father got better in course of time, of course, and went to work on the farm in a discouraged sort of way. But mother was worse, if anything. She never blamed me – never said a word; but her eyes were a living reproach.

"Mother, dear," I begged her, "do forgive me! I'll work till I drop, for you; I'll deny myself everything: I'll do most anything that's decent and honest. But to marry a man you don't love is not honest; and to marry an old invalid like that – it's not decent."

She just sighed – didn't say anything.

"Cheer up mother, do! Father's almost well; we can get through this year somehow. Next year I can make enough to buy a cow, really."

But it wasn't more than a month from that time, I was sitting on the door stone at twilight – thinking of Jimmy, of course – and – there *was* Jimmy. I thought it was his ghost; but if it was it was a very warm-blooded one.

As to old Mr. Robert Grey, Sr., he persuaded little Grace Salters to marry him; a pretty, foolish, plump little thing; and if you'll believe it, she died within a year – she and her baby with her.

Well. If ever anybody was glad I was.

I don't mean glad she was dead, poor girl; but glad I didn't marry him, and did marry Jimmy.

My Astonishing Dodo

She was twenty-six, and owned it cheerfully, the day I met her.

This prejudiced me in her favor at once, for I prize honesty in women, and on this point it is unusual. She did not, it is true, share largely in my special artistic tastes, or, to any great extent, in my social circle; but she was a fine wholesome sweet woman, cheerful and strong, and I wished to make a friend of her. I greatly prized my good friends among women, for I had conscientious views against marrying on a small salary.

Later it appeared that she had other and different views, but she did not mention them then.

Dorothea was her name. Her family called her Dora, her intimate friends, Dolly, but I called her Dodo, just between ourselves.

A very good-looking girl was Dodo, though not showy; and in no way distinguished in dress, which rather annoyed me at first; for I have a great admiration for a well-gowned, well-groomed woman.

My ideas on matrimony were strongly colored by certain facts and figures given me by an old college friend of mine.

He was a nice fellow, and his wife one of the loveliest girls of our set, though rather delicate. They lived very comfortably in a quiet way, with a few good books and pictures, and four little ones.

"It's a thousand dollars a year for the first year for each baby," he told me, "and five hundred a year afterward."

I was astonished. I had no idea the little things cost so much.

"There's the trained nurse for your wife," he went on, "at $25.00 a week for four weeks; and then the trained nurse for your baby, at $15.00 a week for forty-eight weeks; that makes $820.00. Then the doctor's bills, the clothes and so on – with the certified milk – easily take up the rest."

"Isn't fifteen dollars a week a good deal for a child's nurse?" I asked.

"What do you pay a good stenographer?" he demanded.

"Why, a special one gets $20.00," I admitted. "But that work needs training and experience."

"So does taking care of babies!" he cried triumphantly. "Don't try to save on babies, Morton; it's poor economy."

I liked his point of view, and admired his family extremely. His wife was one of those sympathetic appreciative women who so help a man in his work. But the prospects of my own marriage seemed remote. That was why I was so glad of a good wholesome companionable friend like Dodo.

We were so calmly intimate that I soon grew to discuss many of my ideas and plans with her. She was much interested in the figures given by my friend, and got me to set them all down for her. He had twice my salary, and not a cent left at the year's end; and they were not in "society" either. Five hundred dollars was allowed for his personal expenses, and the same for her; little enough to dress on nowadays, he had assured me, with all amusements, travel, books and periodicals, and dentist bills, included.

"I don't think it ought to cost so much," said Dodo.

She was a business woman, and followed the figures closely; and of course she appreciated the high views I held on the subject, and my self-denial, too.

I can't tell to this day how it happened; but before I knew it we were engaged. I was almost sorry, for a long engagement is a strain on both parties; but Dodo cheered me up; she said we were really no worse off than we were before, and in some ways better. At times I fully agreed with her.

So we drifted along for about a year, and then, after a good deal of distant discussion, we suddenly got married.

I don't recall now just why we so hastily concluded to do it; I seemed to be in a kind of dream; but anyway we did, and were absurdly happy about it, too.

"Don't be a Goose, dear boy!" she said. "It isn't wicked to be married.

And we're *quite* old enough!"

"But we can't afford it – you know we can't," I said. This was while we were camping out on our honey-vacation.

"Mr. Morton Howland," said my wife; "don't you worry one bit about affording it. I want you to understand that you've married a business woman."

"But you've given up your position!" I cried, aghast. "Surely, you don't think of going back!"

"I've given up one position," she replied with calmness, "and taken another. And I mean to fill it. Now you go peacefully on earning what you did before, and leave the housekeeping business to me – will you, Dear?"

Naturally I had to; for I couldn't keep house; even if I so desired I didn't know how. But I had read so much and heard so much and seen so much of the difficulties of housekeeping for young married people, that I confess I was a good deal worried.

Toward the end of our trip I began to anticipate the burden of house-hunting.

"About where do you think we are going to live?" I tentatively inquired.

"At 384 Meter Avenue," she promptly answered. I nearly dropped the paddle (we were canoeing at the moment), I was so astonished.

"That's a good location – for cheap flats," I said slowly. "Do you mean to say you've rented one, all by yourself?"

She smiled comfortingly. Lovely teeth had my Dodo, strong and white and even, though not small.

"Not quite so bad as that, Dear," she answered, "but I've got the refusal. My friends the Scallens had it, and are moving out this Fall. It's a new building, they had it all papered very prettily, and if you like it we can move in as soon as they leave – say a week after moving time – it will be cheaper then. We'll look at it as soon as we return."

We did. It seemed suitable enough; pleasant, and cheaper than I had thought possible. Indeed, I demurred a little on the question of style, and accessibility to friends; but Dodo said the people who really cared for us would come, and the people who did not could easily be spared.

We had married so hastily, right on the verge of vacation time, that I had hardly given a thought to furnishing but Dodo seemed to know just where to go and what to get; at much less cost than I had imagined.

She produced $250.00 from her bank account, which she had been saving for years she said. I put up about the same; and we had that little flat as pretty and comfortable as any home I ever saw.

She set her foot down about pictures though. "Time enough for those things when we can afford it," she said, and we certainly could not afford it then.

Then was materialized from some foreign clime a neat, strong young woman to do our house-work, washing and all.

"She's an apprentice," said Dodo. "She is willing to learn housekeeping, and I am willing to teach her."

"How do you come to be so competent in house-work?" said I; "I thought you were a bookkeeper."

Then Dodo smiled her large bright smile. "Morton, dear," she said, "I will now tell you a Secret! I have always intended to marry, and, as far as possible, I learned the business. I am a business woman, you know."

She certainly did know her business. She kept the household accounts like – well, like what she was – an expert accountant. When she furnished the kitchen she installed a good reliable set of weights and measures. She weighed the ice and the bread, she measured the milk and the potatoes, and made firm, definite, accurate protests when things went wrong; even sending samples of queer cream to the Board of Health for analysis. What with my business stationery and her accurate figures our letters were strangely potent, and we were well supplied, while our friends sadly and tamely complained of imposture and extortion.

Her largest item of expense in furnishing was a first-class sewing machine, and a marvellous female figure, made to measure, which stood in a corner and served as a "cloak tree" when not in use.

"You don't propose to make your own clothes, surely?" said I when this headless object appeared.

"Some of 'em," she admitted, "you'll see. Of course I can't dress for society."

Now I had prepared myself very conscientiously to meet the storms and shallows of early married life, as I had read about them; I was bound I would not bring home anybody to dinner without telephoning, and was prepared to assure my wife verbally, at least twice a day, that I loved her. She anticipated me on the dinner business, however.

"Look here!" she said, leading me to the pantry, when it was filled to her liking, and she showed me a special corner all marked off and labelled "For Emergencies." There was a whole outfit of eatables and drinkables in glass and tin.

"Now do your worst!" she said triumphantly. "You can bring home six men in the middle of the night – and I'll feed them! But you mustn't do it two nights in succession, for I'd have to stock up again."

As to tears and nervousness and "did I love her," I was almost, sometimes, a bit disappointed in Dodo, she was so calm. She was happy, and I was happy, but it seemed to require no effort at all.

One morning I almost forgot, and left the elevator standing while I ran back to kiss her and say "I love you, dearest." She held me off from her with her two strong hands and laughed tenderly. "Dear boy!" she said, "I mean you shall."

I meditated on that all the way downtown.

She meant I should. Well, I did. And the next time one of my new-married friends circuitously asked for a bit of light on what was to him a dark and perplexing question, I suddenly felt very light-hearted about my domestic affairs. Somehow we hadn't any troubles at all. Dodo kept well; we lived very comfortably and it cost far less than I had anticipated.

"How did you know how to train a servant?" I asked my wife.

"Dear," said she, "I have admitted to you that I always intended to be married, when I found the man I could love and trust and honor." (Dodo overestimates my virtues, of course.)

"Lots of girls intend to marry," I interposed.

"Yes, I know they do," she agreed, "they want to love and he loved, but they don't learn their business! Now the business of house-work is not so abstruse nor so laborious, if you give your mind to it. I took an evening-course in domestic economy, read and studied some, and spent one vacation with an aunt of mine up in Vermont who 'does her own work.' The next vacation I did ours. I learned the trade in a small way."

We had a lovely time that first year. She dressed fairly well, but the smallness of her expense account was a standing marvel, owing to the machine and the Headless One.

"Did you take a course in dressmaking, too?" I inquired.

"Yes, in another vacation."

"You had the most industrious vacations of anyone I ever knew," said I, "and the most varied."

"I am no chicken, you see, my dear," was her cheerful reply, "and I like to work. You work, why shouldn't I?"

The only thing I had to criticize, if there was anything, was that Dodo wouldn't go to the theatre and things like that, as often as I wanted her to. She said frankly that we couldn't afford it, and why should I want to go out for amusement when we had such a happy home? So we stayed at home a good deal, made a few calls, and played cards together, and were very happy, of course.

All this time I was in more or less anxiety lest that thousand dollar baby should descend upon us before we were ready, for I had only six hundred in the bank now. Presently this dread event loomed awe-inspiringly on our horizon. I didn't say anything to Dodo about my fears, she must on no account be rendered anxious, but I lay awake nights and sometimes got up furtively and walked the floor in my room, thinking how I should raise the money.

She heard me one night. "Dear!" she called softly. "What are you doing? Is it burglars?"

I reassured her on that point and she promptly reassured me on the other, as soon as she had made me tell her what I was worrying about.

"Why, bless you, dear," she said, serenely, "you needn't give a thought to that. I've got money in the bank for my baby."

"I thought you spent all of it for the furnishings," said I.

"Oh, that was the Furnishing Money! Cuddle down here, or you'll get cold, and I'll tell you all about it."

So she explained in her calm strong cheerful way, with a little contented chuckle now and then, that she had always intended to be married.

"This is now no news," I exclaimed severely, "tell me something different."

"Well, in order to prepare for this Great Event," she went on, "I learned about housework, as you have seen. I saved money enough to furnish a small flat and put that in one bank. And I also anticipated this not Impossible Contingency and saved more money and put it in another bank!"

"Why two banks, if a mere man may inquire?"

"It is well," she replied sententiously, "not to have all one's eggs in one basket."

I lay still and meditated on this new revelation.

"Have you got a thousand dollars, if this Remote Relative may so far urge for information?"

"I have just that sum," she replied.

"And, not to be impertinent, have you nine other thousands of dollars in nine other banks for nine other not Impossible Contingencies?"

She shook her head with determination. "Nine is an Impossible Contingency," she replied. "No, I have but one thousand dollars in this bank. Now you be good, and continue to practice your business, into the details of which

I do not press, and let me carry on the Baby Business, which is mine."

It was a great load off my mind, and I slept well from that time on.

So did Dodo. She kept well, busy, placid, and cheerful. Once, I came home in a state of real terror. I had been learning, from one of my friends, and from books, of the terrible experience which lay before her. She saw that I was unusually intense in my affection and constantly regarded her with tender anxiety. "What is the matter with you, Morton?" said she. "I'm – worried," I admitted. "I've been thinking – what if I should lose you! Oh Dodo! I'd rather have you than a thousand babies."

"I should think you would," said she calmly. "Now look here, Dear Boy! What are you worrying about? This is not an unusual enterprise I've embarked on; it's the plain course of nature, easily fulfilled by all manner of lady creatures! Don't you be afraid one bit, I'm not."

She wasn't. She kept her serene good cheer up to the last moment, had an efficient but inexpensive woman doctor, and presently was up again, still serene, with a Pink Person added to our family, of small size but of enormous importance.

Again I rather trembled for our peace and happiness, and mentally girded up my loins for wakeful nights of walking. No such troubles followed. We used separate rooms, and she kept the Pink Person in hers. Occasionally he made remarks in the night, but not for long. He was well, she was well – things went along very much as they did before.

I was "lost in wonder, love and praise" and especially in amazement at the continued cheapness of our living.

Suddenly a thought struck me. "Where's ths nurse?" I demanded.

"The nurse? Why she left long ago. I kept her only for the month."

"I mean the child's nurse," said I, "the fifteen dollar one."

"Oh – I'm the child's nurse," said Dodo.

"You!" said I. "Do you mean to say you take all the care of this child yourself?"

"Why, of course," said Dodo, "what's a mother for?"

"But – the time it takes," I protested, rather weakly.

"What do you expect me to do with my time, Morton?"

"Why, whatever you did before – This arrived."

"I will not have my son alluded to as 'This'!" said she severely. "Morton J. Hopkins, Jr., if you please. As to my time before? Why, I used it in preparing for time to come, of course. I have things ready for this youngster for three years ahead."

"How about the certified milk?" I asked.

Dodo smiled a superior smile; "I certify the milk," said she.

"Can you take care of the child and the house, too?"

"Bless you, Morton, 'the care' of a seven-room flat and a competent servant does not take more than an hour a day. And I market while I'm out with the baby.

"Do you mean to say you are going to push the perambulator yourself?"

"Why not?" she asked a little sharply, "surely a mother need not be ashamed of the company of her own child."

"But you'll be taken for a nurse—"

"I *am* a nurse! And proud of it!"

I gazed at her in my third access of deep amazement. "Do you mean to say that you took lessons in child culture, *too?*"

"*Too*? Why, I took lessons in child culture first of all. How often must I tell you, Morton, that I always intended to be married! Being married involves, to my mind, motherhood, that is what it is for! So naturally I prepared myself for the work I meant to do. I am a business woman, Morton, and this is my business."

* * *

That was twenty years ago. We have five children. Morton, Jr., is in college. So is Dorothea second. Dodo means to put them *all* through, she says. My salary has increased, but not so fast as prices, and neither of them so fast as my family. None of those babies cost a thousand dollars the first year though, nor five hundred thereafter; Dodo's thousand held out for the lot. We moved to a home in the suburbs, of course; that was only fair to the children. I live within my income always – we have but one servant still, and the children are all taught housework in the good old way. None of my friends has as devoted, as vigorous and – and – as successful a wife as I have. She is the incarnate spirit of all the Housewives and House-mothers of history and fiction. The only thing I miss in her – if I must own to missing anything – is companionship and sympathy outside of household affairs. My newspaper work – which she always calls "my business" – has remained a business. The literary aspirations I once had were long since laid aside as impracticable. And the only thing I miss in life beyond my home is, well – as a matter of fact, I don't have any life beyond my home – except, of course, my business.

My friends are mostly co-commuters now. I couldn't keep up with the set I used to know. As my wife said, she could 't dress for society, and, visibly, she couldn't. We have few books, there isn't any margin for luxuries, she says; and of course we can't go to the plays and concerts in town. But these are unessentials – of course – as she says.

I am very proud of my home, my family, and my Amazing Dodo.

An Offender

"Where's Harry?" was Mr. Gortlandt's first question.

"He's gone to the country, to mother. It was so hot this last day or two, I've sent him out, with Miss Colton. I'm going Saturday. Sit down."

"I miss him," said her visitor, "more than I thought I could. I've learned more in these seven years than I thought there was to know. Or in the last two perhaps, since I've found you again."

She looked at him with a little still smile, but there was a puzzled expression behind it, as of one whose mind was not made up.

They sat in the wide window of a top floor apartment, awning-shaded. A fresh breeze blew in upon them, and the city dust blew in upon them also, lying sandy on the broad sill.

She made little wavy lines in it with one finger –

"These windows ought to be shut tight, I suppose, and the blinds, and the curtains. Then we should be cleaner."

"As to furniture," he agreed, "but not as to our lungs."

"I don't know about that," she said; "we get plenty of air – but see what's in it."

"A city is a dirty place at the best; but Mary – I didn't come to consider the ethics of the dust – how much longer must I wait?" he asked, after a little pause. "Isn't two years courting, re-courting – enough? Haven't I learned my lesson yet?"

"Some of it, I think," she admitted, "but not all."

"What more do you ask?" he pursued earnestly. "Can't we come to a definite understanding? You'll be chasing off again in a few days; it's blessed luck that brought you to town just now, and that I happened to be here too."

"I don't how about the luck," said she. "It was business that brought me. I never was in town before when it was so hot."

"Why don't you go to a hotel? This apartment is right under the roof, gets the sun all day."

"It gets the breeze too, and sunlight is good. No, I'm better off in the apartment, with Harry. It was very convenient of the Grants to be away, and let me have it."

"How does Hal stand the weather?"

"Pretty well. But he was getting rather fretful, so I sent him off two hours ago. I do hope he won't run away from Miss Colton again. She's as nervous as I am about him."

"Don't you think he is fond of me?" asked the man. "I've got to catch up, you see. He can't help being mine – half mine," he hastily added, seeing a hint of denial in her look.

"Why yes, he seems fond of you, he is fond of you," she conceded. "I hope he always will be, and I believe you are beginning to love him."

"A pretty strong beginning, Mary," said the man. "Of course I don't pretend to have cared much at first, but now! – why he's so handsome, and quick, and such a good little duffer;

and so affectionate! When he gives a jump and gets his arms around my neck and his legs around my waist and 'hugs me all over' as he calls it, I almost feel as if I was a mother! I can't say more than that, can I?"

"No, you certainly can't say more than that. I believe you, I'm not questioning," for he looked up sharply at her tone.

"I've never had much to do with children, you see," he went on slowly, "no little brothers or sisters, and then only – What astonishes me is how good they feel in your arms! The little fellow's body is so firm and sinewy – he wriggles like a fish – a big fish that you're trying to hold with both hands."

The mother smiled tenderly. She knew the feel of the little body so well! From the soft pink helplessness, the little head falling so naturally into the hollow of the arm or neck, the fumbling little hands; then the gradual gain in size and strength, till now she held that eager bounding little body, almost strong enough to get away from her – but not wanting to. He still loved to nestle up to "Muzz," and was but newly and partially won by this unaccustomed father.

"It's seven years Mary! That makes a man all over, they say. I'm sure it has made me over. I'm an older man – and I think, wiser. I've repented, I've outgrown my folly and seen the justice of my punishment. I don't blame you an atom for divorcing me – I think you did right, and I respect you for it. The biggest lesson I've learned is to love you! I can see – now – that I didn't before.

Her face hardened as she looked at him. "No, you didn't, Harry, you certainly didn't, nor the child – When I think of what I was when you married me! Of my proud health!—"

"*You* are not hurt!" he cried. "I don't mean that you haven't been hurt, I could kill myself when I think of how I made you suffer! But you are a finer woman now than you were then; sweeter, stronger, wiser, and more beautiful. When I found you again in Liverpool two years ago it was a revelation. Now see – I don't even ask you to forgive me! I ask you to try me again and let me prove I can make it up to you and the boy!"

"It's not easy for me to forgive," she answered slowly – "I'm not of the forgiving nature. But there is a good deal of reason in your position. You were my husband, you are Hal's father, there's no escaping that."

"Perhaps, if you will let the rest of my life make up for that time of my Godforsaken meanness, you won't want to escape it, Mary! See – I have followed you about for two years. I accepted your terms, you did not promise me anything, but for the child's sake I might try once more, try only as one of many, to see if I could win you – again. And I love you now a hundred times better than I did when I married you!"

She fanned herself slowly with a large soft fan, and looked out across the flickering roofs. Below them lay the highly respectable street on which the house technically fronted, and the broad, crowded, roaring avenue which it really overlooked.

The rattle of many drays and more delivery wagons rose up to them. An unusual jangle drowned his words just then and she smilingly interpreted "that's railroad iron – or girders, I can tell lots of them now. About four A. M. there is a string of huge milk wagons. But the worst is the cars. Hear that now – that's a flat wheel. How do you like it?"

"Mary – why do you bring up these cars again when I'm trying my best to show you my whole heart? Don't put things like that between us!"

"But they are between us, Henry, all the time. I hear you tell me you love me, and I don't doubt you do in a way; yes, as well as you can, very much indeed! – I know. But when it comes to this car question; when I talk to you of these juggernauts of yours; you are no more willing to do the right thing than you were when I first knew you."

Mr. Cortlandt's face hardened. He drew himself up from the eager position in which he had leaned forward, and evidently hesitated for a moment as to his words.

In spite of his love for this woman, who, as he justly said, was far more beautiful and winsome than the strong, angular, over-conscientious girl he had married, neglected and shamed, his feelings as a business man were strong within him.

"My dear – I am not personally responsible for the condition of these cars."

"You are President of the Company. You hold controlling shares of the stock. It was your vote that turned down the last improvement proposition."

He looked at her sharply.

"I'm afraid someone has been prejudicing you against me Mary. You have more technical information than seems likely to have reached you by accident."

"It's not prejudice, but it is information; and Mr. Graham did tell me, if that's what you mean. But he cares. You know how hard the Settlement has worked to get the Company to make the streets safer for children – and you wouldn't do a thing."

Mr. Cortlandt hesitated. It would never do to pile business details on his suit for a love once lost and not yet regained.

"You make it hard for me Mary," he said. "Hard because it is difficult to explain large business questions to a – to anyone not accustomed to them. I cannot swing the affairs of a great corporation for personal ends, even to please you."

"That is not the point," she said quickly.

He flushed, and hastily substituted "Even to suit the noblest humanitarian feelings."

"Why not?" said she.

"Because that is not what street cars are run for," he pursued patiently. "But why must we talk of this? It seems to put you so far away. And you have given me no answer."

"I am sorry, but I am not ready yet."

"Is it Hugh Graham?" he demanded. The hot color leaped to her face, but she met his eyes steadily. "I am much interested in Mr. Graham," she said, "and in the noble work he is doing. I think I should really be happier with him than with you. We care for the same things, he calls out the best in me. But I have made no decision in his favor yet, nor in yours. Both of you have a certain appeal to my heart, both to my duty. With you the personal need, with him the hope of greater service. But – you are the father of the child, and that gives you a great claim. I have not decided."

The man looked relieved, and again drew his chair a little closer. The sharp clangor of the cars rose between the,.

"You think I dragged in this car question," she said. "Really, I did it because it is that sort of thing which does most to keep us apart, and – I would like to remove it."

He leaned forward, playing with her big fan. "Let's remove it by all means!" he said.

She looked at his bent head, the dark hair growing somewhat thin on top, almost tenderly.

"If I could feel that you were truly on the right side, that you considered your work as social service, that you tried to run your cars to carry people – not to kill them! – If you could change your ground here I think – almost –" she stopped, smiling up at him, her fan in her lap, her firm delicate white hands eagerly clasped; then went on,

"Don't you care at all for the lives lost every day in this great city – under your cars?"

"It cannot be helped, my dear. Our men are as careful as men can be.

But these swarming children will play in the streets—"

"Where else can they play!" she interjected.

"And they get right in front of the cars. We are very sorry; we pay out thousands of dollars in damages: but it cannot be helped!"

She leaned back in her chair and her face grew cold.

"You speak as if you never heard of such things as fenders," she said.

"We have fenders! – almost every car—"

"Fenders! Do you call that piece of rat-trap a fender! Henry Cortlandt! We were in Liverpool when this subject first came up between us! They have fenders there that *fend* and no murder list!"

"Conditions are different there," said he with an enforced quiet. "Our pavement is different."

"Our children are not so different, are they?" she demanded. "Our mothers are made of the same stuff I suppose?"

"You speak at if I wanted to kill them! As if I liked to!"

"I thought at first it would hurt you as it did me," she said warmly. "I turned to you with real hope when we met in Liverpool. I was glad to think I knew you, and I had not been glad of that for long! I thought you would care, would do things."

Do what he would, his mouth set hard in its accustomed lines. "Those English fender are not practicable in this country, Mary. They have been tried."

"When? Where? By whom?" she threw at him. "I have read about it, and heard about it. I know there was an effort to get them adopted, and that they were refused. They cost more than this kind!" and she pointed disdainfully at the rattling bit of stub-toed slat-work in front of a passing car.

"Do you expect me to make a revolution in the street car system of America – to please you? Do you make it a condition? Perhaps I can accomplish it. Is it a bargain? Come—"

"No," she said slowly. "I'm not making bargains. I'm only wishing, as I have wished so often in years past – that you were a different kind of man—"

"What kind do you want me to be?"

"I want you to be – I wish you were – a man who cared to give perfect service to his country, in his business."

"Perhaps I can be yet. I can try. If I had you to help me, with your pure ideals, and the boy to keep my heart open for the children. I don't know much about these things, but I can learn. I can read, you can tell me what to read. We could study together. And in my position perhaps, I could really be of some service after all."

"Perhaps?" She watched him, the strong rather heavy face, the attractive smile, the eyes that interested and compelled. He was an able, masterful man. He surely loved her now. She could feel a power over him that her short miserable marriage had never given her; and her girlhood's attraction toward him reasserted itself.

A new noise rose about them, a dissonant mingled merry outcry, made into a level roaring sound by their height above the street.

"That's when the school up here lets out," she said. "We hear it every day. Just see the crowds of them!"

They leaned on the broad sill and watched the many-colored torrent of juveniles pouring past.

"One day it was different," she said. "A strange jarring shrillness in it, a peculiar sound. I looked out, and there was a fight going on; two boys tumbling about from one side of the street to the other, with a moving ring around them, a big crowd, all roaring in one key."

"You get a birdseye view of life in these streets, don't you. Can you make out that little chap with the red hair down there?"

"No – we are both near-sighted, you know. I can't distinguish faces at this distance. Can you?"

"Not very clearly," he said. "But what a swarm they are!"

"Come away," said she, "I can't bear to look at them. So many children in that stony street, and those cars going up and down like roaring lions!"

They drew back into the big sunny room, and she seated herself at the piano and turned over loose sheets of music.

He watched her with a look of intensest admiration, she was so tall, so nobly formed, her soft rich gown flowed and followed as she walked, her white throat rose round and royal from broad smooth shoulders.

He was beside her; he took away the music, laid it out of reach, possessed himself of her hands.

"Give them back to me, Mary," he pleaded. "Come to me and help me to be a better man! Help me to be a good father. I need you!"

She looked at him almost pleadingly. His eyes, his voice, his hands, – they had their old-time charm for her. Yet he had only said "Perhaps" – and he *might* study, *might* learn.

He asked her to help him, but he did not say "I will do this" – only "I may."

In the steady bright June sunshine, in the sifting dust of a city corner, in the dissonant, confused noise of the traffic below, they stood and looked at one another.

His eyes brightened and deepened as he watched her changing color. Softly he drew her towards him. "Even if you do not love me now, you shall in time, you shall, my darling!"

But she drew back from him with a frightened start, a look of terror.

"What has happened!" she cried. "It's so still!"

They both rushed to the window. The avenue immediately below them was as empty as midnight, and as silent. A great stillness widened and spread for the moment around one vacant motionless open car. Without passenger, driver, or conductor, it stood alone in the glaring space; and then, with a gasp of horror, they both saw.

Right under their eyes, headed towards them, under the middle of the long car – a little child.

He was quite still, lying face downward, dirty and tumbled, with helpless arms thrown wide, the great car holding him down like a mouse in a trap.

Then people came rushing.

She turned away, choking, her hands to her eyes.

"Oh!" she cried, "Oh! It's a child, a little child!"

"Steady, Mary, steady!" said he, "the child's dead. It's all over. He's quite dead. He never knew what hit him." But his own voice trembled.

She made a mighty effort to control herself, and he tried to take her in his arms, to comfort her, but she sprang away from him with fierce energy.

"Very well!" she said. "You are right! The child is dead. We can not save him. No one can save him. Now come back – come here to the window – and see what follows. I want to see with my own eyes – and have you see – what is done when your cars commit murder! Child murder!"

She held up her watch. "It's 12:10 now," she said.

She dragged him back to the window, and so evident was the struggle with which she controlled herself, so intense her agonized excitement, that he dared not leave her.

"Look!" she cried. "Look! See the them crowd now!"

The first horrified rush away from the instrument of death was followed by the usual surging multitude.

From every direction people gathered thickly in astonishing numbers, hustling and pushing about the quiet form upon the ground; held so flat between iron rails and iron wheels, so great a weight on so small a body! The car, still empty, rose like an island from the pushing sea of heads. Men and women cried excited directions. They tried with swarming impotent hands to lift the huge mass of wood and iron off the small broken thing beneath it, so small that it did not raise the crushing weight from the ground.

A whole line of excited men seized the side rail and strove to lift the car by it, lifting only the rail.

The crowd grew momently, women weeping, children struggling to see, men pushing each other, policemen's helmets rising among them. And still the great car stood there, on the body of the child.

"Is there no means of lifting these monsters?" she demanded. "After they have done it, can't they even get off."

He moistened his lips to answer.

"There is a jacking crew," he said. "They will be here presently."

"Presently!" she cried. "Presently! Couldn't these monsters use their own power to lift themselves somehow? not even that?"

He said nothing.

More policemen came, and made a scant space around the little body, covering it with a dark cloth. The motorman was rescued from many would be avengers, and carried off under guard.

"Ten minutes," said she looking at her watch. "Ten minutes and it isn't even off him yet!" and she caught her breath in a great sob.

Then she turned on the man at her side: "Suppose his mother is in that crowd! She may be! Their children go to this school, they live all about below here, she can't even get in to see! And if she could, if she knew it was her child, she can't *get him out*!"

Her voice rose to a cry.

"Don't, Mary," said he, hoarsely. "It's – it's horrible! Don't make it worse!"

She kept her eyes on her watch-face, counting the minutes She looked down at the crowd shudderingly, and said over and over, under breath, "A little child! A little soft child!"

It was twelve minutes and a-half before the jacking crew drove up, with their tools. It was a long time yet before they did their work, and that crushed and soiled little body was borne to a near-by area grating and laid there, wrapped in its dingy shroud, and guarded by a policeman.

It was a full half hour before the ambulance arrived to take it away.

She drew back then and crouched sobbing by the sofa. "O the poor mother! God help his mother!"

He sat tense and white for a while; and when she grew quieter he spoke.

"You were right, Mary. I – naturally, I never – visualized it! It is horrible! I am going to have those fenders on every car of the four systems!"

She said nothing. He spoke again.

"I hate to leave you feeling so, Dear. Must I go?"

She raised a face that was years older, but did not look at him.

"You must go. And you must never come back. I cannot bear to see your face again!"

And she turned from him, shuddering.

Three Thanksgivings

Andrew's letter and Jean's letter were in Mrs. Morrison's lap. She had read them both, and sat looking at them with a varying sort of smile, now motherly and now unmotherly.

> *"You belong with me," Andrew wrote. "It is not right that Jean's husband should support my mother. I can do it easily now. You shall have a good room and every comfort. The old house will let for enough to give you quite a little income of your own, or it can be sold and I will invest the money where you'll get a deal more out of it. It is not right that you should live alone there. Sally is old and liable to accident. I am anxious about you. Come on for Thanksgiving – and come to stay. Here is the money to come with. You know I want you. Annie joins me in sending love. ANDREW."*

Mrs. Morrison read it all through again, and laid it down with her quiet, twinkling smile. Then she read Jean's.

> *"Now, mother, you've got to come to us for Thanksgiving this year. Just think! You haven't seen baby since he was*

three months old! And have never seen the twins. You won't know him – he's such a splendid big boy now. Joe says for you to come, of course. And, mother, why won't you come and live with us? Joe wants you, too. There's the little room upstairs; it's not very big, but we can put in a Franklin stove for you and make you pretty comfortable. Joe says he should think you ought to sell that white elephant of a place. He says he could put the money into his store and pay you good interest. I wish you would, mother. We'd just love to have you here. You'd be such a comfort to me, and such a help with the babies. And Joe just loves you. Do come now, and stay with us. Here is the money for the trip. – Your affectionate daughter, JEANNIE."

Mrs. Morrison laid this beside the other, folded both, and placed them in their respective envelopes, then in their several well-filled pigeon-holes in her big, old-fashioned desk. She turned and paced slowly up and down the long parlor, a tall woman, commanding of aspect, yet of a winningly attractive manner, erect and light-footed, still imposingly handsome.

It was now November, the last lingering boarder was long since gone, and a quiet winter lay before her. She was alone, but for Sally; and she smiled at Andrew's cautious expression, "liable to accident." He could not say "feeble" or "ailing," Sally being a colored lady of changeless aspect and incessant activity.

Mrs. Morrison was alone, and while living in the Welcome House she was never unhappy. Her father had built it, she was born there, she grew up playing on the broad green lawns in front, and in the acre of garden behind. It was the finest house in the village, and she then thought it the finest in the world.

Even after living with her father at Washington and abroad, after visiting hall, castle and palace, she still found the Welcome House beautiful and impressive.

If she kept on taking boarders she could live the year through, and pay interest, but not principal, on her little mortgage. This had been the one possible and necessary thing while the children were there, though it was a business she hated.

But her youthful experience in diplomatic circles, and the years of practical management in church affairs, enabled her to bear it with patience and success. The boarders often confided to one another, as they chatted and tatted on the long piazza, that Mrs. Morrison was "certainly very refined."

Now Sally whisked in cheerfully, announcing supper, and Mrs. Morrison went out to her great silver tea-tray at the lit end of the long, dark mahogany table, with as much dignity as if twenty titled guests were before her.

Afterward Mr. Butts called. He came early in the evening, with his usual air of determination and a somewhat unusual spruceness. Mr. Peter Butts was a florid, blonde person, a little stout, a little pompous, sturdy and immovable in the attitude of a self-made man. He had been a poor boy when she was a rich girl; and it gratified him much to realize – and to call upon her to realize – that their positions had changed. He meant no unkindness, his pride was honest and unveiled. Tact he had none.

She had refused Mr. Butts, almost with laughter, when he proposed to her in her gay girlhood. She had refused him, more gently, when he proposed to her in her early widowhood. He had always been her friend, and her husband's friend, a solid member of the church, and had taken the small mortgage of the house. She refused to allow him at first, but he was convincingly frank about it.

"This has nothing to do with my wanting you, Delia Morrison," he said. "I've always wanted you – and I've always wanted this house, too. You won't sell, but you've got to mortgage. By and by you can't pay up, and I'll get it – see? Then maybe you'll take me – to keep the house. Don't be a fool, Delia. It's a perfectly good investment."

She had taken the loan. She had paid the interest. She would pay the interest if she had to take boarders all her life. And she would not, at any price, marry Peter Butts.

He broached the subject again that evening, cheerful and undismayed. "You might as well come to it, Delia," he said. "Then we could live right here just the same. You aren't so young as you were, to be sure; I'm not, either. But you are as good a housekeeper as ever – better – you've had more experience."

"You are extremely kind, Mr. Butts," said the lady, "but I do not wish to marry you."

"I know you don't," he said. "You've made that clear. You don't, but I do. You've had your way and married the minister. He was a good man, but he's dead. Now you might as well marry me."

"I do not wish to marry again, Mr. Butts; neither you nor anyone."

"Very proper, very proper, Delia," he replied. "It wouldn't look well if you did – at any rate, if you showed it. But why shouldn't you? The children are gone now – you can't hold them up against me any more."

"Yes, the children are both settled now, and doing nicely," she admitted.

"You don't want to go and live with them – either one of them – do you?" he asked.

"I should prefer to stay here," she answered.

"Exactly! And you can't! You'd rather live here and be a grandee – but you can't do it. Keepin' house for boarders isn't any better than keepin' house for me, as I see. You'd much better marry me."

"I should prefer to keep the house without you, Mr. Butts."

"I know you would. But you can't, I tell you. I'd like to know what a woman of your age can do with a house like this – and no money? You can't live eternally on hens' eggs and garden truck. That won't pay the mortgage."

Mrs. Morrison looked at him with her cordial smile, calm and non-committal. "Perhaps I can manage it," she said.

"That mortgage falls due two years from Thanksgiving, you know."

"Yes – I have not forgotten."

"Well, then, you might just as well marry me now, and save two years of interest. It'll be my house, either way – but you'll be keepin' it just the same."

"It is very kind of you, Mr. Butts. I must decline the offer none the less. I can pay the interest, I am sure. And perhaps – in two years' time – I can pay the principal. It's not a large sum."

"That depends on how you look at it," said he. "Two thousand dollars is considerable money for a single woman to raise in two years – *and* interest."

He went away, as cheerful and determined as ever; and Mrs. Morrison saw him go with a keen, light in her fine eyes, a more definite line to that steady, pleasant smile.

Then she went to spend Thanksgiving with Andrew. He was glad to see her. Annie was glad to see her. They proudly installed her in "her room," and said she must call it "home" now.

This affectionately offered home was twelve by fifteen, and eight feet high. It had two windows, one looking at some pale gray clapboards within reach of a broom, the other giving a view of several small fenced yards occupied by cats, clothes and children. There was an ailanthus tree under the window, a lady ailanthus tree. Annie told her how profusely it bloomed. Mrs. Morrison particularly disliked the smell of ailanthus flowers. "It doesn't bloom in November," said she to herself. "I can be thankful for that!"

Andrew's church was very like the church of his father, and Mrs. Andrew was doing her best to fill the position of minister's wife – doing it well, too – there was no vacancy for a minister's mother.

Besides, the work she had done so cheerfully to help her husband was not what she most cared for, after all.

She liked the people, she liked to manage, but she was not strong on doctrine. Even her husband had never known how far her views differed from his. Mrs. Morrison had never mentioned what they were.

Andrew's people were very polite to her. She was invited out with them, waited upon and watched over and set down among the old ladies and gentlemen – she had never realized so keenly that she was no longer young. Here nothing recalled her youth, every careful provision anticipated age. Annie brought her a hot-water bag at night, tucking it in at the foot of the bed with affectionate care. Mrs. Morrison thanked her, and subsequently took it out – airing the bed a little before she got into it. The house seemed very hot to her, after the big, windy halls at home.

The little dining-room, the little round table with the little round fern-dish in the middle, the little turkey and the little carving-set – game-set she would have called it – all made her feel as if she was looking through the wrong end of an opera-glass.

In Annie's precise efficiency she saw no room for her assistance; no room in the church, no room in the small, busy town, prosperous and progressive, and no room in the house. "Not enough to turn round in!" she said to herself. Annie, who had grown up in a city flat, thought their little parsonage palatial. Mrs. Morrison grew up in the Welcome House.

She stayed a week, pleasant and polite, conversational, interested in all that went on.

"I think your mother is just lovely," said Annie to Andrew.

"Charming woman, your mother," said the leading church member.

"What a delightful old lady your mother is!" said the pretty soprano.

And Andrew was deeply hurt and disappointed when she announced her determination to stay on for the present in her old home. "Dear boy," she said, "you mustn't take it to heart. I love to be with you, of course, but I love my home, and want to keep it is long as I can. It is a great pleasure to see you and Annie so well settled, and so happy together. I am most truly thankful for you."

"My home is open to you whenever you wish to come, mother," said Andrew.

But he was a little angry.

Mrs. Morrison came home as eager as a girl, and opened her own door with her own key, in spite of Sally's haste.

Two years were before her in which she must find some way to keep herself and Sally, and to pay two thousand dollars and the interest to Peter Butts. She considered her assets. There was the house – the white elephant. It *was* big – very big. It was profusely furnished. Her father had entertained lavishly like the Southern-born, hospitable gentleman he was; and the bedrooms ran in suites – somewhat deteriorated by the use of boarders, but still numerous and habitable. Boarders – she abhorred them. They were people from afar, strangers and interlopers. She went over the place from garret to cellar, from front gate to backyard fence.

The garden had great possibilities. She was fond of gardening. and understood it well. She measured and estimated.

"This garden," she finally decided, "with the hens, will feed us two women and sell enough to pay Sally. If we make plenty of jelly, it may cover the coal bill, too. As to clothes – I don't need any. They last admirably. I can manage. I can *live* – but two thousand dollars – *and* interest!"

In the great attic was more furniture, discarded sets put there when her extravagant young mother had ordered new ones. And chairs – uncounted chairs. Senator Welcome used to invite numbers to meet his political friends – and they had delivered glowing orations in the wide, double parlors, the impassioned speakers standing on a temporary dais, now in the cellar; and the enthusiastic listeners disposed more or less comfortably on these serried rows of "folding chairs," which folded sometimes, and let down the visitor in scarlet confusion to the floor.

She sighed as she remembered those vivid days and glittering nights. She used to steal downstairs in her little pink wrapper and listen to the eloquence. It delighted her young soul to see her father rising on his toes, coming down sharply on his heels, hammering one hand upon the other; and then to hear the fusilade of applause.

Here were the chairs, often borrowed for weddings, funerals, and church affairs, somewhat worn and depleted, but still numerous. She mused upon them. Chairs – hundreds of chairs. They would sell for very little.

She went through her linen room. A splendid stock in the old days; always carefully washed by Sally; surviving even the boarders. Plenty of bedding, plenty of towels, plenty of napkins and tablecloths. "It would make a good hotel – but I *can't* have it so – I *can't!* Besides, there's no need of another hotel here. The poor little Haskins House is never full."

The stock in the china closet was more damaged than some other things, naturally; but she inventoried it with care. The countless cups of crowded church receptions were especially prominent. Later additions these, not very costly cups, but numerous, appallingly.

When she had her long list of assets all in order, she sat and studied it with a clear and daring mind. Hotel – boarding-house – she could think of nothing else. School! A girls' school! A boarding school! There was money to be made at that, and fine work done. It was a brilliant thought at first, and she gave several hours, and much paper and ink, to its full consideration. But she would need some capital for advertising; she must engage teachers – adding to her definite obligation; and to establish it, well, it would require time.

Mr. Butts, obstinate, pertinacious, oppressively affectionate, would give her no time. He meant to force her to marry him for her own good – and his. She shrugged her fine shoulders with a little shiver. Marry Peter Butts! Never! Mrs. Morrison still loved her husband. Some day she meant to see him again – God willing – and she did not wish to have to tell him that at fifty she had been driven into marrying Peter Butts.

Better live with Andrew. Yet when she thought of living with Andrew, she shivered again. Pushing back her sheets of figures and lists of personal property, she rose to her full graceful height and began to walk the floor. There was plenty of floor to walk. She considered, with a set deep thoughtfulness, the town and the townspeople, the surrounding country, the hundreds upon hundreds of women whom she knew – and liked, and who liked her.

It used to be said of Senator Welcome that he had no enemies; and some people, strangers, maliciously disposed, thought it no credit to his character. His daughter had no enemies, but no one had ever blamed her for her unlimited friendliness. In her father's wholesale entertainments the whole town knew and admired his daughter; in her husband's popular church she had come to know the women of the countryside about them. Her mind strayed off to these women, farmers' wives, comfortably off in a plain way, but starving for companionship, for occasional stimulus and pleasure. It was one of her joys in her husband's time to bring together these women – to teach and entertain them.

Suddenly she stopped short in the middle of the great high-ceiled room, and drew her head up proudly like a victorious queen. One wide, triumphant, sweeping glance she cast at the well-loved walls – and went back to her desk, working swiftly, excitedly, well into the hours of the night.

* * *

Presently the little town began to buzz, and the murmur ran far out into the surrounding country. Sunbonnets wagged over fences; butcher carts and pedlar's wagon carried the news farther; and ladies visiting found one topic in a thousand houses.

Mrs. Morrison was going to entertain. Mrs. Morrison had invited the whole feminine population, it would appear, to meet Mrs. Isabelle Carter Blake, of Chicago. Even Haddleton had heard of Mrs. Isabelle Carter Blake. And even Haddleton had nothing but admiration for her.

She was known the world over for her splendid work for children – for the school children and the working children of the country. Yet she was known also to have lovingly and wisely reared six children of her own – and made her husband happy in his home. On top of that she had lately written a novel, a popular novel, of which everyone was talking; and on top of that she was an intimate friend of a certain conspicuous Countess – an Italian.

It was even rumored, by some who knew Mrs. Morrison better than others – or thought they did – that the Countess was coming, too! No one had known before that Delia Welcome was a school-mate of Isabel Carter, and a lifelong friend; and that was ground for talk in itself.

The day arrived, and the guests arrived. They came in hundreds upon hundreds, and found ample room in the great white house.

The highest dream of the guests was realized – the Countess had come, too. With excited joy they met her, receiving impressions that would last them for all their lives, for those large widening waves of reminiscence which delight us the more as years pass. It was an incredible glory – Mrs. Isabelle Carter Blake, *and* a Countess!

Some were moved to note that Mrs. Morrison looked the easy peer of these eminent ladies, and treated the foreign nobility precisely as she did her other friends.

She spoke, her clear quiet voice reaching across the murmuring din, and silencing it.

"Shall we go into the east room? If you will all take chairs in the east room, Mrs. Blake is going to be so kind as to address us. Also perhaps her friend—"

They crowded in, sitting somewhat timorously on the unfolded chairs.

Then the great Mrs. Blake made them an address of memorable power and beauty, which received vivid sanction from that imposing presence in Parisian garments on the platform by her side. Mrs. Blake spoke to them of the work she was interested in, and how it was aided everywhere by the women's clubs. She gave them the number of these clubs, and described with contagious enthusiasm the inspiration of their great meetings. She spoke of the women's club houses, going up in city after city, where many associations meet and help one another. She was winning and convincing and most entertaining – an extremely attractive speaker.

Had they a women's club there? They had not.

Not *yet*, she suggested, adding that it took no time at all to make one.

They were delighted and impressed with Mrs. Blake's speech, but its effect was greatly intensified by the address of the Countess.

"I, too, am American," she told them; "born here, reared in England, married in Italy." And she stirred their hearts with a vivid account of the women's clubs and associations all over Europe, and what they were accomplishing. She was going back soon, she said, the wiser and happier for this visit to her native land, and she should remember particularly this beautiful, quiet town, trusting that if she came to it again it would have joined the great sisterhood of women, "whose hands were touching around the world for the common good."

It was a great occasion.

The Countess left next day, but Mrs. Blake remained, and spoke in some of the church meetings, to an ever widening circle of admirers. Her suggestions were practical.

"What you need here is a 'Rest and Improvement Club,'" she said. "Here are all you women coming in from the country to do your shopping – and no place to go to. No place to lie down if you're tired, to meet a friend, to eat your lunch in peace, to do your hair. All you have to do is organize, pay some small regular due, and provide yourselves with what you want."

There was a volume of questions and suggestions, a little opposition, much random activity.

Who was to do it? Where was there a suitable place? They would have to hire someone to take charge of it. It would only be used once a week. It would cost too much.

Mrs. Blake, still practical, made another suggestion. Why not combine business with pleasure, and make use of the best place in town, if you can get it? I *think* Mrs. Morrison could be persuaded to let you use part of her house; it's quite too big for one woman."

Then Mrs. Morrison, simple and cordial as ever, greeted with warm enthusiasm by her wide circle of friends.

"I have been thinking this over," she said. "Mrs. Blake has been discussing it with me. My house is certainly big enough for all of you, and there am I, with nothing to do but entertain you. Suppose you formed such a club as you speak of – for Rest and Improvement. My parlors are big enough for all manner of meetings; there are bedrooms in plenty for resting. If you form such a club I shall be glad to help with my great, cumbersome house, shall be delighted to see so many friends there so often; and I think I could furnish accommodations more cheaply than you could manage in any other way.

Then Mrs. Blake gave them facts and figures, showing how much clubhouses cost – and how little this arrangement would cost. "Most women have very little money, I know," she said, "and they hate to spend it on themselves when they have; but even a little money from each goes a long way when it is put together. I fancy there are none of us so poor we could not squeeze out, say ten cents a week. For a hundred women that would be ten dollars. Could you feed a hundred tired women for ten dollars, Mrs. Morrison?"

Mrs. Morrison smiled cordially. "Not on chicken pie," she said, "But I could give them tea and coffee, crackers and cheese for that, I think. And a quiet place to rest, and a reading room, and a place to hold meetings."

Then Mrs. Blake quite swept them off their feet by her wit and eloquence. She gave them to understand that if a share in the palatial accommodation of the Welcome House, and as good tea and coffee as old Sally made, with a place to meet, a place to rest, a place to talk, a place to lie down, could be had for ten cents a week each, she advised them to clinch the arrangement at once before Mrs. Morrison's natural good sense had overcome her enthusiasm.

Before Mrs. Isabelle Carter Blake had left, Haddleton had a large and eager women's club, whose entire expenses, outside of stationary and postage, consisted of ten cents a week *per capita,* paid to Mrs. Morrison. Everybody belonged. It was open at once for charter members, and all pressed forward to claim that privileged place.

They joined by hundreds, and from each member came this tiny sum to Mrs. Morrison each week. It was very little money, taken separately. But it added up with silent speed. Tea and coffee, purchased in bulk, crackers by the barrel, and whole cheeses – these are not expensive luxuries. The town was full of Mrs. Morrison's ex-Sunday-school boys, who furnished her with the best they had – at cost. There was a good deal of work, a good deal of care, and room for the whole supply of Mrs. Morrison's diplomatic talent and experience. Saturdays found the Welcome House as full as it could hold, and Sundays found Mrs. Morrison in bed. But she liked it.

A busy, hopeful year flew by, and then she went to Jean's for Thanksgiving.

The room Jean gave her was about the same size as her haven in Andrew's

home, but one flight higher up, and with a sloping ceiling. Mrs.

Morrison whitened her dark hair upon it, and rubbed her head confusedly.

Then she shook it with renewed determination.

The house was full of babies. There was little Joe, able to get about, and into everything. There were the twins, and there was the new baby. There was one servant, over-worked and cross. There was a small, cheap, totally inadequate nursemaid. There was Jean, happy but tired, full of joy, anxiety and affection, proud of her children, proud of her husband, and delighted to unfold her heart to her mother.

By the hour she babbled of their cares and hopes, while Mrs. Morrison, tall and elegant in her well-kept old black silk, sat holding the baby or trying to hold the twins. The old silk was pretty well finished by the week's end. Joseph talked to her also, telling her how well he was getting on, and how much he needed capital, urging her to come and stay with them; it was such a help to Jeannie; asking questions about the house.

There was no going visiting here. Jeannie could not leave the babies. And few visitors; all the little suburb being full of similarly overburdened mothers. Such as called found Mrs. Morrison charming. What she found them, she did not say. She bade her daughter an affectionate good-bye when the week was up, smiling at their mutual contentment.

"Good-bye, my dear children," she said. "I am so glad for all your happiness. I am thankful for both of you."

But she was more thankful to get home.

Mr. Butts did not have to call for his interest this time, but he called none the less.

"How on earth'd you get it, Delia?" he demanded. "Screwed it out o' these club-women?"

"Your interest is so moderate, Mr. Butts, that it is easier to meet than you imagine," was her answer. "Do you know the average interest they charge in Colorado? The women vote there, you know."

He went away with no more personal information than that; and no nearer approach to the twin goals of his desire than the passing of the year.

"One more year, Delia," he said; "then you'll have to give in."

"One more year!" she said to herself, and took up her chosen task with renewed energy.

The financial basis of the undertaking was very simple, but it would never have worked so well under less skilful management. Five dollars a year these country women could not have faced, but ten cents a week was possible to the poorest. There was no difficulty in collecting, for they brought it themselves; no unpleasantness in receiving, for old Sally stood at the receipt of custom and presented the covered cash box when they came for their tea.

On the crowded Saturdays the great urns were set going, the mighty array of cups arranged in easy reach, the ladies filed by, each taking her refection and leaving her dime. Where the effort came was in enlarging the membership and keeping up the attendance, and this effort was precisely in the line of Mrs. Morrison's splendid talents.

Serene, cheerful, inconspicuously active, planning like the born statesman she was, executing like a practical politician, Mrs. Morrison gave her mind to the work, and thrived upon it. Circle within circle, and group within group, she set small classes and departments at work, having a boys' club by and by in the big room over the woodshed, girls' clubs, reading clubs, study clubs, little meetings of every sort that were not held in churches, and some that were – previously.

For each and all there was, if wanted, tea and coffee, crackers and cheese; simple fare, of unvarying excellence, and from each and all, into the little cashbox, ten cents for these refreshments. From the club members this came weekly; and the club members, kept up by a constant variety of interests, came every week. As to numbers, before the first six months was over The Haddleton Rest and Improvement Club numbered five hundred women.

Now, five hundred times ten cents a week is twenty-six hundred dollars a year. Twenty-six hundred dollars a year would not be very much to build or rent a large house, to furnish five hundred people with chairs, lounges, books, and magazines, dishes and service; and with food and drink even of the simplest. But if you are miraculously supplied with a club-house, furnished, with a manager and servant on the spot, then that amount of money goes a long way.

On Saturdays Mrs. Morrison hired two helpers for half a day, for half a dollar each. She stocked the library with many magazines for fifty dollars a year. She covered fuel, light, and small miscellanies with another hundred. And she fed her multitude with the plain viands agreed upon, at about four cents apiece.

For her collateral entertainments, her many visits, the various new expenses entailed, she paid as well; and yet at the end of the first year she had not only her interest, but a solid thousand dollars of clear profit. With a calm smile she surveyed it, heaped in neat stacks of bills in the small safe in the wall behind her bed. Even Sally did not know it was there.

The second season was better than the first. There were difficulties, excitements, even some opposition, but she rounded out the year triumphantly. "After that," she said to herself, "they may have the deluge if they like."

She made all expenses, made her interest, made a little extra cash, clearly her own, all over and above the second thousand dollars.

Then did she write to son and daughter, inviting them and their families to come home to Thanksgiving, and closing each letter with joyous pride: "Here is the money to come with."

They all came, with all the children and two nurses. There was plenty of room in the Welcome House, and plenty of food on the long mahogany table. Sally was as brisk as a bee, brilliant in scarlet and purple; Mrs. Morrison carved her big turkey with queenly grace.

"I don't see that you're over-run with club women, mother," said

Jeannie.

"It's Thanksgiving, you know; they're all at home. I hope they are all as happy, as thankful for their homes as I am for mine," said Mrs. Morrison.

Afterward Mr. Butts called. With dignity and calm unruffled, Mrs.

Morrison handed him his interest – and principal.

Mr. Butts was almost loath to receive it, though his hand automatically grasped the crisp blue check.

"I didn't know you had a bank account," he protested, somewhat dubiously.

"Oh, yes; you'll find the check will be honored, Mr. Butts."

"I'd like to know how you got this money. You *can't* 'a' skinned it out o' that club of yours."

"I appreciate your friendly interest, Mr. Butts; you have been most kind."

"I believe some of these great friends of yours have lent it to you.

You won't be any better off, I can tell you."

"Come, come, Mr. Butts! Don't quarrel with good money. Let us part friends."

And they parted.

When I Was a Witch

If I had understood the terms of that one-sided contract with Satan, the Time of Witching would have lasted longer – you may be sure of that. But how was I to tell? It just happened, and has never happened again, though I've tried the same preliminaries as far as I could control them.

The thing began all of a sudden, one October midnight – the 30th, to be exact. It had been hot, really hot, all day, and was sultry and thunderous in the evening; no air stirring, and the whole house stewing with that ill-advised activity which always seems to move the steam radiator when it isn't wanted.

I was in a state of simmering rage – hot enough, even without the weather and the furnace – and I went up on the roof to cool off. A top-floor apartment has that advantage, among others – you can take a walk without the mediation of an elevator boy!

There are things enough in New York to lose one's temper over at the best of times, and on this particular day they seemed to all happen at once, and some fresh ones. The night before, cats and dogs had broken my rest, of course. My morning paper was more than usually mendacious; and my neighbor's morning paper – more visible than my own as I went down town – was more than usually salacious. My cream wasn't cream – my egg was a relic of the past. My "new" napkins were giving out.

Being a woman, I'm supposed not to swear; but when the motorman disregarded my plain signal, and grinned as he rushed by; when the subway guard waited till I was just about to step on board and then slammed the door in my face – standing behind it calmly for some minutes before the bell rang to warrant his closing – I desired to swear like a mule-driver.

At night it was worse. The way people paw one's back in the crowd! The cow-puncher who packs the people in or jerks them out – the men who smoke and spit, law or no law – the women whose saw-edged cart-wheel hats, swashing feathers and deadly pins, add so to one's comfort inside.

Well, as I said, I was in a particularly bad temper, and went up on the roof to cool off. Heavy black clouds hung low overhead, and lightning flickered threateningly here and there.

A starved, black cat stole from behind a chimney and mewed dolefully.

Poor thing! She had been scalded.

The street was quiet for New York. I leaned over a little and looked up and down the long parallels of twinkling lights. A belated cab drew near, the horse so tired he could hardly hold his head up.

Then the driver, with a skill born of plenteous practice, flung out his long-lashed whip and curled it under the poor beast's belly with a stinging cut that made me shudder. The horse shuddered too, poor wretch, and jingled his harness with an effort at a trot.

I leaned over the parapet and watched that man with a spirit of unmitigated ill-will.

"I wish," said I, slowly – and I did wish it with all my heart – "that every person who strikes or otherwise hurts a horse unnecessarily, shall feel the pain intended – and the horse not feel it!"

It did me good to say it, anyhow, but I never expected any result. I saw the man swing his great whip again, and – lay on heartily. I saw him throw up his hands – heard him scream – but I never thought what the matter was, even then.

The lean, black cat, timid but trustful, rubbed against my skirt and mewed.

"Poor Kitty" I said; "poor Kitty! It is a shame!" And I thought tenderly of all the thousands of hungry, hunted cats who stink and suffer its a great city.

Later, when I tried to sleep, and up across the stillness rose the raucous shrieks of some of these same sufferers, my pity turned cold. "Any fool that will try to keep a cat in a city!" I muttered, angrily.

Another yell – a pause – an ear-torturing, continuous cry. "I wish," I burst forth, "that every cat in the city was comfortably dead!"

A sudden silence fell, and in course of time I got to sleep.

Things went fairly well next morning, till I tried another egg. They were expensive eggs, too.

"I can't help it!" said my sister, who keeps house.

"I know you can't," I admitted. "But somebody could help it. I wish the people who are responsible had to eat their old eggs, and never get a good one till they sold good ones!"

"They'd stop eating eggs, that's all," said my sister, "and eat meat."

"Let 'em eat meat!" I said, recklessly. "The meat is as bad as the eggs! It's so long since we've had a clean, fresh chicken that I've forgotten how they taste!"

"It's cold storage," said my sister. She is a peaceable sort; I'm not.

"Yes, cold storage!" I snapped. "It ought to be a blessing – to tide over shortages, equalize supplies, and lower prices. What does it do? Corner the market, raise prices the year round, and make all the food bad!"

My anger rose. "If there was any way of getting at them!" I cried. "The law don't touch 'em. They need to be cursed somehow! I'd like to do it! I wish the whole crowd that profit by this vicious business might taste their bad meat, their old fish, their stale milk – whatever they ate. Yes, and feel the prices as we do!"

"They couldn't you know; they're rich," said my sister.

"I know that," I admitted, sulkily. "There's no way of getting at 'em. But I wish they could. And I wish they knew how people hated 'em, and felt that, too – till they mended their ways!"

When I left for my office I saw a funny thing. A man who drove a garbage cart took his horse by the bits and jerked and wrenched brutally. I was amazed to see him clap his hands to his own jaws with a moan, while the horse philosophically licked his chops and looked at him.

The man seemed to resent his expression, and struck him on the head, only to rub his own poll and swear amazedly, looking around to see who had hit him. the horse advanced a step, stretching a hungry nose toward a garbage pail crowned with cabbage leaves, and the man, recovering his sense of proprietorship, swore at him and kicked him in the ribs. That time he had to sit down, turning pale and weak. I watched with growing wonder and delight.

A market wagon came clattering down the street; the hard-faced young ruffian fresh for his morning task. He gathered the ends of the reins and brought them down on the horse's back with a resounding thwack. The horse did not notice this at all, but the boy did. He yelled!

I came to a place where many teamsters were at work hauling dirt and crushed stone. A strange silence and peace hung over the scene where usually the sound of the lash and sight of brutal blows made me hurry by. The men were talking together a little, and seemed to be exchanging notes. It was too good to be true. I gazed and marvelled, waiting for my car.

It came, merrily running along. It was not full. There was one not far ahead, which I had missed in watching the horses; there was no other near it in the rear.

Yet the coarse-faced person in authority who ran it, went gaily by without stopping, though I stood on the track almost, and waved my umbrella.

A hot flush of rage surged to my face. "I wish you felt the blow you deserve," said I, viciously, looking after the car. "I wish you'd have to stop, and back to here, and open the door and apologize. I wish that would happen to all of you, every time you play that trick."

To my infinite amazement, that car stopped and backed till the front door was before me. The motorman opened it. holding his hand to his cheek. "Beg your pardon, madam!" he said.

I passed in, dazed, overwhelmed. Could it be? Could it possibly be that – that what I wished came true. The idea sobered me, but I dismissed it with a scornful smile. "No such luck!" said I.

Opposite me sat a person in petticoats. She was of a sort I particularly detest. No real body of bones and muscles, but the contours of grouped sausages. Complacent, gaudily dressed, heavily wigged and ratted, with powder and perfume and flowers and jewels – and a dog.

A poor, wretched, little, artificial dog – alive, but only so by virtue of man's insolence; not a real creature that God made. And the dog had clothes on – and a bracelet! His fitted jacket had a pocket – and a pocket-handkerchief! He looked sick and unhappy.

I meditated on his pitiful position, and that of all the other poor chained prisoners, leading unnatural lives of enforced celibacy, cut off from sunlight, fresh air, the use of their limbs; led forth at stated intervals by unwilling servants, to defile our streets; over-fed, under-exercised, nervous and unhealthy.

"And we say we love them!" said I, bitterly to myself. "No wonder they bark and howl and go mad. No wonder they have almost as many diseases as we do! I wish –" Here the thought I had dismissed struck me agin. "I wish that all the unhappy dogs in cities would die at once!"

I watched the sad-eyed little invalid across the car. He dropped his head and died. She never noticed it till she got off; then she made fuss enough.

The evening papers were full of it. Some sudden pestilence had struck both dogs and cats, it would appear. Red headlines struck the eye, big letters, and columns were filled out of the complaints of those who had lost their "pets," of the sudden labors of the board of health, and interviews with doctors.

All day, as I went through the office routine, the strange sense of this new power struggled with reason and common knowledge. I even tried a few furtive test "wishes" – wished that the waste basket would fall over, that the inkstand would fill itself; but they didn't.

I dismissed the idea as pure foolishness, till I saw those newspapers, and heard people telling worse stories.

One thing I decided at once – not to tell a soul. "Nobody'd believe me if I did," said I to myself. "And I won't give 'em the chance. I've scored on cats and dogs, anyhow – and horses."

As I watched the horses at work that afternoon, and thought of all their unknown sufferings from crowded city stables, bad air and insufficient food, and from the wearing strain of asphalt pavements in wet and icy weather, I decided to have another try on horses.

"I wish," said I, slowly and carefully, but with a fixed intensity of purposes, "that every horse owner, keeper, hirer and driver or rider, might feel what the horse feels, when he suffers at our hands. Feel it keenly and constantly till the case is mended."

I wasn't able to verify this attempt for some time; but the effect was so general that it got widely talked about soon; and this "new wave of humane feeling" soon raised the status of horses in our city. Also it diminished their numbers. People began to prefer motor drays – which was a mighty good thing.

Now I felt pretty well assured in my own mind, and kept my assurance to my self. Also I began to make a list of my cherished grudges, with a fine sense of power and pleasure.

"I must be careful," I said to myself; "very careful; and, above all things, make the punishment fit the crime."

The subway crowding came to my mind next; both the people who crowd because they have to, and the people who make them. "I mustn't punish anybody, for what they can't help," I mused. "But when it's pure meanness!" Then I bethought me of the remote stockholders, of the more immediate directors, of the painfully prominent officials and insolent employees – and got to work.

"I might as well make a good job of it while this lasts," said I to myself. "It's quite a responsibility, but lots of fun." And I wished that every person responsible for the condition of our subways might be mysteriously compelled to ride up and down in them continuously during rush hours.

This experiment I watched with keen interest, but for the life of me I could see little difference. There were a few more well-dressed persons in the crowds, that was all. So I came to the conclusion that the general public was mostly to blame, and carried their daily punishment without knowing it.

For the insolent guards and cheating ticket-sellers who give you short change, very slowly, when you are dancing on one foot and your train is there, I merely wished that they might feel the pain their victims would like to give them, short of real injury. They did, I guess.

Then I wished similar things for all manner of corporations and officials. It worked. It worked amazingly. There was a sudden conscientious revival all over the country. The dry bones rattled and sat up. Boards of directors, having troubles enough of their own, were aggravated by innumerable communications from suddenly sensitive stockholders.

In mills and mints and railroads, things began to mend. The country buzzed. The papers fattened. The churches sat up and took credit to themselves. I was incensed at this; and, after brief consideration, wished that every minister would preach to his congregation exactly what he believed and what he thought of them.

I went to six services the next Sunday – about ten minutes each, for two sessions. It was most amusing. A thousand pulpits were emptied forthwith, refilled, re-emptied, and so on, from week to week. People began to go to church; men largely – women didn't like it as well. They had always supposed the ministers thought more highly of them than now appeared to be the case.

One of my oldest grudges was against the sleeping-car people; and now I began to consider them. How often I had grinned and borne it – with other thousands – submitting helplessly.

Here is a railroad – a common carrier – and you have to use it. You pay for your transportation, a good round sum.

Then if you wish to stay in the sleeping car during the day, they charge you another two dollars and a half for the privilege of sitting there, whereas you have paid for a seat when you bought your ticket. That seat is now sold to another person – twice sold! Five dollars for twenty-four hours in a space six feet by three by three at night, and one seat by day; twenty-four of these privileges to a car – $120 a day for the rent of the car – and the passengers to pay the porter besides. That makes $44,800 a year.

Sleeping cars are expensive to build, they say. So are hotels; but they do not charge at such a rate. Now, what could I do to get even? Nothing could ever put back the dollars into the millions of pockets; but it might be stopped now, this beautiful process.

So I wished that all persons who profited by this performance might feel a shame so keen that they would make public avowal and apology, and, as partial restitution, offer their wealth to promote the cause of free railroads!

Then I remembered parrots. This was lucky, for my wrath flamed again. It was really cooling, as I tried to work out responsibility and adjust penalties. But parrots! Any person who wants to keep a parrot should go and live on an island alone with their preferred conversationalist!

There was a huge, squawky parrot right across the street from me, adding its senseless, rasping cries to the more necessary evils of other noises.

I had also an aunt with a parrot. She was a wealthy, ostentatious person, who had been an only child and inherited her money.

Uncle Joseph hated the yelling bird, but that didn't make any difference to Aunt Mathilda.

I didn't like this aunt, and wouldn't visit her, lest she think I was truckling for the sake of her money; but after I had wished this time, I called at the time set for my curse to work; and it did work with a vengeance. There sat poor Uncle Joe, looking thinner and meeker than ever; and my aunt, like an overripe plum, complacent enough.

"Let me out!" said Polly, suddenly. "Let me out to take a walk!"

"The clever thing!" said Aunt Mathilda. "He never said that before."

She let him out. Then he flapped up on the chandelier and sat among the prisms, quite safe.

"What an old pig you are, Mathilda!" said the parrot.

She started to her feet – naturally.

"Born a Pig – trained a Pig – a Pig by nature and education!" said the parrot. "Nobody'd put up with you, except for your money; unless it's this long-suffering husband of yours. He wouldn't, if he hadn't the patience of Job!"

"Hold your tongue!" screamed Aunt Mathilda. "Come down from there!

Come here!"

Polly cocked his head and jingled the prisms. "Sit down, Mathilda!" he said, cheerfully. "You've got to listen. You are fat and homely and selfish. You are a nuisance to everybody about you. You have got to feed me and take care of me better than ever – and you've got to listen to me when I talk. Pig!"

I visited another person with a parrot the next day. She put a cloth over his cage when I came in.

"Take it off!" said Polly. She took it off.

"Won't you come into the other room?" she asked me, nervously.

"Better stay here!" said her pet. "Sit still – sit still!"

She sat still.

"Your hair is mostly false," said pretty Poll. "And your teeth – and your outlines. You eat too much. You are lazy. You ought to exercise, and don't know enough. Better apologize to this lady for backbiting! You've got to listen."

The trade in parrots fell off from that day; they say there is no call for them. But the people who kept parrots, keep them yet – parrots live a long time.

Bores were a class of offenders against whom I had long borne undying enmity. Now I rubbed my hands and began on them, with this simple wish: That every person whom they bored should tell them the plain truth.

There is one man whom I have specially in mind. He was blackballed at a pleasant club, but continues to go there. He isn't a member – he just goes; and no one does anything to him.

It was very funny after this. He appeared that very night at a meeting, and almost every person present asked him how he came there. "You're not a member, you know," they said. "Why do you butt in? Nobody likes you."

Some were more lenient with him. "Why don't you learn to be more considerate of others, and make some real friends?" they said. "To have a few friends who do enjoy your visits ought to be pleasanter than being a public nuisance."

He disappeared from that club, anyway.

I began to feel very cocky indeed.

In the food business there was already a marked improvement; and in transportation. The hubbub of reformation waxed louder daily, urged on by the unknown sufferings of all the profiters by iniquity.

The papers thrived on all this; and as I watched the loud-voiced protestations of my pet abomination in journalism, I had a brilliant idea, literally.

Next morning I was down town early, watching the men open their papers. My abomination was shamefully popular, and never more so than this morning. Across the top was printing in gold letters:

> *All intentional lies, in adv., editorial, news, or any*
>   *other column... Scarlet*
> *All malicious matter... Crimson*
> *All careless or ignorant mistakes... Pink*
> *All for direct self-interest of owner... Dark green*
> *All mere bait – to sell the paper... Bright green*
> *All advertising, primary or secondary... Brown*
> *All sensational and salacious matter... Yellow*
> *All hired hypocrisy... Purple*
> *Good fun, instruction and entertainment... Blue*
> *True and necessary news and honest editorials...*
>   *Ordinary print*

You never saw such a crazy quilt of a paper. They were bought like hot cakes for some days; but the real business fell off very soon. They'd have stopped it all if they could; but the papers looked all right when they came off the press. The color scheme flamed out only to the bona-fide reader.

I let this work for about a week, to the immense joy of all the other papers; and then turned it on to them, all at once. Newspaper reading became very exciting for a little, but the trade fell off. Even newspaper editors could not keep on feeding a market like that. The blue printed and ordinary printed matter grew from column to column and page to page. Some papers – small, to be sure, but refreshing – began to appear in blue and black alone.

This kept me interested and happy for quite a while; so much so that I quite forgot to be angry at other things. There was *such* a change in all kinds of business, following the mere printing of truth in the newspapers. It began to appear as if we had lived in a sort of delirium – not really knowing the facts about anything. As soon as we really knew the facts, we began to behave very differently, of course.

What really brought all my enjoyment to an end was women. Being a woman, I was naturally interested in them, and could see some things more clearly than men could. I saw their real power, their real dignity, their real responsibility in the world; and then the way they dress and behave used to make me fairly frantic. 'Twas like seeing archangels playing jackstraws – or real horses only used as rocking-horses. So I determined to get after them.

How to manage it! What to hit first! Their hats, their ugly, inane, outrageous hats – that is what one thinks of first. Their silly, expensive clothes – their diddling beads and jewelry – their greedy childishness – mostly of the women provided for by rich men.

Then I thought of all the other women, the real ones, the vast majority, patiently doing the work of servants without even a servant's pay – and neglecting the noblest duties of motherhood in favor of house-service; the greatest power on earth, blind, chained, untaught, in a treadmill. I thought of what they might do, compared to what they did do, and my heart swelled with something that was far from anger.

Then I wished – with all my strength – that women, all women, might realize Womanhood at last; its power and pride and place in life; that they might see their duty as mothers of the world – to love and care for everyone alive; that they might see their dirty to men – to choose only the best, and then to bear and rear better ones; that they might see their duty as human beings, and come right out into full life and work and happiness!

I stopped, breathless, with shining eyes. I waited, trembling, for things to happen.

Nothing happened.

You see, this magic which had fallen on me was black magic – and I had wished white.

It didn't work at all, and, what was worse, it stopped all the other things that were working so nicely.

Oh, if I had only thought to wish permanence for those lovely punishments! If only I had done more while I could do it, had half appreciated my privileges when I was a Witch!

A Word in Season

"Children pick up words like pigeons peas,

And utter them again as God shall please."

When Grandma came to the breakfast table with her sour little smile and her peremptory "Good morning," every one said "good morning" as politely and pleasantly as they could, but they didn't say very much else. They attempted bravely.

"A fine morning, Mother," Papa observed, but she only answered "Too cold."

"Did you sleep well, Mother?" ventured Mama; and the reply to that was,

"No, I never do!"

Then Uncle John tried – he always tried once.

"Have you heard of our new machine, Mrs. Grey? We've got one now that'll catch anything in a room – don't have to talk right into it."

Mrs. Grey looked at him coldly.

"I do not take the least interest in your talking machines, Henry, as I have told you before."

She had, many times before, but Uncle Henry never could learn the astonishing fact. He was more interested in his machines than he was in his business, by far; and spent all his spare time in tinkering with them.

"I think they are wonderful," said little Josie.

"You're my only friend, Kid! I believe you understand 'em almost as well is I do," her Uncle answered gaily; and finished his breakfast as quickly as possible.

So did everybody. It was not appetizing to have Grandma say "How you do dawdle over your meals, Louise!"

Little Josephine slipped down from her chair, with a whispered "Scuse me Mama!" and whisked into her play room.

"How you do spoil that child!" said Grandma, and Mama closed her lips tight and looked at her husband.

"Now Mother, don't you fret about Josie," said he. "She's a good little girl and quiet as a mouse."

"Anything I can do for you downtown, Mother?"

"No thank you Joseph. I'll go to my room and be out of Louise's way."

"You're not in my way at all, Mother – won't you sit down stairs?"

Young Mrs. Grey made a brave effort to speak cordially, but old Mrs. Grey only looked injured, and said "No thank you, Louise," as she went upstairs.

Dr. Grey looked at his wife. She met his eyes steadily, cheerfully.

"I think Mother's looking better, don't you dear?" she said.

"There's nothing at all the matter with my mother – except –" he shut his mouth hard. "There are things I cannot say, Louise," he continued, "but others I can. Namely; that for sweetness and patience and gentleness you – you beat the

Dutch! And I do appreciate it. One can't turn one's Mother out of the house, but I do resent her having another doctor!"

"I'd love your Mother, Joseph, if – if she was a thousand times worse!" his wife answered; and he kissed her with grateful love.

Sarah came in to clear the table presently, and Ellen stood in the pantry door to chat with her.

"Never in my life did I see any woman wid the patience of her!" said

Ellen, wiping her mouth on her apron.

"She has need of it," said Sarah. "Any Mother-in-law is a trial I've heard, but this wan is the worst. Why she must needs live with 'em I don't see – she has daughters of her own."

"'Tis the daughter's husbands won't put up wid her," answered Ellen, "they havin' the say of course. This man's her son – and he has to keep her if she will stay."

"And she as rich as a Jew!" Sarah went on. "And never spendin' a cent!

And the Doctor workin' night and day!" –

Then Mama came in and this bit of conversation naturally came to an end.

A busy, quiet, sweet little woman was Mama; and small Josie flew into her arms and cuddled there most happily.

"Mama Dearest," she said, "How long is it to Christmas? Can I get my mat done for Grandma? And *do* you think she'll like it?"

"Well, well dear – that's three *questions!* It's two weeks yet to Christmas; and I think you can if you work steadily; and I hope she'll like it."

"And Mama – can I have my party?"

"I'm afraid not, dearest. You see Grandma is old, and she hates a noise and confusion – and parties are expensive. I'm sorry, childie. Can't you think of something else you want, that Mother can give you?"

"No," said the child, "I've wanted a party for three years, Mama! Grandma just spoils everything!"

"No, no, dear – you must always love Grandma because she is dear Papa's mother; and because she is lonely and needs our love.

"We'll have a party some day, Dearest – don't feel badly. And *we* always have a good time together, don't we?"

They did; but just now the child's heart was set on more social pleasures, and she went sadly back to her playroom to work on that mat for Grandma.

It was a busy day. Mama's married sister came to see her, and the child was sent out of the room. Two neighbors called, and waited, chatting, some time before Mama came down.

Grandma's doctor – who was not Papa – called; and her lawyer too; and they had to wait some time for the old lady to dress as she thought fitting.

But Grandma's doctor and lawyer were very old friends, and seemed to enjoy themselves.

The minister came also, not Grandma's minister, who was old and thin and severe and wore a long white beard; but Mama's minister, who was so vigorous and cheerful, and would lift Josephine way up over his head – as if she was ten years old. But Mama sent her out of the room this time, which was a pity.

To be sure Josephine had a little secret trail from her playroom door – behind several pieces of furniture – right up to the back of the sofa where people usually sat, but she was not often interested in their conversation. She was a quiet child, busy with her own plans and ideas; playing softly by herself, with much imaginary conversation. She set up her largest doll, a majestic personage known as "The Lady Isobel," and talked to her.

"Why is my Grandma so horrid? And why do I have to love her? How can you love people – if you don't, Lady Isobel?

"Other girls' Grandmas are nice. Nelly Elder's got a lovely Grandma! She lets Nelly have parties and everything. Maybe if Grandma likes my mat she'll – be pleasanter.

"Maybe she'll go somewhere else to live – sometime. Don't you think so, Lady Isobel?"

The Lady Isobel's reply, however, was not recorded.

Grandma pursued her pious way as usual, till an early bedtime relieved the family of her presence. Then Uncle Harry stopped puttering with his machines and came out to be sociable with his sister. If Papa was at home they would have a game of solo – if not, they played cribbage, or quiet.

Uncle Harry was the life of the household – when Grandma wasn't around.

"Well, Lulu," he said cheerfully, "What's the prospect? Can Joe make it?"

"No," said Mama. "It's out of the question. He could arrange about his practice easily enough but it's the money for the trip. He'll have to send his paper to be read."

"It's a shame!" said the young man, "He ought to be there. He'd do those other doctors good. Why in the name of reason don't the old lady give him the money – she could, easy enough."

"Joe never'll ask her for a cent," answered Mrs. Grey, "and it would never occur to her to give him one! Yet I think she loves him best of all her children."

"Huh! *Love!*" said Uncle Harry.

* * *

Grandma didn't sleep well at night. She complained of this circumstantially and at length.

"Hour after hour I hear the clock strike," she said. "Hour after hour!"

Little Josephine had heard the clock strike hour after hour one terrible night when she had an earache. She was really sorry for Grandma.

"And nothing to take up my mind," said Grandma, as if her mind was a burden to her.

But the night after this she had something to take up her mind. As a matter of fact it woke her up, as she had napped between the clock's strikings. At first she thought the servants were in her room – and realized with a start that they were speaking of her.

"Why she must live with 'em I don't see – she has daughters of her own—"

With the interest of an eavesdropper she lay still, listening, and heard no good of herself.

"How long is it to Christmas?" she presently heard her grandchild ask, and beg her mother for the "party "—still denied her.

"Grandma spoils everything!" said the clear childish voice, and the mother's gentle one urged love and patience.

It was some time before the suddenly awakened old lady, in the dark, realized the source of these voices – and then she could not locate it.

"It's some joke of that young man's" she said grimly – but the joke went on.

It was Mrs. Grey's sister now, condoling with her about this mother-in-law.

"Why do you have to put up with it Louise? Won't any of her daughters have her?"

"I'm afraid they don't want her," said Louise's gentle voice. "But Joe is her son, and of course he feels that his home is his mother's. I think he is quite right. She is old, and alone – she doesn't *mean* to be disagreeable."

"Well, she achieves it without effort, then! A more disagreeable old lady I never saw, Louise, and I'd like nothing better than to tell her so!"

The old lady was angry, but impressed. There is a fascination in learning how others see us, even if the lesson is unpleasant. She heard the two neighbors who talked together before Mama came down, and their talk was of her – and of how they pitied young Mrs. Grey.

"If I was in her shoes," said the older of the two, "I'd pick up and travel! She's only sixty-five – and sound as a nut."

"Has she money enough?" asked the other.

"My, yes! Money to burn! She has her annuity that her father left her, and a big insurance – and house rents. She must have all of three thousand a year."

"And doesn't she pay board here?"

"Pay board! Not she. She wouldn't pay anything so long as she has a relative to live on. She's saved all her life. But nobody'll get any good of it till she's dead."

This talk stopped when their hostess entered, changing to more general themes; but the interest revived when men's voices took up the tale.

"Yes – wants her will made again. Always making and unmaking and remaking. Harmless amusement, I suppose."

"She wastes good money on both of us – and I tell her so. But one can't be expected to absolutely refuse a patient."

"Or a client!"

"No. I suppose not."

"She's not really ill then?"

"Bless you, Ruthven, I don't know a sounder old woman anywhere. All she needs is a change – and to think of something besides herself! I tell her that, too – and she says I'm so eccentric."

"Why in all decency don't her son do her doctoring?"

"I suppose he's too frank – and not quite able to speak his mind. He's a fine fellow. That paper of his will be a great feature of our convention. Shame he can't go."

"Why can't he? Can't afford it?"

"That's just it. You see the old lady don't put up – not a cent – and he has all he can do to keep the boys in college." And their conversation stopped, and Grandma heard her own voice – inviting the doctor up to her room – and making another appointment for the lawyer.

Then it was the young minister, a cheerful, brawny youth, whom she had once described as a "Godless upstart!"

He appeared to be comforting young Mrs. Grey, and commending her. "You are doing wonders," he said, as their voices came into hearing, "and not letting your right hand know it, either."

"You make far too much of it, Mr. Eagerson," the soft voice answered, "I am so happy in my children – my home – my husband. This is the *only tr*ouble – I do not complain."

"I know you don't complain, Mrs. Grey, but I want you to know that you're appreciated! 'It is better to dwell in a corner of the housetop, than with a woman in a wide house' – especially if she's your mother-in-law."

"I won't allow you to speak so – if you are my minister!" said young Mrs. Grey with spirit; and the talk changed to church matters, where the little lady offered to help with time and service, and regretted that she had no money to give.

There was a silence, save for small confused noises of a day time household; distant sounds of doors and dishes; and then in a sad, confidential voice – "Why is Grandma so horrid? And why do I have to love her? How can you love people you don't, Lady Isobel?"

Grandma was really fond of quiet little Josephine, even if she did sometimes snub her as a matter of principle. She lay and listened to these strictly private remarks, and meditated upon them after they had ceased. It was a large dose, an omnibus dose, and took some time to assimilate; but the old lady had really a mind of her own, though much of it was uninhabited, and this generous burst of light set it to working.

She said nothing to anyone, but seemed to use her eyes and ears with more attention than previously, and allowed her grand-daughter's small efforts toward affection with new receptiveness. She had one talk with her daughter-in-law which left that little woman wet-eyed and smiling with pleasure, though she could not tell about it – that was requisite.

But the family in general heard nothing of any change of heart till breakfast time on Christmas morning. They sat enjoying that pleasant meal, in the usual respite before the old lady appeared, when Sarah came in with a bunch of notes and laid one at each plate, with an air of great importance.

"She said I was to leave 'em till you was all here – and here they are!" said Sarah, smiling mysteriously, "and that I was to say nothing – and I haven't!" And the red-cheeked girl folded her arms and waited – as interested as anybody.

Uncle Harry opened his first. "I bet it's a tract!" said he. But he blushed to the roots of his thick brown hair as he took out, not a tract, but a check.

"A Christmas present to my son-in-law-by-marriage; to be spent on the improvement of talking machines – if that is necessary!"

"Why bless her heart!" said he, "I call that pretty handsome, and I'll tell her so!"

Papa opened his.

"For your Convention trip, dear son," said this one, "and for a new dress suit – and a new suit case, and a new overcoat – a nice one. With Mother's love."

It was a large check, this one. Papa sat quite silent and looked at his wife. She went around the table and hugged him – she had to.

"You've got one, too, Louise," said he – and she opened it.

"For my dear daughter Louise; this – to be spent on other people; and *this*" (*this* was much bigger) "to be inexorably spent on herself – every cent of it! On her own special needs and pleasures – if she can think of any!"

Louise was simply crying – and little Josephine ran to comfort her.

"Hold on Kiddie – you haven't opened yours," said Uncle Harry; and they all eagerly waited while the child carefully opened her envelope with a clean knife, and read out solemnly and slowly, "For my darling Grand-child Josephine, to be spent by herself, for herself, with Mama's advice and assistance; and in particular to provide for her party!"

She turned over the stiff little piece of paper – hardly understanding.

"It's a check, dear," said Papa. "It's the same as money. Parties cost money, and Grandma has made you a Christmas present of your party."

The little girl's eyes grew big with joy.

"Can I? – Is there really – a party?"

"There is really a party – for my little daughter, this afternoon at four!"

"O where is Grandma!" cried the child – "I want to hug her!"

They all rose up hurriedly, but Sarah came forward from her scant pretense of retirement, with another note for Dr. Grey.

"I was to give you this last of all," she said, with an air of one fulfilling grave diplomatic responsibility.

"My dear ones," ran the note, "I have gathered from my family and friends, and from professional and spiritual advisers the idea that change is often beneficial. With this in mind I have given myself a Christmas present of a Cook's Tour around the world – and am gone. A Merry Christmas and a Happy New Year to you all!"

She was gone.

Sarah admitted complicity.

"Sure she would have no one know a thing – not a word!" said Sarah. "And she gave us something handsome to help her! And she's got that young widder Johnson for a companion – and they went off last night on the sleeper for New York!"

The gratitude of the family had to be spent in loving letters, and in great plans of what they would do to make Grandma happy when she came back.

No one felt more grateful than little loving Josephine, whose dearest wishes were all fulfilled. When she remembered it she went very quietly, when all were busy somewhere else, climbed up on the step ladder, and took down the forgotten phonograph from the top of the wardrobe.

"Dear Grandma!" she said. "I do hope she liked it!"

Christmas Love

When the Writer or the Preacher or one who chances to be both considers a Christmas sermon, a Christmas story, what is the idea that comes uppermost?

Love, of course. Not sex-love: that's for every day. Not Mother-love: that's always and always. Not any of the minor brands of admiring devotion, gratitude, sympathy, friendship, attraction of any sort. No. When we say "Love" at Christmas time we mean Love, the Spirit of Life.

About once a year we give thought to it. About once a year we seek to express it; and, pitiful and limited though that expression be, its forms are right.

These main forms of Christmas expressions are two-fold: the Spirit of Joy, of Celebration, of High Festival – the highest of all; and the Spirit of Giving. These are found wherever Christmas is kept, and make it, as it should be, the glory of the year. In joy and in giving we are most absolutely in line with the mainspring of the Universe: unmeasured happiness – happiness that cannot be quenched – cannot be kept to ourselves. What must run over and pour forth on other people: that is real Love, Christmas Love – and that, of course, finds physical expression in gay festivities and showering gifts.

Light, color, music – all that is sweet and gay and comforting; games, dances and performances that show the happy heart; and always the overflow – giving, giving, giving. That is the Spirit of Life.

It is the children's festival because children are more in line with the Life Spirit than weazened old folk: the child has the passionate thirst for joy which marks his high parentage.

Whatever else is true about the Central Power of the Universe, this is true: it *is* power. And it pours forth in Radiant Energy. All "inanimate nature," so called, expresses this Power, each form after its kind; and all animate nature, crowned with consciousness, not only expresses it, but *feels* it, – which is called "Living."

We human beings are the highest, finest, subtlest instrument on this planet to receive and to transmit these waves of pouring Power. When we feel it most we call it Happiness. In two ways it reaches our consciousness, as it comes in and as it goes out, via the sensory and motor nerves. The joy of receiving power is great: "stimulus" we call it. It comes to us along the avenues of sense and thrills us with increased well being. But this kind of pleasure is sadly limited by those sense nerves of ours. We are but a little tea-cup: we cannot hold much. The Music of the Spheres might pour round us; the light of a thousand suns, the sweetness of piled banks of flowers, and all honey and sugar and rich food: every sense can be fed to its little limit only – and there the Happiness stops.

We can only feel so much – coming in. But there seems to be no limit to the joy we feel when Power goes out through us. It seems so self-evident, so needless, to say "It is more blessed to give than to receive." Why *of course* it is: any child even knows that.

True, a child, having a fresh, unsated sensorium, can receive with more vivid pleasure than an adult – for a while. But it is easily over-tired, easily over-fed with sensation, easily bored and weary with receiving.

Not with giving! Every child delights to let out the Power which is in him – in her; delights to make and delights to give. Therefore, to children is this their festival: the busy weeks of happiness in making gifts, the swelling, glowing pride of giving them!

It's all right as far as it goes, but why, when such a thing is such transcendent splendid blessedness, why only once a year? Why should this beautiful experience in which we not only remember the birth of the man who taught the world most of love but even try to practise what He preached – why should it be limited to a mere memorial of His birthday, plastered over the remnants of ancient festivals of the return of the Sun God – the Goodness of the Earth Mother?

If Christmas is good, why not more of it? Then we smile, wryly, and say, "Why, of course, we couldn't. The rest of life isn't like that – and we have to live, you see."

Ah, that is where we are wrong – utterly wrong. The rest of life *is* like that. That is *life* – Loving and Giving.

"Tut! Tut!" says the Practical Man. "That's emotional nonsense. That's womanish." Two-thirds right, my practical friend. It is not nonsense, but it is "emotional" and it is "womanish."

Emotion is *consciousness under pressure*. When we feel Power, we call it emotion. Emotions vary: some are helpful and some hateful, according to the nature of the instrument; but not to be emotional at all is not to be alive. Those who spend their lives lit by a blaze of emotion, warmed by a deep, slow-burning fire of emotion, pouring forth that emotion in great works – we call Geniuses. Genius is simply more Power.

As to being womanish: that word is no longer a term of reproach or belittlement. To be womanish is to be human, and we may now turn round and pitifully dismiss much old world folly and passion as merely "mannish." To be womanish – and practical – let us repeat, Life *is* Loving and Giving. When we realize this, intelligently and completely, we shall have a "continuous performance" of Christmases and a higher level of happiness the year round, varied by greater heights. At present the natural flood of Life Force, pouring through us in unbounded creative energy, resulting in the myriad forms of human achievement and manufacture, is sadly thwarted in its output by lingering remains of our old period.

For a long time we lived by getting: to hunt, to catch, to kill, to eat was all we knew: no loving or giving there save as the mother fulfilled the law. But since our Humaness began, since all our thousand powers and talents grew for mutual service, since we learned to do things for each other – to make things for each other, to give things to each other

– then grew in us that rising tide of Power which lives out in expression.

In spite of our old world perverseness, that Power pours on. Though we scorn the gifts of those who make the comforts of life for us, though we despise their service and so cruelly use them as to greatly thwart their love – still we are fed and housed and clothed and carried by the love and service of our kind, the daily, hourly gifts of those who work.

"They are not gifts," cries the Practical Man. "They are paid for – every bit of 'em." Yes, Brother. And how paid for? Paid how much? What scant reward, what meagre living, what miserable houses, what stinted food, what limited education, and what poisoned pleasures do we pay to those who make every necessity, comfort, convenience and luxury for us!

Pay indeed! If a man "saves your life" once, and you give him twenty cents an hour for his exertions in your behalf – have you paid him? By the life-long labor of the human race – all those dead workers who built up the structure of our present world, all those living workers who keep the wheels revolving now – by these labors we live, all of us, all the time.

Pay? Pay for daily – hourly – maintenance, protection, food, shelter, safety, comfort? Pay for being kept alive?

Life is giving – Loving and Giving. You can't pay for it. You don't pay for it. But this you do: you hinder it, by your paying. This pitiful trickle of measurement, this ticking and pricing and holding back the world's flood of outpouring energy by our wretched turnstiles – this is what keeps us poor!

We need to let loose the Power that is in us. We need to Love more and Give more – a plain truth, Jesus taught some centuries ago, largely in vain. We have but to let out the love that is in us: there is no limit to its flood.

To so love every child that is born on earth as to provide that child with all that it needs for richest growth, for full appreciation of the splendor of human life – of conscious citizenship! Children so reared will have a thousandfold more to give, and a thousandfold greater joy in giving. Then life will roll out through our glad hearts and willing hands as the sun's light pours abroad – only that we are conscious, we feel this light, this heat, this radiant energy. We call it – *love*.

The End

A Life & Works

Charlotte Perkins Gilman

Perhaps best known for her fascinating and seminal short story, 'The Yellow Wallpaper', Charlotte Perkins Gilman was a pioneering social reformer, lecturer and editor as well as a feminist literary icon who spent much of her adult life striving for equal rights and opportunities for women. Her thought-provoking, important and often controversial works still resonate and inspire today, nearly a hundred years after her death.

Childhood and Education

Born on 3 July 1860 to Frederic and Mary Perkins, Gilman spent her early life in Hartford, Connecticut. Frederic abandoned his family when Charlotte was just an infant, leaving Mary to raise her children in reduced financial circumstances. She received support from family, including her father's aunts, one of whom was Harriet Beecher Stowe, the author of *Uncle Tom's Cabin* (1852), a novel which highlighted the plight of slaves in North America. Other prominent females in Gilman's life were her aunts Catherine Beecher and Isabella Beecher Hooker, both advocates for women's rights and education, and women whom Gilman greatly admired.

Despite the support of her extended family, Gilman and her brother, Thomas, received little affection from their mother, who insisted that her children avoided close relationships to keep them from being as devastated as she had been by Frederic's betrayal. Gilman did keep up some contact with her father, but his presence in her life was as inconstant as her general upbringing, with the family moving many times during her formative years. As a result, Gilman's formal education was erratic and brief, and she was not a strong student despite her natural intelligence and curiosity. She did however attend the Rhode Island School of Design from 1878 to 1880, also taking on work designing greeting and trade cards.

Relationships and First Marriage

In her late teens to early twenties, Gilman grew close to a woman called Martha Luther, with whom she shared a deep and happy friendship until Martha married in 1881. Gilman avoided relationships for a time until she married the artist Charles Walter Stetson on 2 May, 1884. This relationship did not give Gilman the security and happiness she might have longed for as a girl. Following the birth of their only child, Katherine Beecher Stetson, in 1885, Gilman suffered from serious post-partum depression. At the time, such illnesses were often not taken seriously or were dismissed as hysterical diseases. Gilman was eventually treated by Dr. Silas Weir Mitchell in 1887. He pioneered the rest cure treatment, in which people were expected to spend their time being as sedentary as possible. Gilman was encouraged to spend little or no time in intellectual pursuits, to avoid any potentially useful outlets such as writing or drawing, and to rest as much as possible inside the home. She was even bathed and fed by others for a time.

After a few months, Gilman's treatment led to further mental decline and talks of suicide. In order to preserve what was left of her sanity, she removed herself from the situation and spent the winter with a friend, the writer and poet Grace Channing, during which she improved mentally and physically. Gilman then separated from Charles in 1888 before taking the brave decision to divorce him in 1894, an act which was seen as unusual and even scandalous at the time.

Shortly after Gilman and Charles' divorce was finalised in 1894, Charles married Grace Channing. Despite the breakup, the three remained friends, with Gilman even sending Katherine to live with Charles and Grace as she felt it was important for Katherine to have a meaningful relationship with her father. This would unfortunately be seen by some of her critics as her abandonment of her husband and child, causing problems later in her career.

Career and Second Marriage

Determined to be financially independent after separating from Charles, Gilman moved to Pasadena, California, with Katherine. For a time, she worked as a door-to-door soap seller, but soon began to make a name for herself as a noted lecturer, travelling the US lecturing on social reform, human rights and gender politics. She was instrumental in expanding the women's movement in America, with her analogy of the female mind being like the female liver – that is, no different to the male mind or liver – expressing her frustration at the expectation of women to do little more than marry well, bear children and spend their lives working towards the goals and comfort of others rather than themselves. An advocate for economic freedom for women, she encouraged women to seek roles outside of the home to financially support themselves.

Following the death of her mother in 1893, Gilman re-established contact with her cousin, the attorney George Houghton Gilman. Over time, they grew closer and fell in love, marrying in 1900 and giving Gilman the happy, secure relationship she wanted, as well as the freedom to pursue her chosen career as a significant and celebrated writer, lecturer and editor. The couple remained happily married until his death in 1934.

Short Stories

While touring and lecturing, Gilman also wrote avidly, penning essays, poems and numerous short stories, including one of her best-known works, 'The Yellow Wallpaper', originally published in January 1892 in *The New England Magazine*. The story explores an unnamed woman's plummet into mental illness as she endures treatment for her 'temporary nervous depression' in the form of a rest cure. John, her husband and physician, restricts her movements to a single room, ordering her to rest and do nothing. With no stimulus to distract her, she becomes increasingly obsessed by the ugly yellow wallpaper in the room and eventually breaks away from her family and her own sanity. 'The Yellow Wallpaper' reflects Gilman's own experiences with post-partum depression after the birth of her daughter. Tellingly, Gilman sent a copy of 'The Yellow Wallpaper' to Dr Silas Weir Mitchell when it was published, but received no response.

Some of Gilman's most poignant and original stories are collated in *When I Was a Witch & Other Stories*. The title story, first published in *Forerunner* magazine in 1910, explores the results of a woman's wishes being temporarily granted. While addressing elements of social reform, the story casts its own spell on the reader with its irreverence and joie de vivre. The collection addresses the role of women in the home and in the workplace, social reform and animal rights, among other issues.

Editing and Writing

Gilman edited *The Impress* magazine from 1894 to 1895, a weekly publication for which Gilman herself wrote many articles and poems. It was her own status as a divorced woman and 'unnatural' mother which was thought to have led to social condemnation and the failure of the magazine, despite her growing fame as an important advocate for women's rights.

Unwilling to be silenced, Gilman penned *Women and Economics: A Study of the Economic Relation Between Men and Women as a Factor in Social Evolution* (1898) in which she argued for reforms to the role and expectations of women, especially as wives, mothers and homemakers. At a time when many women were fighting to enter the workforce, her argument for their financial independence and recognition of their contributions made her ideas both pioneering and highly relevant. This was followed by worldwide recognition with many critics praising her work even as others continued to condemn her private life. Gilman would continue to explore gender politics in other non-fiction works, including *The Home: Its Work and Influence* (1903) and *The Man-Made World* (1911).

In 1909 Gilman began her own publication, *The Forerunner* – a magazine aimed at presenting thought-provoking material to inspire change. The magazine ran for seven years and two months, and was largely Gilman's sole creation. In it, she serialised many of her works, both non-fiction and fiction, such as *Herland*, first published in 1915 in serial form. This novel is an enthralling study of a female-only utopian society whose inhabitants have created a highly evolved society of peace, companionship and order in which women take on all roles necessary for the survival and, essentially, the improvement of their society for the benefit of all. In Herland, women are able to make their own choices and the result is a place that is not not blighted by war, suffering, extreme poverty and which suffers hardly any crime. Its key difference to any other society? There are no men. Gilman could not have been clearer in her aim to challenge traditional gender stereotypes and present women as just as – or even more capable – than men.

Death and Legacy

Public interest in Gilman's lectures and books started to fade in the following decades, with her message appearing to some as slightly dated. Gilman was diagnosed with breast cancer in January 1932 and soon found out it was incurable. She lost her beloved husband George in 1934, a blow which – possibly coupled with her feelings of no longer being relevant and her own failing health – prompted her to commit suicide by taking an overdose of chloroform on 17 August 1935, ending her life as she had lived it, on her own terms.

Received in her lifetime as wildly popular, relevant and exciting, and yet controversial and unorthodox, the resurgence in Gilman's works in the 1960s, which shows no sign of diminishing, means that she has continued to inspire thought, provoke discussion and be an important voice for women.

Other Contributors

Ruth Robbins (Series Foreword) is Professor of English Literature and Director of Research for Cultural Studies at Leeds Beckett University. She has published widely on both feminism and the literature of the period 1870–1940. Her books include *Literary Feminisms, Pater to Forster, Subjectivity, Oscar Wilde* and *The British Short Story*. She is currently working on *Virginia Woolf: A Writer's Life*.

Catherine J. Golden (Introduction and Further Reading) is Professor of English and the Tisch Chair in Arts and Letters (2017–22) at Skidmore College. She is author of *Serials to Graphic Novels: The Evolution of the Victorian Illustrated Book* (2017), *Posting It: The Victorian Revolution in Letter Writing* (2009), and *Images of the Woman Reader in Victorian British and American Fiction* (2003). She is editor of *Charlotte Perkins Gilman's The Yellow Wall-Paper: A Sourcebook and Critical Edition* (2004), co-editor of *The Mixed Legacy of Charlotte Perkins Gilman* (with Joanna Zangrando, 2000), and a regular contributor to the *Victorian Web* and *Illustration Magazine*, a British arts journal.

Judith John (Life & Works and Glossary) is a writer and editor specializing in literature and history. A former secondary school English Language and Literature teacher, she has subsequently worked as an editor on major educational projects, including *English A: Literature* for the Pearson International Baccalaureate series. Judith's major research interests include Romantic and Gothic literature, and Renaissance drama.

Victorian, Gothic, Sci-Fi & Literary

A Glossary of Terms

A

abbess: nun in charge of a convent; female brothel keeper, a madame

abhorrence: feeling of loathing or revulsion

abode: place where people live; period of living somewhere

abominable: causing revulsion or disgust

aggrandizement: self-promotion; increase in power or status air-blebs: air heads, empty-headed people

afterlife: existence after death; eternal life

alchemy: mythical practice of turning base metals into gold, prolonging life or finding a universal remedy for disease

alderman: term for a half-Crown; senior local government official

ale: alcoholic drink made from hops and fermented malt, stronger and heavier than beer

almanac: annual calendar which contains information on important dates, tides, astronomical data, etc.

almshouse: lodgings for the poor, privately funded (often by the church), as opposed to the workhouse, which was publicly funded

amorphous: undefined, without clear shape

anatomical: relating to the structure of the body

antagonist: enemy or adversary

antinomianism: policy which allows Christians freedom from moral obligations

apoplexy: a crippling cerebral stroke, sometimes fatal; a fit of anger

apothecary: pharmacist; one who prepares drugs and medicines and gives medical advice; lowest order of medical man

apprentice: someone who works under a skilled professional for a specific amount of time (usually seven years) in order to learn a trade. When one finished his apprenticeship, he became a journeyman and would get paid for work himself

Armageddon: the final battle between good and evil

asylum: institution for people with mental health problems, often referred to as lunatic asylums

athwart: across; in opposition to

atone: to make amends for a crime or offence

automaton: someone who resembles a machine by going through motions repetitively, but without feeling or emotion

B

Babylonian finger: that which spells out the writing on the wall; delivering a judgement

balderdash: nonsense, senseless or exaggerated speech or writing

banns: announcement or notice of a forthcoming marriage in a parish church, proclaimed on three consecutive Sundays

beak: magistrate

bearer up: thief with a female accomplice who would distract the victim so the crime could be performed

beating: repeatedly hitting someone; scaring birds from bushes out into the open for shooting parties

Bedlam: nickname for the Hospital of St Mary of Bethlehem, a London psychiatric hospital; place or situation full of noise, frenzy and confusion

beg to: wish to

berserker: traditionally an ancient and ferocious Norse warrior known for savagery

bizarre: unusual or strange

blackleg: someone who works during a strike, often criticized by those who obey the strike (also known as a 'scab')

blag: to steal something, often by smash-and-grab; to trick or con someone

blasphemy: sacrilegious talk concerning God or religion

blighter: annoying or contemptible person

bloodletting: reducing the volume of blood in the body by either opening a vein or applying leeches as a way of restoring health, used from ancient times up to the nineteenth century

bloofer: vampire, usually female; term possibly comes from the mispronunciation of 'beautiful'

bludger: violent criminal who often used a bludgeon or heavy, stout weapon

blue bottle: policeman

blunderbuss: musket, used at close-range; clumsy or awkward person

boarder: person paying rent for a bed, a room and usually meals in a private home or boarding house

bob: cockney slang for a shilling or five-pence piece

Boche: German person; the term was often used to describe soldiers

body-snatching: the act of stealing corpses from graves, tombs or morgues, usually for dissection or scientific study

borough: town that had been given the right to self-govern by royal charter; in Victorian London, Southwark was referred to as 'the borough'

Bow Street Runners: detective force in London who pre-dated the police, organized by novelist Henry Fielding and his brother John in 1750 up to 1829, when Robert Peel founded London's first police force

brackish: slightly salty, usually refers to water

buck cabbie: dishonest cab driver

bug hunting: stealing from or cheating drunks, especially at night in drinking dens

bull: cockney slang for five shillings

C

calamity: accident or distressing event

cant: a free meal; language or vocabulary spoken by thieves or groups of people perceived to be common

caper: criminal act; dangerous activity

caravanserai: roadside inn for travellers, often found along the Asian trade routes

cash carrier: pimp or whore's minder, who would literally hold the money earned by soliciting

casuist: skilled orator, who uses clever but potentially deceptive reasoning

cavalier: Royalist soldier; often used to describe a chivalrous man or gentleman

census: official list of the British population, including address and details of age, gender, occupation and birthplace, carried out every ten years since 1841

charlatan: person who assumes false skills or knowledge; also known as a mountebank

charnel-house: vault containing the remains of dead bodies or skeletons

cherubim: winged celestial beings (singular: cherub)

chilblains: red, itchy swelling to parts of face, fingers and toes caused by exposure to cold and damp

chimera: something wished for but impossible; a fire-breathing monster from Greek mythology

chink: money (from the noise coins make when they knock against each other)

chiv/shiv: knife, razor or sharpened stick used as a weapon

chivvied: harassed or annoyed by attacks; to be encouraged to do something

choker: clergyman, referring to the clerical collar worn around the neck

cholera: disease of the small intestine, often fatal, marked by symptoms of thirst, cramps, vomiting and diarrhoea, caused by drinking water tainted with human waste. Victorians were hit with several cholera epidemics before sanitation conditions were improved

choused: to have been cheated

christen: to remove identifying marks from; to use for the first time; to make something like new again

chronometer: tool for measuring accurate time

claustrophobia: abnormal dread of being imprisoned or confined in a close or narrow space

cly faking: to pick someone's pocket

coal scuttle: metal pail for carrying and pouring coal

colonial: native of a colony; something characteristic of or relating to a colony

commencement: the beginning or start of something

comrade: term used for someone with shared interests or beliefs, commonly used among communist or socialist parties

confabulation: to cause confusion on purpose by filling in memory gaps with untruths

connubial: conjugal; relating to marriage

contagion: spread of disease caused by close contact

cop/copper: policeman

costermonger: street peddler, usually selling fruits or vegetables

cracksman: safecracker, someone who cracks or breaks locks

cravat: scarf or band of fabric worn around the neck and tied in a bow

creator: someone who makes something come alive

crib: building, house or lodging; location of a gaol

crossgrained: bad tempered or stubborn

crow: lookout during criminal activities; doctor

crusher: policeman

cudgel: heavy stick used as a weapon

cursory: quick, superficial and not very thorough

cypher: coded message; secret way of writing

D

daguerreotype: photograph taken by an early process, now obsolete

dandy: a man very concerned with his appearance and clothing; something excellent or agreeable

daresay: venture to say; think probable

day boarder: someone who spends the day at school but lives at home, as opposed to someone who boards at the school

deadlurk: empty premises

deaner: shilling

debouchment: narrow, confined opening or area; the act of moving from a confined area into an open space

deformity: disfigurement or malformation, often of a body part but can also refer to morals or the mind

deity: god or goddess; supreme being

depraved: wicked, immoral or corrupt

deputation: group of people charged with a mission or to represent other people

despatch: send something; to send someone to carry out a task

despotism: oppressive and often tyrannical rule or authority

deuce: euphemism for 'devil', used to express annoyance; the two on a die or playing card

deuce hog: two shillings

device: tuppence; an emblem or motto

Devil: the Devil, as depicted in Christianity and some other religions, stands as the enemy or opposite to God and tempts people to sin so that they go to Hell; the actual term 'Devil' comes from the Latin *diabolus*, meaning slanderous. Gothic characters are often tempted by agents of the Devil

dewskitch: a beating (bodily assault)

diligence: public stagecoach; taking care or attention over something

ding: to throw something away; to take something that has been thrown away

diphtheria: infectious disease caused by germs in the throat, causing difficulty in breathing, fever and damage to the heart and nervous system

dirge: funeral hymn, mournful lament for the dead

dispatches: loaded dice; sends someone to carry out a task

do down: to beat someone with fists, especially as a punishment

dogmatism: emphatic belief presented as fact without consideration of truth or others' opinions

dollyshop: unlicensed, often cheap, loan or pawn shop

don: eminent, professional or clever person; leader or head of a group

Doppelgänger: literally translated from German as 'doublegoer'; the ghostly apparition of another, living person; double or alter ego

double-knock: applied to the door by a confident visitor, one who was known to the family and comfortable with the purpose of his visit (a single-knock signified a more timid caller, often of an inferior class)

dowager: widow with an inherited title or property from her deceased husband; distinguished, respected older woman

down: cause suspicion or doubt; to inform on a person, when used in the expression 'to put down on someone'

dragsman: someone who steals from carriages or coaches

draught: cheque or bill of exchange; a small quantity of liquid drunk in one mouthful

duckett: street dealer or vendor's licence

duffer: someone who sells allegedly stolen or worthless goods, also known as a 'hawker'

E

ecod: mild curse, most likely derived from 'My God'

economy: cheapness; giving better value

eldritch: ghostly or sinister

Elysian Fields: from Greek mythology, term for the afterlife of the blessed; blissful or heavenly place

employ: to hire someone to work for you; if you were in the employ of or employed by someone, you worked for them

entrapment: imprisoning someone; incarcerating or trapping someone, often in dark, strange or claustrophobic surroundings

epidemic: illness that spreads rapidly and extensively, affecting most of the people who come in contact with it

epoch: period of time marked by particular events

equinoctial: occurring at the time of or near to the equinox, a twice-yearly event when the sun crosses the celestial equator

erethism: extreme excitement or stimulation

escop/eslop: policeman

establishment: shop, place of business

exculpation: exoneration; being cleared from guilt

exorcism: act of forcing the Devil, a demon or evil spirits from the body of someone who is possessed, done through religious prayer or rituals

expectations: chance of coming into an inheritance, property or money

extant: living or existing

extermination: destruction of an entire group or civilization

extra-terrestrial: existing outside of the earth's atmosphere

F

fadge: slang term for farthing

fakement: sham or trick, often used when begging

fan: to feel surreptitiously under someone's clothing while they are wearing it, searching for objects to steal

fanatical: zealous or single-minded

farthing: monetary unit worth a quarter of a penny; something almost worthless or of the lowest value

fawney-dropping: trick where a criminal pretends to find a ring (which has no actual value) and sells it as an item of possible worth

fiend: evil demon; evil or wicked person

finny: slang term for five-pound note

flam: lie or deception

flash: to show off or try to impress; something special or expensive-looking

flash house: public house with criminals as clientele

flimp: snatch stealing or pickpocketing from a crowd

flue faker: chimney sweep, usually young boys

footman: servant in livery, usually in a mansion or palace; a servant who serves at table, tends the door or carriage, runs errands

forebodings: feelings of apprehension or anxiety

forfeits: parlour games where each player needs to supply a correct answer and has a forfeit if the answer is not given

fossicking: rummaging or searching, usually for something valuable. The term is often used to describe searching for gold or valuable stones

foundling: orphan or abandoned child raised by someone else

furlong: unit of measurement equal to 201 m (660 ft), the length of the traditional furrow or plough trench on a farm

furtherance: helping or advancing the progress of something

fusillade: volleys of shots fired simultaneously or in rapid succession

G

gable: triangular end of a building where the wall meets the roof

gaff: show or exhibition; cheap, smutty theatre; hoax or trick

gainsay: contradict; deny

galvanize: to shock someone or something into action

gammon: misleading comment, meant to deceive

gammy: someone false who is not to be trusted

gaol: jail

garniture: decorative ornament or embellishment

garret: fob pocket in a waistcoat; room at the top of the house

gattering: public house

general post: mail that was sent from the London Post Office to the rest of England

ghost: phantom or spirit of somebody who has died and who has possibly not gone on to the afterlife, which often inspires fear or terror

gibbet: post with a projecting beam for hanging executed criminals, often done publicly as a warning to the public

gig: light, open, two-wheeled carriage drawn by a single horse

gill: unit of liquid equalling a quarter of a pint

gimlety: piercing, sharp-eyed

glim: light or fire; a source of light; begging by saying you are homeless due to fire; venereal disease

gloaming: dusk or twilight

glock: slow, half-witted person

gonoph: petty, small-time criminal

Gordian knot: an impossible or extremely complex problem; from the legend of Gordius, king of Phrygia, who tied a knot that could only be cut by the future ruler of Asia and which was cut by Alexander the Great

Gorgon: female monster from Greek mythology with snakes for hair

gothic: style of architecture, music, art or fiction generally associated with strange, frightening occurrences and mysterious or supernatural plots, characters or locations

gout: disease mainly affecting men, causing inflammation and swelling of the hands and feet, arthritis and deformity; caused by excess uric acid production

governess: woman employed to teach and care for children in a school or home

greatcoat: long, heavy overcoat worn outdoors, often with a short cape worn over the shoulders

grog: mixture of alcohol, often rum, and water, named after an English admiral who diluted sailors' rum

grotesque: misshapen or mutated character; something or someone unexpected, monstrous or bizarre

gruel: watery, unappetizing porridge, popular with the owners of the workhouse or orphanage due to its cheapness

guinea: gold coin, monetary value of twenty-one shillings or one pound and one shilling

gulpy: someone gullible or easy to fool

H

haberdasher: someone who sells personal items, often accessories such as thread or ribbons

habiliments: clothing

hackney coach: carriage for hire

hagiology: literature about the lives of saints or venerated people

hansom cab: two-wheeled, horse-drawn carriage where the driver sat on a high seat at the back so that the passengers had a clear view of the road

harbinger: something that signals or foreshadows an event or person

haybag: derogatory term for a woman

hedonism: the pursuit of pleasure

heliograph: signalling device that works by moving a mirror to reflect sunlight

heresy: belief that contradicts generally accepted or official religious teaching

hob: metal shelf or rack over a fireplace where the pans or kettle could be warmed

hoisting: shoplifting; to lift something up

hopping: picking hops, used for making beer

humbug: something insincere or nonsensical, meant to deceive or cheat people; used to express disbelief or disgust; a hoax or fraud

hykey: pride, arrogance

I

inchoate: partly or imperfectly formed; not fully in existence

incubus: name for a male demon, thought to be a fallen angel, who forces himself sexually upon sleeping women, which often resulted in the birth of a demon or deformed, half-human child

infusoria: single-celled organisms

indefatigable: tirelessly persistent; not giving in to fatigue

influenza/flu: viral illness causing aching joints, fever, headaches, sore throat, cough and sneezing, even followed by death in Victorian times

inmate: someone confined to an institution such as a lunatic asylum or prison

Inquisition: organization founded by the Catholic Church charged with the eradication of heresy or acting against God, by which those found guilty were often put to death; (lowercase) period of extended questioning, often associated with violence and torture

insensate: lacking understanding, sense or reason; without sensitivity or feeling

insurrection: uprising in revolt or rebellion, usually against an established government or authority

integument: tough, protective outer layer

interred: buried

invidious: unpleasant or undesirable

ironclad: armoured warship

ironmonger: someone who sells metal goods, tools and hardware

irons: guns, usually pistols or revolvers

J

jolly: disturbance or brawl; cheerful or happy

journeyman: skilled worker who has finished an apprenticeship and is qualified to hire himself out for work

Judgement Day: the end of the world when God judges humanity and the dead come back to life; also known as doomsday

Judy: term for a woman, usually a prostitute

juggernaut: massive and destructive force that is almost impossible to stop

jump: ground-floor window, or a burglary committed by entering through the window

K

kecks: slang term for trousers

ken: house, lodging or public house

keystone: wedge-shaped stone placed at the summit of an arch, which locks the other stones in place; a central principle or policy

kidsman: organizer of child thieves

kismet: fate or destiny

kith: someone's friends, neighbours or relatives

knacker: someone who disposes of injured, unwanted or dead animals, often turning their carcasses into by-products such as animal food, fat or glue

knaves: jacks in a deck of cards

knee breeches: trousers that reach the knee

knock up: to bang loudly on someone's door to wake them up

know life: to be familiar with criminal ways; to be street-wise

kopjes: small hill, South African term meaning 'little head'

L

lag: convict; someone sentenced to transportation or gaol

lassitude: feeling of weariness, lack of energy

laudanum: solution of opium and alcohol used as pain relief or to aid sleep, highly addictive

lavender, lay in: to hide from the police; to pawn something for money; to be dead

league: group or association with mutual interests, such as individuals, states or countries

leg: dishonest person, cheat

Lethean: forgetfulness or oblivion; from the river Lethe, one of the rivers of Hades in Greek mythology. Drinking from the river Lethe made people completely forget their past

leviathan: sea monster; large and powerful object or thing

liberal: generous; tolerant or open-minded

link boy: boy who carries a torch to light a person's way through the dark streets

liverish: feeling unwell, especially bilious; feeling disagreeable or peevish

lodger: person paying rent to stay in a room (or bed) in somebody else's house

logbook: book in which a teacher would comment on pupils' attendance, behaviour, learning progress, etc.

lumber: wood used for building or woodworking, often second-hand furniture; to pawn something; to go to gaol

Lunnun: slag term for London

lurker: criminal; beggar or someone who dresses as a beggar for money

lush: alcoholic drink; someone who drinks too much alcohol; luxurious

M

macaroni: term used to describe young men dressed in the fashionable continental style

macer: cheat

mag: slang term for a ha'pence piece

magistrate: judge over trials of misdemeanours; civil officer who upholds the law

maid-of-all-work: usually a young girl, hired as the only servant in the house and required to do any job asked of her

mail coach: carrier of the mail and a limited number of passengers, replaced in the mid-nineteenth century by the railroad

malefactor: someone who commits a crime or wrongdoing

malignity: malevolence, bad feeling towards someone

malt: grain, such as barley, that has been allowed to ferment, used for brewing beer and sometimes whisky

mandrake: homosexual; type of plant

mania: mental obsession or abnormality which can cause mood swings

manifestation: a sign or visual proof of existence

manifesto: declaration of policy or intent, often published by a political party

mark: the victim of a crime

market day: the regular day each week when country people would bring their livestock and goods to sell in town

market town: town that regularly held a market, usually the largest town of a farming area

masochism: psychosexual perversion where someone gains erotic pleasure by having pain, abuse or humiliation inflicted on them

materially reduced: having your circumstances and/or finances reduced or lessened

maxim: statement or saying

mead: fermented alcoholic drink made of water, honey, malt, yeast and sometimes spices

mecks: alcohol, usually wine or spirits

mesmeric: causing someone to be entranced or rendered unaware of their surroundings

Messrs: plural of Mr., used when referring to more than one man

metamorphosis: change or complete transformation in physical form, shape or structure, thought to be caused by supernatural powers

miasma: unpleasant smell or vapour, often related to disease or death

Michaelmas: Christian festival celebrating the archangel Michael, celebrated on 29 September, one of the four quarters of the year

middle class: people who earn enough money to live comfortably, often in a skilled profession, such as doctors and lawyers

misanthropy: hatred of humankind

mist: cloud of water particles that condense in the atmosphere, often used in Gothic literature to obscure objects or to prelude something or someone terrifying

mizzle: steal or disappear; fine rain

moniker/monniker: signature; first name

monolithic: something huge and impenetrable, often describing a building or an organization

mortality: death rate; the number of deaths in a given time or given group

moucher/moocher: rural vagrant or beggar, someone who lives on the road

mourning clothes: black garments worn after a relative dies, the length of which depended on your relationship to the deceased

muck snipe: someone down on their luck

muffler: scarf

mug-hunter: street thief or pickpocket, from which the modern term 'mugger' comes

mutcher: pickpocket who usually steals from drunks

myrmidons: loyal follower or acolyte, often someone who follows orders blindly or who acts with few scruples

N

nail: steal; to catch someone who is guilty of a crime

narcissism: egotism or self-idolatry; term comes from Greek mythology where the boy Narcissus fell in love with his own reflection in a lake

natural philosophy: the science of nature

nebulous: hazy; vague

necromancy: black art of conversing with the spirits of the dead, usually done to predict or influence the future, also for making the dead perform tasks for you; witchcraft or sorcery

nethers: charges or rent for lodgings

netherskens: cheap, unsavoury lodging houses, flophouses

new-fangled: new or original, not necessarily an improvement over a previous version

nib: point of a pen, often a fountain pen

nibbed: arrested

nickey: slow or simple-minded

nightmare: frightening or unsettling dream, often used in Gothic literature to heighten drama or fear; a malign spirit thought to haunt or suffocate people during sleep

nobble: to inflict severe pain or bodily harm

nocturne: romantic or reflective musical composition; night scene

nonpareil: unequalled or unsurpassed, often used to describe the most popular person of the season

nose: informant or spy; to try to find something out

O

occult: relating to the supernatural, witchcraft or magic; something not capable of being understood by ordinary people, but known only by the initiated

occupation: job, means of earning a living

odour: smell

Old Country: country of origin or of ones' ancestors, usually used to describe European countries

omen: sign or portent of a future event

omnibus: single or double-decker bus which was pulled by horses, capable of carrying lots of people

omnipotent: having unlimited power, god-like, infinite

on the fly: while in motion, moving quickly; done quickly or spontaneously

opium: drug extracted from the dried juice and seeds of the opium poppy which is highly addictive

orthodox: following established rules of religion or society; proper way of behaving

outdoor relief: charity for the poor which did not require them to enter the workhouse, eliminated in 1834 by the New Poor Law to stop people playing the system

outsider: instrument used for opening a lock from the wrong side; stranger or interloper

P

pacifist: someone who is against war or violence for any reason

page: boy or young man working as a servant or running errands

palanquin: box-shaped travelling conveyance, usually carrying one person and borne on horizontal poles by four or six others

pall: detect; become dull or fade; gloomy atmosphere or mood

palmer: shoplifter; someone who 'palms' items to steal them

palsy: medical condition producing uncontrollable shaking of the muscles

pandemonium: wild disorder, chaos

panegyric: impassioned speech or text praising something or someone

parlour: living room, usually for guests

patterer: someone who earns a living by recitation or hawker's sales talk, convincing people to buy goods

peach: inform against someone or give information against someone, often leading to imprisonment

pea-coat: short, heavy, double-breasted overcoat worn by seamen, usually dark blue or black

peelers: nickname for the new London police force, organized by Sir Robert Peel in 1829

perdition: eternal damnation following death; loss of the soul

pertaining to: concerning or to do with

phantasm: ghost or apparition

phenomenon: fact or occurrence that is out of the ordinary or hard to believe, even though it can be seen, felt, heard, etc.

phonograph: gramophone; machine for recording or playing sound

picnic: any informal social gathering for which each guest provided a share of the food; informal meal eaten outside

pidgeon: victim; also known as a plant

pig: policeman, usually a detective

pig in a poke: something for sale at more than its true value

pile: a fortune; large amount of money

pistoles: Spanish gold coin, used until the late 1800s

pleurisy: inflammation of the lungs producing a fever, hacking cough, sharp chest pain and difficulty in breathing

polyglot: someone who can speak or understand several languages

poorhouse: place where poor, old or sick people lived, where anyone able was put to work; also known as the workhouse

portrait: likeness of an individual or group created through photography or in paintings

possession: being controlled by an evil, demonic or supernatural force

post chaise: enclosed, four-wheeled, horse-drawn carriage, used to transport mail and passengers

post-human: class of humans who have evolved or changed to be beyond human, such as the Eloi and Morlocks in *The Time Machine*

premonitory: premonition or warning

prig: self-righteous or superior person

proctor: court officer who manages the affairs of others, answering to an attorney or solicitor

prodigious: great in amount or size; a lot

profane: disrespectful of religious beliefs

prognathous: projecting chin or lower jaw

prolixities: speeches or utterances of tedious or unnecessary length

Prometheus: a Titan who stole fire from the Greek god, Zeus, in order to give it to humankind

proprietor: owner of a commercial or business enterprise

puckering: jabbering; speaking in an incomprehensible manner

pugilistic: relating to the practice of boxing or fist fighting

punishers: men hired to give beatings or 'nobblings'

pursuit: the act of chasing after someone, usually to attack or catch them, often inspiring fear

push: slang term for money

putrefactive: causing decay or putrefaction

Q

quadrille: card game for four players using forty cards; dance

quarter days: four days of the year when quarterly payments were made: Lady Day (25 March), Midsummer (24 June), Michaelmas (29 September) and Christmas (25 December)

quay: wharf or platform in a port or harbour where ships are loaded or unloaded

quick-lime: white, corrosive, alkaline substance consisting of calcium oxide, acquired by heating limestone

quid: slang term for pound

quidnunc: gossip or busy body

quixotic: something unrealistic or improbable

R

racket: illicit or dishonest occupation or activity

ream: someone superior, real or genuine

rebellion: resistance and overthrow of authority, such as a leader or government, in order to change the way things are run

red planet: name for the planet Mars, given due to its red colour

remembrance: memory

repeater: pocket watch that chimed on the hour or quarter past the hour, making it easier to tell the time in the dark

republic: state or country in which the people elect representatives via elections rather than being run by a monarchy

reservist: reserve member of the military

resurrectionist: body snatcher; someone who steals corpses from graves, usually to sell to medical students. Legally, only the bodies of criminals could be used, but demand for corpses was so high that resurrectionists dug up the graves of the recently dead

revenant: dead person who has returned to terrorize or to avenge a score with someone living

revenge: act of avenging or repaying someone for a harm that the person has caused; to punish someone in retaliation for something done to them or to a loved one, carried out by humans or by spirits; a popular theme in Gothic literature

revery: daydream or musing; state of abstraction, also spelt reverie

ribald: description for vulgar, lewd humour, often involving jokes about sex

roller: thief who robs drunks; prostitute who steals from her (usually drunk) customers

Romanticism: arts and literature of the Romantic movement, characterized by the passion, emotion and often danger of love and associated feelings

Romany: gypsy or traveller; language spoken by gypsies

rookery: urban slum or ghetto; nesting place for rooks

rozzers: policemen

ruffles: slang term for handcuffs

ruin: to go out of business; lose all your money or possessions

runic: inscriptions on runes; written in the runic alphabet

S

saddle: loaf; cut of meat

sadism: perversion where one person gains sexual gratification by causing others physical or mental pain, first coined to describe the writings of the Marquis de Sade; delight in torment or excessive cruelty

salubrity: health or well-being

Salvation Army: worldwide religious organization founded by William Booth in 1865; it provided aid to the poor, helped those in need and sought to bring people back to God

sanctum sanctorium: holiest of holy places; place of secret or vital work, also spelt sanctum sanctorum

sapper: military engineer

savan: scientist or learned person

sawbones: physician or surgeon

scarlet fever: infection usually suffered by children, causing a red rash and high fever; also called Scarlatina

screever: forger; writer of fake documents

sealing wax: wax that is soft when heated, used to seal letters – red for business letters, black for mourning and other colours for general correspondence

sentient: able to feel and respond to sensations

sentinel: guard or soldier who keeps watch

sepulture: act of burial or interment

servant's lurk: public house used primarily by crooked or dismissed servants

sharp: conman, card swindler

shilling: unit of money equal to five pence in today's money

shirkster: layabout, work-shy

shofulman: someone who makes or passes bad money

silicious: consisting of silica, a crystalline compound

slap-bang job: public house frequented by thieves, where no credit is given

slate: used to teach children to write; they would write on black slates with white chalk, instead of the paper used today

slum: ghetto; false or faked document; to cheat someone or pass money you know to be bad or false

smasher: someone who passes bad or false money

snakesman: small boy used for housebreaking, as they could enter a house through a small gap

snoozer: someone who steals from sleeping guests in hotels

snowing: stealing clothes that have been hung out on a washing line to dry

somnambulism: sleepwalking, a dissociated mental state that occurs during deep sleep during which, in Gothic literature, people would do things they would not normally do

spectroscope: tool for recording and measuring spectra of light or radiation

spike: slang term for the workhouse

sponging-house: temporary prison for those who cannot pay their debts, prior to them being sent to a prison such as the Marshalsea in London

srew: skeleton key, for use in burglaries

stratagem: scheme or plan that has been carefully worked out

stricken: affected by; suffering or struck by

sublime: the concept of being awed, moved or transported by something, such as religion, beauty or emotions; used in Gothic literature for the thrill of being terrified, because fear inspires such strong emotions

substratum: underlying layer

succubus: female demon, counterpart of the incubus (*q.v.*)

supernatural: used to describe phenomena or events that seem unbelievable or cannot be explained by natural laws or occurrences relating to magic or the occult

superstition: deep-seated but often irrational belief in something, such as an action or ritual, that is thought to bring good or bad luck

supplication: asking for or begging humbly, often to a deity

surreal: bizarre or fantastical

sweetmeat: sweet treat, such as candy or candied fruit, often served at the end of a meal

swell: elegantly or stylishly dressed gentleman; expensive dress

T

tallow: hard, fatty substance from sheep or oxen, used to make candles or soap

taper: small, slim wax candle, narrower at the top than at the bottom

taproom: bar room in a public house where working-class people ate and drank, as opposed to the parlour, used by the middle classes

terrestrial: an inhabitant of, or relating to, the earth

thick 'un: slang term for sovereign

thicker: slang for sovereign or pound

thriving: to be profitable or successful; flourishing

thwart: to prevent someone from doing something

timorous: timid or nervous

Titan: name for the giants from Greek mythology; one of Saturn's moons

tocsin: warning signal or bell

toff: elegant or stylish gentleman; someone rich or upper-class

toffken: house in which well-to-do, upper-class people lived

tonneau: rear compartment of a car, usually consisting of the back seats

topped: to be hung

torpidity: mental inactivity; feeling sluggish or lacking in vigour

tradesman: man in a skilled trade, such as a carpenter or plumber; shopkeeper; someone who buys and sells goods

transfigure: to transform

transportation: when exiled British criminals were sent to the colonies, usually Australia, as punishment

trephining: surgery on the skull to remove sections of bone, sometimes used to treat mental illness

troglodytic: to describe a cave-dweller; bestial or brutal of character

turnkey: jailor; keeper of keys

typhoid: serious, often fatal, illness caused by drinking polluted water (contaminated by sewage)

U

ululation: howling or crying out, often from pain

ulster: long, heavy coat with a cape covering the shoulders and upper arms

umbrageous: providing or creating shade; also describes someone who is angry or has taken offense

unanimity: consensus or agreement

uncanny: something or someone too strange, weird or eerie to be natural or human; supernatural

unclean: dirty, impure

union workhouse: workhouse for the poor, which parishes were obligated to provide after the 1834 New Poor Law

unhallowed: unholy or not consecrated ground

unprovided for: left with no money or security

upper class: people from rich, moneyed families, such as landowners or aristocracy

utopia: imaginary society, place or period in which everything is perfect

V

vamp: to steal; to pawn something; to brazenly seduce or manipulate someone

vampire: supernatural being of a malignant nature, believed to leave its coffin at night to suck the blood of the living for sustenance, from European folklore

vapour: steam

vaporize: to convert something or someone into vapour; to destroy someone or something

veld: open country or grassland in southern Africa

venal: corrupt, capable of being bribed

vespers: evening church service, prayers

vicissitude: contrast or change, often unwelcome

vintner: wine maker or merchant

vivisection: surgery performed upon living organisms for scientific research or investigation

volplaning: gliding

W

watch: men chosen to guard the streets at night, periodically calling out the time and ensuring that no crimes were being committed

werewolf: someone who is human by day and turns into a wolf at night, living off humans, animals or even corpses, from European folklore

whist: popular card game, a variant of which developed into contract bridge

witchcraft: spells and magic performed by a witch; in Gothic fiction the witch is usually depicted as an old, hag-like crone or a beautiful, seductive young woman

without: outside, usually referring to outside the house in which someone is

woe-begone: sad or miserable in appearance

worldling: sophisticated or worldly person

work capitol: crime punishable by death

workhouse: place where the sick, poor, old and those in debt went or were sent for food and shelter. The New Poor Law (1834) made the workhouse almost a prison for the poor, who had to work hard in miserable conditions, often fed on gruel only and separated from their families

working class: those in heavy manual labour, usually for low, hourly wages, such as farm labourers, factory workers and builders

worrit: worry; worry-wort

wretch: miserable or unhappy person

Y

yack: slang term for a watch

Z

zenith: peak; most powerful or successful point

zombie: corpse, believed by voodoo followers to be reanimated by witchcraft; often presented as a monster who bites living people to infect them and spread the disease

zoophagous: carnivorous, feeding on animal flesh

A Selection of
Fantastic Reads

A range of Gothic novels, horror, crime,
mystery, fantasy, adventure, dystopia,
utopia, science fiction and more: available
and forthcoming from Flame Tree 451

Categories: Bio = Biographical, BL = Black Literature, C = Crime,
F = Fantasy, FL = Feminist Literature, G = Gothic, H = Horror, L = Literary,
M = Mystery, MF = Myth & Folklore, P = Political, SF = Science Fiction,
TH = Thriller. Organized by year of first publication.

1764	*The Castle of Otranto*, Horace Walpole	G
1786	*The History of the Caliph Vathek*, William Beckford	G
1768	*Barford Abbey*, Susannah Minifie Gunning	G
1783	*The Recess Or, a Tale of Other Times*, Sophia Lee	G
1791	*Tancred: A Tale of Ancient Times*, Joseph Fox	G
1872	*In a Glass Darkly*, Sheridan Le Fanu	C, M
1794	*Caleb Williams*, William Godwin	C, M
1794	*The Banished Man*, Charlotte Smith	G
1794	*The Mysteries of Udolpho*, Ann Radcliffe	G
1795	*The Abbey of Clugny*, Mary Meeke	G
1796	*The Monk*, Matthew Lewis	G
1798	*Wieland*, Charles Brockden Brown	G
1799	*St. Leon*, William Godwin	H, M
1799	*Ormond, or The Secret Witness*, Charles Brockden Brown	H, M
1801	*The Magus,* Francis Barrett	H, M
1807	*The Demon of Sicily*, Edward Montague	G
1811	*Undine*, Friedrich de la Motte Fouqué	G
1814	*Sintram and His Companions*, Friedrich de la Motte Fouqué	G
1818	*Northanger Abbey*, Jane Austen	G
1818	*Frankenstein*, Mary Shelley	H, G
1820	*Melmoth the Wanderer*, Charles Maturin	G
1826	*The Last Man*, Mary Shelley	SF
1828	*Pelham*, Edward Bulwer-Lytton	C, M
1831	*Short Stories & Poetry*, Edgar Allan Poe (to 1949)	C, M
1838	*The Amber Witch*, Wilhelm Meinhold	H, M

1842	*Zanoni*, Edward Bulwer-Lytton	H, M
1845	*Varney the Vampyre*, Thomas Preskett Prest	H, M
1846	*Wagner, the Wehr-wolf*, George W.M. Reynolds	H, M
1847	*Wuthering Heights*, Emily Brontë	G
1850	*The Scarlet Letter*, Nathaniel Hawthorne	H, M
1851	*The House of the Seven Gables*, Nathaniel Hawthorne	H, M
1852	*Bleak House*, Charles Dickens	C, M
1853	*Twelve Years a Slave*, Solomon Northup	Bio, BL
1859	*The Woman in White*, Wilkie Collins	C, M
1859	*Blake, or the Huts of America*, Martin R. Delany	BL
1860	*The Marble Faun*, Nathaniel Hawthorne	H, M
1861	*East Lynne*, Ellen Wood	C, M
1861	*Elsie Venner*, Oliver Wendell Holmes	H, M
1862	*A Strange Story*, Edward Bulwer-Lytton	H, M
1862	*Lady Audley's Secret*, Mary Elizabeth Braddon	C, M
1864	*Journey to the Centre of the Earth*, Jules Verne	SF
1868	*The Huge Hunter*, Edward Sylvester Ellis	SF
1868	*The Moonstone*, Wilkie Collins	C, M
1870	*Twenty Thousand Leagues Under the Sea*, Jules Verne	SF
1872	*Erewhon*, Samuel Butler	SF
1874	*The Temptation of St. Anthony*, Gustave Flaubert	H, M
1874	*The Expressman and the Detective*, Allan Pinkerton	C, M
1876	*The Man-Wolf and Other Tales*, Erckmann-Chatrian	H, M
1878	*The Haunted Hotel*, Wilkie Collins	C, M
1878	*The Leavenworth Case*, Anna Katharine Green	C, M
1886	*The Mystery of a Hansom Cab*, Fergus Hume	C, M
1886	*Robur the Conqueror*, Jules Verne	SF
1886	*The Strange Case of Dr Jekyll & Mr Hyde*, R.L. Stevenson	SF
1887	*She*, H. Rider Haggard	F

1887	*A Study in Scarlet*, Arthur Conan Doyle	C, M
1890	*The Sign of Four*, Arthur Conan Doyle	C, M
1891	*The Picture of Dorian Gray*, Oscar Wilde	G
1892	*The Big Bow Mystery*, Israel Zangwill	C, M
1894	*Martin Hewitt, Investigator*, Arthur Morrison	C, M
1895	*The Time Machine*, H.G. Wells	SF
1895	*The Three Imposters*, Arthur Machen	H, M
1897	*The Beetle*, Richard Marsh	G
1897	*The Invisible Man*, H.G. Wells	SF
1897	*Dracula*, Bram Stoker	H
1898	*The War of the Worlds*, H.G. Wells	SF
1898	*The Turn of the Screw*, Henry James	H, M
1899	*Imperium in Imperio*, Sutton E. Griggs	BL, SF
1899	*The Awakening*, Kate Chopin	FL
1899	*The Conjure Woman*, Charles W. Chesnutt	H
1902	*The Hound of the Baskervilles*, Arthur Conan Doyle	C, M
1902	*Of One Blood: Or, The Hidden Self*, Pauline Hopkins	FL, BL
1903	*The Jewel of Seven Stars*, Bram Stoker	H, M
1904	*Master of the World*, Jules Verne	SF
1905	*A Thief in the Night*, E.W. Hornung	C, M
1906	*The Empty House & Other Ghost Stories*, Algernon Blackwood	G
1906	*The House of Souls*, Arthur Machen	H, M
1907	*Lord of the World*, R.H. Benson	SF
1907	*The Red Thumb Mark*, R. Austin Freeman	C, M
1907	*The Boats of the 'Glen Carrig'*, William Hope Hodgson	H, M
1907	*The Exploits of Arsène Lupin*, Maurice Leblanc	C, M
1907	*The Mystery of the Yellow Room*, Gaston Leroux	C, M
1908	*The Mystery of the Four Fingers*, Fred M. White	SF
1908	*The Ghost Kings*, H. Rider Haggard	F
1908	*The Circular Staircase*, Mary Roberts Rinehart	C, M

1908	*The House on the Borderland*, William Hope Hodgson	H, M
1909	*The Ghost Pirates*, William Hope Hodgson	H, M
1909	*Jimbo: A Fantasy*, Algernon Blackwood	G
1909	*The Necromancers*, R.H. Benson	SF
1909	*Black Magic*, Marjorie Bowen	H, M
1910	*The Return*, Walter de la Mare	H, M
1911	*The Lair of the White Worm*, Bram Stoker	H
1911	*The Innocence of Father Brown*, G.K. Chesterton	C, M
1911	*The Centaur*, Algernon Blackwood	G
1912	*Tarzan of the Apes*, Edgar Rice Burroughs	F
1912	*The Lost World*, Arthur Conan Doyle	SF
1913	*The Return of Tarzan*, Edgar Rice Burroughs	F
1913	*Trent's Last Case*, E.C. Bentley	C, M
1913	*The Poison Belt*, Arthur Conan Doyle	SF
1915	*The Valley of Fear*, Arthur Conan Doyle	C, M
1915	*Herland*, Charlotte Perkins Gilman	SF, FL
1915	*The Thirty-Nine Steps*, John Buchan	TH
1917	*John Carter: A Princess of Mars*, Edgar Rice Burroughs	F
1917	*The Terror*, Arthur Machen	H, M
1917	*The Job*, Sinclair Lewis	L
1917	*The Sturdy Oak*, Ed. Elizabeth Jordan	FL
1918	*When I Was a Witch & Other Stories,* Charlotte Perkins Gilman	FL
1918	*Brood of the Witch-Queen*, Sax Rohmer	H, M
1918	*The Land That Time Forgot*, Edgar Rice Burroughs	F
1918	*The Citadel of Fear*, Gertrude Barrows Bennett (as. Francis Stevens)	FL, TH
1919	*John Carter: A Warlord of Mars*, Edgar Rice Burroughs	F
1919	*The Door of the Unreal*, Gerald Biss	H
1919	*The Moon Pool*, Abraham Merritt	SF
1919	*The Three Eyes*, Maurice Leblanc	SF
1920	*A Voyage to Arcturus*, David Lindsay	SF

1920	*The Metal Monster*, Abraham Merritt	SF
1920	*Darkwater*, W.E.B. Du Bois	BL
1922	*The Undying Monster*, Jessie Douglas Kerruish	H
1925	*The Avenger*, Edgar Wallace	C
1925	*The Red Hawk*, Edgar Rice Burroughs	SF
1926	*The Moon Maid*, Edgar Rice Burroughs	SF
1927	*Witch Wood*, John Buchan	H, M
1927	*The Colour Out of Space*, H.P. Lovecraft	SF
1927	*The Dark Chamber*, Leonard Lanson Cline	H, M
1928	*When the World Screamed*, Arthur Conan Doyle	F
1928	*The Skylark of Space*, E.E. Smith	SF
1930	*Last and First Men*, Olaf Stapledon	SF
1930	*Belshazzar*, H. Rider Haggard	F
1934	*The Murder Monster*, Brant House (Emile C. Tepperman)	H
1934	*The People of the Black Circle*, Robert E. Howard	F
1935	*Odd John*, Olaf Stapledon	SF
1935	*The Hour of the Dragon*, Robert E. Howard	F
1935	*Short Stories Selection 1*, Robert E. Howard	F
1935	*Short Stories Selection 2*, Robert E. Howard	F
1936	*The War-Makers*, Nick Carter	C, M
1937	*Star Maker*, Olaf Stapledon	SF
1936	*Red Nails*, Robert E. Howard	F
1936	*The Shadow Out of Time*, H.P. Lovecraft	SF
1936	*At the Mountains of Madness*, H.P. Lovecraft	SF
1938	*Power*, C.K.M. Scanlon writing in *G-Men*	C, M
1939	*Almuric*, Robert E. Howard	SF
1940	*The Ghost Strikes Back*, George Chance	SF
1937	*The Road to Wigan Pier*, George Orwell	P, Bio
1938	*Homage to Catalonia*, George Orwell	P, Bio,
1945	*Animal Farm*, George Orwell	P, F
1949	*Nineteen Eighty-Four*, George Orwell	P, F

| 1953 | *The Black Star Passes*, John W. Campbell | SF |
| 1959 | *The Galaxy Primes*, E.E. Smith | SF |

New Collections of Ancient Myths, Early Modern and Contemporary Stories

2014	*Celtic Myths*, J.K. Jackson (ed.)	MF
2014	*Greek & Roman Myths*, J.K. Jackson (ed.)	MF
2014	*Native American Myths*, J.K. Jackson (ed.)	MF
2014	*Norse Myths*, J.K. Jackson (ed.)	MF
2018	*Chinese Myths*, J.K. Jackson (ed.)	MF
2018	*Egyptian Myths*, J.K. Jackson (ed.)	MF
2018	*Indian Myths*, J.K. Jackson (ed.)	MF
2018	*Myths of Babylon*, J.K. Jackson (ed.)	MF
2019	*African Myths*, J.K. Jackson (ed.)	MF
2019	*Aztec Myths*, J.K. Jackson (ed.)	MF
2019	*Japanese Myths*, J.K. Jackson (ed.)	MF
2020	*Arthurian Myths*, J.K. Jackson (ed.)	MF
2020	*Irish Fairy Tales*, J.K. Jackson (ed.)	MF
2020	*Polynesian Myths*, J.K. Jackson (ed.)	MF
2020	*Scottish Myths*, J.K. Jackson (ed.)	MF
2021	*Viking Folktales*, J.K. Jackson (ed.)	MF
2021	*West African Folktales*, J.K. Jackson (ed.)	MF
2022	*East African Folktales*, J.K. Jackson (ed.)	MF
2022	*Persian Myths*, J.K. Jackson (ed.)	MF
2022	*The Tale of Beowulf*, J.K. Jackson (ed.)	MF
2022	*The Four Branches of the Mabinogi*, J.K. Jackson (ed.)	MF
2022	*American Ghost Stories*, Brett Riley (Intro.)	H, G
2022	*Irish Ghost Stories*, Maura McHugh (Intro.)	H, G
2022	*Scottish Ghost Stories*, Helen McClory (Intro.)	H, G
2022	*Victorian Ghost Stories*, Reggie Oliver (Intro.)	H, G
2023	*Slavic Myths*, Ema Lakinska (Intro.)	MF
2023	*Turkish Folktales*, Nathan Young (Intro.)	MF

A TASTE FOR THE FANTASTIC

Herland by *Charlotte Perkins Gilman*

A lost world fantasy in the tradition of Arthur Conan Doyle and the
Utopianism of William Morris, *Herland* inverted expectations with its
exclusively female society visited by three men from the Edwardian era.
An early example of feminist science fiction, this utopian fantasy explores
miracle births, role reversals and concepts of peace and freedom.

The Job by *Sinclair Lewis*

A statement of female empowerment, and self-determination over societal
expectation. Una Golden gains work in an exclusively male world of
commercial real estate. Golden struggles for the recognition of her male
peers while balancing romantic and work life; she marries, divorces,
continues to work hard and finally emerges triumphant on her own terms.

The Awakening by *Kate Chopin*

Edna Pontellier is a wife and mother of two who struggles to submit to the
prevalent views of women in late nineteenth-century Southern Louisiana.
Her unconventional ideas of motherhood and femininity have got her
in trouble more than once. When she meets Robert and falls in love, it
is the beginning of her journey to stepping away from her life of purely
maternal duties, reclaiming her individuality and finding happiness. This is
a touching story of self-discovery that was very much ahead of its time.

**For information on these as paperbacks and
ebooks please visit flametreepublishing.com**